LOVE BEYOND BOUNDARIES

BOOK 12 OF MORNA'S LEGACY SERIES

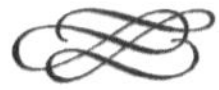

BETHANY CLAIRE

For Jason

A NOTE FROM THE AUTHOR

A Quick Recap

First, let me begin by saying how pleased I am that you've picked up this book. These characters and this world that Morna has helped me build are such a big part of my life, and I'm thrilled to share them with you.

If you're this far into the series, I'm sure you've noticed that things get a little more complicated as we go on. There are so many characters to keep track of, and as time passes between books, it gets harder to keep track of what's going on. So I thought it might be helpful to give you a quick rundown of where we're at, and who is involved with this story, so you can dive right in and enjoy it. :) So…in case you haven't picked up on where I'm going yet – there are SPOILERS ahead. Stop reading now if you haven't read the previous books in the series.

The last book, *Love Beyond Destiny*, ended with Machara's defeat – the evil fae who'd cursed The Eight so long ago. You may also recall that the thought-to-be widowed Silva, wasn't so widowed after all. Her husband, Ross, was actually alive and well, and we saw a little bit of him in *Destiny*. The last we saw of him, he had taken

Laurel up on her offer to reside in her Boston apartment while he tried to get his feet under him and figure out what his life would look like without magic and Silva.

And that's where we pick up with this book – just shortly after the end of *Destiny*, with Ross living in present-day Boston, picking up the pieces of his life. If you've been with these stories for a long time, you'll remember that Laurel's husband, Raudrich, is best friends with Sydney, the chef at Cagair Castle and one of the only one of Morna's ladies that doesn't live in the past. She's in this story as well, enlisted by Raudrich to check in on his old friend.

Okay…now that you're aware of where we are, and we've quickly recapped some old characters, I think you're ready to dig in.

I loved writing this story. It was one of only a handful that I really felt myself get lost in while I was writing it. That's when this work is the absolute best—when the story sweeps me away as I make it. It's my hope that it does the same for you—that for at least a little while you're able to disappear into Morna's world. I hope you enjoy every minute.

With love,
    Bethany

agair Castle
    4 Months After Machara's Defeat
Present Day

With the rest of Cagair Castle's residents tucked away for the night, Sydney kissed her sleeping baby and husband, quietly withdrawing from the comfort of her bed. By the time she made it down to her beloved kitchen, it would be seven in the evening in Boston—time for her weekly check-in with Ross.

Her weekly phone calls were part of the agreement Laurel made with Ross prior to his departure from the Isle of Eight Lairds after their successful defeat of Machara. In exchange for a place to live for the duration of Laurel's lease and access to her rather hefty savings account, Ross was expected to visit with Sydney each week to ensure he was making good on the opportunity to make a new life for himself. As far as she could tell, he wasn't.

While she'd happily agreed to be the go-between, she now dreaded these chats. Every week, they left her sad and exhausted.

Ross was always kind to her. He would converse because he knew it was expected of him, but nothing he ever said rang true. Any bit of cheer in his voice sounded forced, and she often wondered if he made up stories to make his days sound more varied than they were just to placate her. She knew he continued to struggle to find his way, and honestly, from what Sydney could see, it wasn't any wonder.

She knew where Laurel was coming from. She understood the impulse to solve other people's problems, but providing Ross a place to live and giving him enough money that he needn't seek out a way to make a living on his own was the last thing someone like him needed. It took away all necessity for him to solve his own problems.

With any luck, all of that would change soon. She'd visited with Laurel last week, and it had been clear that they had come to the same conclusion—life was a bit too easy for Ross now. Since Laurel still occasionally kept in touch with a few of her friends in Boston via Morna's magic, Laurel had told her she had something in mind that might change things. Sydney couldn't wait to see what it was.

She glanced at the clock as she flipped on the kitchen light and shuffled over to the small round table at the end of her favorite room in the castle. It was time.

Ross' number was at the top of her call history. He was one of the few people she still visited with on the phone. She was so used to waiting for him to pick up until the last ring that it surprised her when she heard his voice after only the second ring.

"Sydney, good evening to ye."

His voice sounded distorted—his tone muffled by the soft crunch of something in his mouth.

"Same to you. Are you eating?"

"Aye, apologies. Give me just a moment."

Sydney smiled as she listened to him swallow. Whatever was in his mouth, he seemed to be enjoying it very much.

As if reading her mind, he confirmed her last thought. "'Twas the best meal I've had in at least five years."

"Did you order out, then?"

He chuckled in response to her question, and the sound of it startled her. It was the first time she'd heard him laugh. It was a glorious sound that loosened the knot of dread that had settled in her stomach.

"No, lass. Believe it or not, I dinna order out. 'Twas a delivery from a neighbor. Said her name was Beth, and that she'd been meaning to come for a while, only she just had a babe a few months ago and couldna find the time until now. She's the wife of the building manager, or I suppose I should say she is the wife of the former manager. He just bought the building and is looking for someone to replace him as manager now."

Sydney thought of the first few months with her baby and nodded. "Ah, well, a new baby does have a way of taking up every minute of your day. That was kind of her to stop by and introduce herself to you. You visited with her, then?"

"Aye."

There was a slight pause, and Sydney suspected he was shoveling another bite of food into his mouth.

"She dinna give me any choice, really. She stepped right into the apartment the moment I opened the door."

I like her, Sydney thought, but kept the opinion to herself. If Ross liked her, she didn't want to say anything that might make him push her away. Ross needed friends as badly as anyone she'd ever known.

"What did you two talk about?"

"*We* dinna talk at all. I mayhap said fifteen words the whole half hour she was here. She, however, spoke extensively about a manner of things."

Sydney laughed. "She's been trapped in her house with a new baby and is probably starved for some conversation. I'm sure she's not always so chatty."

Ross didn't sound convinced. "I doona know about that. It seemed to be her personality. She somehow got me to agree to join her and her husband for dinner one week from today."

Sydney smiled once again, and her worry dissipated a little bit more.

Clearly, whatever Laurel's new plan was, it had just taken effect.

*S*pring

*A*fter three unanswered phone calls, Sydney was convinced that Ross had just successfully skipped out on their scheduled conversation for the first time. Just as she was about to give up and go back to bed, her phone lit up with his number.

She didn't even have a chance to speak before he leapt into an explanation.

"My apologies. Caleb, Beth's husband, asked if I would work on Ms. Jenkins' drain. It took me far longer than I imagined."

That was the sort of excuse Sydney would always be pleased with. Hard work was exactly what Ross needed. She would never give him a hard time for that.

"He's been asking you to do quite a bit for him lately."

"Aye. He's said nothing, but I canna help but feel as if I am unknowingly being interviewed for a job."

"What do you mean?"

"I told ye some time back that Caleb purchased the building. Beth's dental practice has really grown in the past year, and they want Caleb to be able to be at home with their girls more. I believe Beth wants me to take over as building manager."

It shocked Sydney to realize that the idea hadn't occurred to her. The job would be perfect for Ross. Working on a farm for several years when he first traveled to the twenty-first century had made him handy, and from what she knew about Ross, he would never work well under any one else. Managing such a large building would keep him busy, but in many ways, he would be on his own.

"If Caleb ends up offering you the job, will you take it?"

"Aye. I know that I need to work. 'Tis not as if I've ever had any desire not to. I just havena been able to figure out how to go about it. I have no past work history, no education to show prospective employers, no references that anyone can call. On paper, I am not the most appealing candidate for any sort of job. And with my magic now gone, I canna even falsify such documents. If such an opportunity presents itself, I will jump at the chance."

Sydney smiled as Callum entered the kitchen dressed in sweatpants and a white t-shirt. She always thought he looked sexiest just before bed. Quietly, he walked over to her and bent to press a light kiss on her forehead as she did her best to reassure Ross.

"I suspect that they will. Perhaps you should hint to him that you're looking for work? It might spur him on."

"Aye, I will."

There was a slight pause as Ross' breath caught, and a knot grew in Sydney's stomach. She suspected she knew which direction their conversation was about to go.

"Sydney?"

"Yes, Ross. It's done."

"They're married then, aye?"

"Yes. Silva and Marcus left on their honeymoon a week ago."

Silence hung between them for a long moment, and Sydney didn't rush to fill the silence. Instead she gave him the room he needed. She didn't know what to say to him anyway. After thirty-odd seconds, he spoke.

"I hope he makes her far happier than I did. Will ye do me a favor, Sydney?"

"If I can."

"If I write Silva a letter and send it to ye, will ye make sure she gets it somehow?"

"Ross, I don't know..." Sydney started to protest, but Ross quickly interrupted her.

"There's no need for ye to worry, lass. I'll not say anything to upset her, but she was the most important part of my life for a verra long time. It doesna seem right that such a monumental event should occur without me acknowledging it. She'll expect something from me. I'm sure of it."

His use of the word 'was' made her hopeful. It meant that some part of him had begun to heal. He could see that what had once been true no longer was, and from that place, there was room to move on.

"Okay. Yes. I'll get it to her."

***

Fall

"*How* is the new job going?"

It had taken little time for Caleb to offer Ross the position of building manager, but Ross' full takeover of the position had only been complete for about a month.

"While I canna say I expected there to be quite as much work as there is, I am thankful for the learning period Caleb provided."

"I suspect he knew what he was doing. And how do you like the new apartment? Has anyone else moved into Laurel's old place now that she's finally given up her lease?"

"I love it. 'Tis much larger. It has an office so I can keep up with the necessary paperwork, and it connects to a storeroom that is large enough to hold all of my tools and equipment. As for Laurel's old apartment, no, 'tis still vacant. There've been many applicants, but Caleb has asked that I keep it open for a while. I doona know why."

Ross had lived in modern times far longer than her own husband, but the speed with which Ross had learned everything that should have been so foreign to him—computers, cell phones, paperwork—still astonished her.

"How did you learn everything when you first came forward to this time? It doesn't matter what we talk about, you seem to have knowledge of it."

Ross gave her a slight chuckle before answering. "I read extensively and became quick friends with the farmer's wife who employed me. I believe she thought of me as the son she never had. While I'm sure she must've thought I'd been raised in a cave, she took great pride in teaching me much that I didn't know."

"Sounds like you lucked out."

"Aye. I did."

Sydney smiled as she glanced over at the calendar. One year had passed since Ross had traveled back to help The Eight defeat Machara. She wondered if Ross even realized it. He'd come so far in the past year. The man she looked forward to speaking to now bore no resemblance to the man she'd conversed with one year ago.

"Where'd ye go, lass? Ye grew quiet on me."

"Sorry. I'm here. I was looking at the calendar. Can you believe it's been a year, Ross? Please don't take this the wrong way, but when you first moved to Boston, I was half worried you would drink yourself to death within six months."

There was a soft, somber chuckle from the other end of the phone.

"So was I. I doona know if I've told ye before, but I will never be able to repay the kindness ye have shown me, lass. I doona deserve the friendship I've received from ye and others. I've slowly begun to find myself again. For a long time, I dinna think I ever would."

Sydney swallowed the lump in her throat. She didn't want him to hear her cry. The depth of her own affection for Ross frequently took her by surprise. It had taken so long for him to let her in, but now that she'd cracked Ross' tough exterior, she could see just how utterly warm and gooey he was on the inside.

"I'm proud of you, Ross. And there's no need for you to thank me. I look forward to visiting with you as much as you do with me."

A sudden shrill yipping sound reached her, and she pulled the phone away from her ear reflexively.

"Hush yer yappin' now, Tink. Ye know that Ms. Jenkins is right frightened of ye. We canna have her telling Caleb that ye are here."

Sydney listened on in fascination, waiting until he stopped before speaking.

"Did you get a dog, Ross?"

"Ach, no. I canna stand the little rascal. 'Twas Beth's doing. She adopted the wee, ornery rat as a Christmas gift for her girls, but she doesna wish for them or Caleb to see her until Christmas Day. I suspect she knows that once Caleb sees how excited his girls are, he willna be able to say no. So…she's placed the pup under my care until then."

Sydney shook her head, wishing Ross could see her.

"That's the worst idea I've ever heard. Do you have any idea how difficult it is going to be for you to give her up after taking care of her for that long?"

He quickly dismissed her. "'Twill be no trouble at all, I promise ye that. The creature is driving me mad. My only regret in having agreed to care for the wee beastie is that I underestimated what a pain in the arse she would be."

Sydney pinched the phone between her ear and shoulder, struggling to keep it still as she reached out for the small babe Callum extended in her direction. Nothing she said would change Ross' mind. He would just have to learn the lesson for himself.

"Whatever you say, Ross. My bet is that you're at the dog shelter five minutes after you drop Tink off with Beth and Caleb on Christmas morning."

Ross laughed as their conversation drew to a close. "Doona hold your breath, lass."

Two Weeks Later

"Sydney, wake up, lass. Yer phone is ringing. 'Tis Ross."

Startled by the sound of her husband's voice and the obnoxious ping from her cell phone, Sydney sat up in bed and reached to turn on the bedside lamp.

"What time is it?"

"Four in the morning. Something must be wrong. He wouldna call ye at this time of day otherwise. Ye best answer it."

A sick, cold, foreboding enveloped her as she reached for her cell phone and stumbled out of bed. Adrenaline fully waking her, she hurried from the room, ringing phone in hand. Once she was out in the hallway, she slid her thumb across the screen to answer his call.

"Ross? Is everything okay? What's…"

He interrupted her; the sound of his voice enough to make her grip the doorway.

"She's dead, Sydney. Beth has died. A car hit her as she was walking across the parking lot at her office."

Ross broke down into a string of strangled sobs, and Sydney closed her eyes as she slowly slid to the floor. She didn't know this woman, didn't even have the slightest idea what she looked like, but Ross' affection for her was enough to break her heart.

God, what about her two little girls? Sydney couldn't bear the thought of how her husband might be feeling. There were so many people that would be devastated by this loss, but her only priority was the man on the telephone.

He'd come so far in the past year, and now the friend who had helped him so much was gone. She couldn't let him backslide.

"Ross...I'll start looking at flights right now. Don't worry. You don't have to go through this alone. I'll be there as soon as I can."

CHAPTER 1

Boston, Massachusetts

The motorized whirl of the blender kept me from hearing my grandfather's footsteps as he approached me in the kitchen. When I turned away from the counter to see him two steps away, I jumped back with such force that I nearly knocked it off of the counter. Thankful that I hadn't sloshed our daily spinach and banana smoothie all over myself and the kitchen floor, I did my best to recover from the shock of seeing him up and about before I left for work. Most mornings when I left, the sound of Gramps' loud snoring was still echoing down the hallway. I hadn't seen him up this early since I'd moved in with him two years ago.

"Gramps, you're..." I started to remark on how early it was, but then my eyes finally caught up with my brain as I took in the sight of him. It was enough to stop me short. He looked so stinking adorable I could hardly stand it.

With his pink, button-down dress shirt tucked into his navy corduroy pants, his ensemble was finished with a pink and white polka dot bow tie. He'd combed his white hair neatly to the left and pulled out his most eccentric pair of eyeglasses—his especially large and especially round ones in tortoise-shell print.

On anyone else, his outfit would've looked ridiculous, but he pulled it off perfectly.

"Early morning date?"

He smiled at me and nodded mischievously. "How'd you know?"

"I can think of nothing else that would have you up this early, and you only wear your bow ties when you're trying to impress one of your dates."

"Well, that's not true. I've been known to wear bow ties on a few other occasions."

I laughed and shook my head. "You wore them to chemo, but that was only to bait the nurses into giving you a compliment so you could flirt with them."

He made a small gruff noise and stepped around me to get us each a glass. For the first six months of his cancer treatment, he'd detested my morning smoothies, but as time passed, he'd grown accustomed to me shoving at least a handful of greens into him at the beginning of each day.

He held the glasses toward me as I poured the now-blended drink.

"I'll only drink a little today. I want to have plenty of room to enjoy breakfast in a little bit."

I nodded and placed the container in the kitchen sink, filling it with water before I moved to join him at the small dining table just off the kitchen.

"What time is your date?"

"Ten."

It was just a quarter to seven.

"Then why are you up so early?"

"Allanah, I need to talk to you, sweetheart."

Allanah was my first name, the same as my late grandmother, and

Gramps was the only person in the whole world who called me by it. Most people called me by my middle name, Sue. It was a name I'd always hated, but for some reason that was entirely beyond me, it had stuck at a young age. Gramps knew how much I loved that he called me Allanah, and it didn't get by me that he used it now because he was buttering me up for whatever was about to come next.

"Okay..." I said the word hesitantly. Everyone that knew and loved Gramps knew to be fearful of the words 'I need to talk to you' if they came from him. It meant something was about to change, and regardless, you better just strap in for the ride. He was a dreamer—always had been. The scariest thing that differentiated him from most people with big ideas was that he tended to actually go through with them. There was no stopping him once he put his mind to something.

I think that's probably why I wasn't especially frightened when he'd received his cancer diagnosis a few years earlier. Gramps wasn't scared, so I figured there was no reason for me to be either. While I'd insisted on moving in with him to help take care of him during his treatments, I'd never doubted that he would get through it. And so he had. For the past three months, he'd been in remission.

"This morning will be my fifth date with Gladys."

My eyes lit up. I'd never known anyone to make it past three dates with him. His legendary love for the grandmother I'd never known had made him especially picky.

"Whoa. That's big, Gramps. So, you like her, huh?"

He nodded. "Yes. I do. I think she might be the real deal. We've decided to only see one another."

"That's fantastic. Am I ever going to get to meet Gladys?"

He shrugged. "Maybe, but not for quite a long while."

I laughed. At least he was honest.

"Okay. Well, it's your life. I can respect that."

"Which leads me to what I really need to speak to you about. I'm healthy now, sweetheart. I want my house back, and I need you out of here by date number twelve."

I inwardly cringed as I thought about what might be so significant about date number twelve and did my best to skirt that topic of conversation as quickly as possible.

"Alright. Done. You know I never intended to stay here forever. I've just been super busy with work. I'll call Caleb tonight and see if there are any vacancies in his building."

Once it had become clear that Gramps' treatments were going to last longer than we'd first anticipated, I'd given up my apartment and moved everything into storage.

"Thank you." He took one last sip of his smoothie and stood to go and rinse his glass. He paused as he passed my chair and bent to kiss the top of my head. "And Allanah, you know I'm going to miss you, don't you?"

I nodded. Despite the fact that living with my grandfather had caused my social life to decline significantly, I was going to miss the hell out of him too.

I started to stand to put my own glass away but hesitated when the phone in my pocket began to buzz. I could hardly believe it when I saw the name that popped up on my phone.

"That's weird."

"Who is it?"

"It's Ethan."

The mention of Ethan was enough to send Gramps off on a tangent.

"Ethan, huh? You want me to answer it? I'd love to speak to him."

Gramps had compassion for everyone except those who hurt me. So even though Ethan was certainly due some, he needn't expect any from my grandfather.

As I stared down at his name, it only took a second for my surprise to turn to dread. I held up a hand to stop my grandfather from talking.

"Gramps. He wouldn't call me unless..." Nausea swam up my center as I gripped at the edge of the table and sat back down.

The sound of my voice was enough to send Gramps rushing over to me.

"You're pale, Allanah. You don't know that anything is wrong."

I did know. I could feel it. And the very last thing I wanted to do in the whole world was answer that phone.

"Answer it, sweetheart. Either way, you gotta know."

Nodding at him, I shakily answered the phone, "Ethan?"

I knew it was her before he said a word.

"Sue. Something terrible has happened! Beth is dead."

CHAPTER 2

The drive to Caleb and Beth's house was too short. I wasn't ready. It had taken every ounce of effort to drag myself to my car. I'd somehow assumed that once I arrived at my late friend's house, I would have gathered the strength I needed to face Caleb. I hadn't. I didn't know how to do this. My mind still couldn't process that she was gone.

Beth. My best friend in the entire world. My old roommate. The best mother I'd ever seen to her two beautiful young girls was gone. In a flash. Killed in an instant by a distracted driver. I could barely stand to think of it.

It was foolish, I knew, but some part of me had always believed, or perhaps I'd just always hoped, that people could sense that their time was near before their death. They didn't. Not at all. I'd spoken to Beth an hour before she left her office for the last time, and all she could talk about was how close she was to talking Caleb into trying for another baby. You don't plan for more children if you have any sense that you're not going to be there to raise them. I couldn't place my finger on precisely why, but the thought that you could just be gone with no premonition of it chilled me through.

Shaking, I cracked open the door to my car and vomited all over the curb. I had the weakest stomach of anyone I knew. Scared—I would vomit. Angry—vomit. Heartbroken and more grief stricken than I knew was possible—apparently that made me vomit too.

A hand touched my shoulder, and I was pulled from the nightmarish images that kept playing inside my mind back into the car with Gramps.

"Breathe, Allanah. That's always what makes you ill. You forget to breathe."

I tried to draw in a deep breath, but it shook on the inhale and released the sob I'd been trying so hard to hold back. Collapsing against the steering wheel, I began to cry hysterically once again.

"I can't do this, Gramps. I can't. I shouldn't be here. How am I supposed to comfort Caleb when I can't go thirty seconds without collapsing into hysterics again?"

"You don't have to comfort him. You just need to be there with him."

"I don't want him to feel like he has to tend to me. He's the one that just lost his wife. He's the one that now has to raise two little girls all on his own. I'm just the old roommate. I don't have a right to the pain I'm feeling right now."

Gramps reached for my chin and gently turned my head so I faced him.

"Hogwash. You and Beth were as close as friends get. You have every right to the way you feel. Now...close your eyes, take five deep breaths, wipe your eyes, and let's go up there. You know you need to be here. Ethan was right when he said Beth would expect you to be. Sitting in this car isn't going to make it any easier."

Gramps' stern voice pulled me out of my grief for just a moment. I knew he was right. I'd put off this visit for as long as I could. I should've been here the day Ethan called me. Instead, I'd spent yesterday in bed, shaking, vomiting, and crying more than I knew I could.

"You don't have to be here, Gramps. Really, you don't. I can drive you back home if you want me to."

"Allanah." The tone of his voice told me that there was no point in arguing with whatever he was about to say. "You're not taking me home. I need to be in that house too. Caleb needs to know that he'll survive this. While I'm sure there are lots of people telling him that now, he might actually believe it if it comes from me."

As usual, he was right. My mother was the youngest of four, but her oldest sibling was only five years older than her. My gramps and grandmother had given birth to four children in five years, but she'd passed away while giving birth to my mother. On the day he gained his only daughter, my grandfather had also lost his wife and became a single father to four children under the age of six. There was no one who could relate to Caleb's pain in the same way that my grandfather could.

"Okay." I reached out to squeeze his hand. "Let's go."

*than, not Caleb, opened the door. I'd known I would see him. Still...it was strange to see my ex-boyfriend, Beth's brother, standing in the doorway. I'd not laid eyes on him since he ended our relationship four years earlier. He looked different. Leaner. More put together. Although the lines in his face were tight with grief, I expected that under different circumstances, I would have found him to look much more peaceful than the tormented man I'd known years ago.

"Sue..." He bent his tall frame down to hug me before stepping aside to let us in the house. "Caleb will be so glad you're here."

"Are the girls here?"

I felt like a coward for hoping that they weren't. I just didn't think I could bear to look at them yet. While Maddie wouldn't show grief, I knew that the one-year-old would already be missing her mother. But Hannah, who was five going on thirty, would be devastated. If I were to look at them, all I would think about was all that they'd lost, and I would fall apart all over again.

"No. Caleb's mother took them for the day so we could finalize the arrangements for the funeral. I hope the people from the funeral home don't arrive until the afternoon. Caleb has finally allowed himself to fall apart. I don't want him to have to pull himself together right away."

Gramps gave Ethan a curt nod. Slipping past us, I assumed that he was going in search of Caleb so Ethan and I could have a few minutes to speak alone.

I waited until Gramps was out of sight, and then gave Ethan's arm a gentle squeeze.

"What about you? You don't always have to keep your feelings so close to the vest, either. Please tell me you've allowed yourself some time to fall totally apart, as well."

He nodded. "In private, I have. You know me. I'm not good at letting others in on how I feel. Too many years of practice, I guess."

I knew the statement was his attempt at self-deprecation. A way of feeling me out to see if I still held any ill feelings toward him.

The truth was, I'd never been angry with him. Even when it had felt like I was, I was really only angry with myself for not seeing what was really so plain to see if only I'd been paying attention. I would never want anyone to deny who they are—especially not for my sake.

"How's Ben?"

He looked at me hesitantly. "Good. He's flying down tonight."

"Ethan…I'm happy for you two. I've been happy for you for quite a while now."

His eyes softened and I knew my words had given him some sense of relief. He pulled me into a hug.

"Thank you. It's good to see you, Sue. I just wish it wasn't for this."

His voice caught, and he quickly pulled away.

"Why don't you and I slip into the kitchen for a drink while your grandfather spends some time with Caleb. Believe me, you're going to need something to numb the pain a little when you see Caleb's face."

---

*G*ramps' conversation with Caleb lasted long enough for me to get a thoroughly decent buzz going. The moment I walked into the living room and laid eyes on Caleb, I wanted to turn around and personally thank Ethan for getting me a little bit drunk. The sight of him—his face red, his eyes sunken with shock and grief—was one of the worst things I'd ever seen in my life.

Whatever grief I felt, it was nothing compared to the hole that had been blown directly through the center of Caleb's chest. I moved to the couch where he sat. The moment I lowered myself down next to him, he collapsed into my arms. I held him as he sobbed.

We stayed that way for what seemed like hours until his sobs finally came a little more slowly, and he was ready to talk.

"Can you get me a glass of water, Sue?"

"Absolutely."

I hurried back into the kitchen where Gramps sat alone.

"This is going to take a while. If you want to take my car back to your house, I'll Uber over there when I'm done."

He shook his head. "I'm fine. Take all the time you need with him."

Getting the water, I quickly made my way back to the living room. Caleb drank the entire glass. When he set it down and looked at me, there was determination in his eyes.

"I'm not going to let this ruin my girls' lives. I don't know how I'm going to do it. I certainly don't have the strength today, but I will find a way to be all that they need."

"Of course you will. You are the only man I've ever known that was worthy of Beth. Your girls adore you. They're going to be okay."

"Your grandfather thinks he has the solution for me."

I looked at him hesitantly. There was no telling what Gramps had told him.

"Oh yeah? What's that?"

"Running. He said it was the only thing that saved him when your grandmother died. He talked me into training for the Boston Marathon with him."

There were certainly worse things he could've suggested. I shrugged.

"Maybe he's right. He's the only one I know that's been through something like this."

Caleb nodded solemnly. "Same. I think I'd do anything he told me to right now."

A brief moment of silence followed, and then Caleb steered our conversation in another direction.

"Hannah wants to go. To the funeral, I mean. Should I let her?"

"Absolutely." I didn't hesitate with my answer. I was not an expert in children by any stretch of the imagination, but intuitively this seemed like a no-brainer to me. "She's young, but if she's telling you she wants to go, you can't deny her that. She needs to be able to say goodbye."

"I don't think I'll be able to keep it together during the funeral."

"You don't need to. It's okay for Hannah to see how much you loved her mother, how much you'll miss her. It will let her know that her own feelings are okay, too."

He nodded, as he reached for a tissue. "You're right, I know. It's going to be the worst day of my life."

I shook my head. "No. You've already survived the worst day of your life. It's going to be a terrible day, that much is true, but it's not going to be as terrible as the day you got that call. And if it helps you at all, just remember that you've already survived the worst."

He nodded, but I wasn't sure he believed me.

"I have to find someone to watch Maddie during the funeral. Everyone there needs to be able to grieve. Their attention doesn't need to be on caring for a baby. I know it doesn't make sense, but I don't want to hire a babysitter. She will never remember Beth. I know that. But I want someone who loves her to be holding her while the rest of us say goodbye to her mother."

I knew he wasn't asking, but I knew immediately what I needed to do.

"I'll watch her, Caleb. I'll say my private goodbyes to Beth in my own way, and I'll watch Maddie here, in her home, on Saturday."

Missing her funeral was the exact thing Beth would want me to do. There was absolutely no question in my mind.

CHAPTER 3

*R*oss sat on the end of his couch watching as Sydney rolled a ball across the living room floor. Every time the tiny, obnoxious ball of fluff clumsily ran to fetch the ball for her, it lit some small light of joy inside him despite the overwhelming heaviness of his heart. He couldn't believe Sydney had dropped everything to fly halfway across the world for him. He didn't deserve her friendship.

"Ye truly dinna need to come all this way, Sydney. There is nothing ye can do. And ye needn't play with her. I know ye must be exhausted."

Sydney waved a dismissive hand at him and rolled the ball once more. "Nonsense. I can be here for you. Sometimes that's all we need. And I'm not nearly as tired as I should be. I may have overdone the coffee on the way over."

This time when Tink waddled toward her, Sydney leaned forward to pick the pup up, lifting her and kissing the side of the pup's face.

"Come on, Ross. Just listen to that little puppy pant. And oh my God, those eyes! You can't honestly tell me that you don't find her a little bit adorable?"

"She is not an ugly dog, I'll admit that. Nothing more."

Still holding the squirming pup, Sydney pushed herself off the floor and moved to sit by him on the couch.

"Are you hungry? I might be a cook, but I'm also pretty good at navigating a take-out menu. How about I order us some dinner?"

He shook his head. "Please order ye something. I know ye must be hungry, but I've no appetite."

She looked at him and sighed. "I'm going to order two entrees—just in case you change your mind."

She left Tink on the couch as she stood to sort through the collection of menus in the kitchen. It took all of two seconds for the pup to launch herself at him, climbing up his chest to lick his face profusely.

He knew it was just his need for comfort that kept him from pushing the dog away. Instead, to his own surprise, he squeezed Tink tightly and allowed her to settle onto his chest.

The grief hit him in waves. For a moment he would feel fine, then the cold disbelief of knowing Beth was gone would hit him, and he would sink into it once more.

He jumped when Sydney's hand gently touched his shoulder, and Tink let out a short yippy bark as if she meant to protect him.

Sydney laughed and leaned down toward Tink's face. "Oh, I'm not scared of you. You'd never hurt a fly, would you, Tink?"

He frowned at the baby voice Sydney used every time she talked to the dog. "Do ye think that tone helps her understand ye? I can assure ye, it doesna."

She shrugged and settled down beside him once again. "Habit, I guess. Come on, Ross. Talk to me. What are you thinking?"

He looked at her squarely and said the first thing that came to his mind. "I'm thinking that I finally understand what I put Silva through. I dinna understand it before. I dinna know true grief myself. Now I do. I will never forgive myself for what I did to her."

"She's forgiven you, Ross. You should forgive yourself, too."

"Mayhap so, but I doubt I ever will." Mentioning Silva made him think of the others—those in the past who had known Beth.

"Sydney, have ye spoken with Laurel and Kate? They do know, aye?"

Sydney nodded somberly. "Yes. Morna contacted them before I had the chance to reach out to her. I bet she knew about what happened before any of us did. I'd never heard her so upset about anything."

He'd only been around the old witch a couple of times. He couldn't imagine why she would've had any attachment to Beth.

"I can understand her having some empathy for the rest of us, but why do ye think she seemed so upset?"

Sydney looked at him with an expression that told him he should've already guessed the answer to that. "She cares about you, Ross. Just like she cares about pretty much everyone that has ever crossed her path. She's been watching things from afar since you moved here, probably waiting for the opportune time to meddle in your life, if I were to guess. But Beth stepped in to do that for her. She didn't see Beth's death coming. I believe she's upset with herself for not having stopped it."

Although his own magic was now gone, he'd had powers long enough to know that there were some things that shouldn't be changed even if one has the power to do so. Morna bore no responsibility for Beth's death.

"'Twould have been wrong for Morna to do so. Do ye have a way for me to contact her? Mayhap when things have settled a little and I am not so weepy myself, I can reach out to her."

"Of course. I'll leave you with the number we all use before I leave here."

"And what of Laurel and Kate?"

"Heartbroken, but they have support around them. Ross, would you like me to go to the funeral with you tomorrow? I know I didn't know her, but I truly wouldn't mind being there to support you."

He shook his head. "No. Ye can stay and watch Tink if ye doona mind. The wee pup finds trouble if left alone for more than a few hours."

A sudden knock on the door interrupted their conversation.

"That can't be the food already. It's not been long enough. I guess you should get it."

He nodded and stood. "'Tis most likely a tenant with some maintenance issue or question."

Peeking through the peephole, he was shocked to find Caleb standing on the other side of the door. While he'd spoken to him, he'd not seen him since Beth's death. He'd not wanted to be in the way of the family's preparations.

Caleb didn't need to see Tink yet. While he knew he would have to tell Caleb about what Beth had done before Christmas Day, there was no need to burden him with such news right now.

Opening the door, he stepped out into the hall and closed the door to his apartment so Caleb wouldn't have an opportunity to step inside.

"Caleb…"

Wordlessly, he moved to hug his friend. Caleb clung on to him for a long moment before stepping away.

"I'm sorry to interrupt your evening."

"Doona apologize, lad. Ye've interrupted nothing."

Silence followed, and Ross didn't hurry to fill the space between them. There was nothing he could say to help his friend.

Eventually…Caleb spoke again. "I've a favor to ask of you, Ross."

"O'course. Whatever ye need."

"Will you say a few words at the funeral tomorrow? Beth's family wants me to speak, but I can't do it. I've spent all afternoon trying to put together some words, and I just can't. You meant so much to her. I've never seen her take to anyone as fast as she did you. I know it would mean so much to her if you did. It would mean so much to me, as well."

A sinking dread filled him. Talking wasn't his strong suit. And there would be so many others there who had known Beth much longer than he had. He would feel awkward and out of place, but he knew there was no way he could say no.

"O'course."

Caleb nodded. "Thank you." He hesitated briefly before continuing. "I hope you don't take this the wrong way, but I was hesitant when Beth seemed to take you on as her pet project, but I am as grateful for your friendship as she was."

Ross allowed himself a soft chuckle. He'd always known that Beth had seen him as someone she could *fix* with her friendship and love. "I will be forever honored to call ye a friend, Caleb." And so she had.

Caleb pointed at the closed door behind him. "Do you mind if I come in? I just don't want to go back home right now."

Caleb would just have to see Tink. There was no getting around it. Of course Caleb didn't want to go back to the house he and Beth had shared.

"Aye. Come on in."

Opening the door for his friend, he didn't miss Sydney's startled expression as Caleb stepped into the apartment.

He watched as she quickly stood to greet him, extending her hand.

"Hello. I'm Sydney. You must be Caleb, yes? I'm so, so sorry for your loss."

"Thank you, and yes. Are you…" Caleb paused and turned his head toward Ross. "Do you have a girlfriend you've been hiding from us?"

Before he could answer, Sydney interrupted, answering Caleb's question. "Oh, definitely not. I'm married. Just a friend."

An odd expression flashed across Caleb's face as he closed his eyes and nodded. Ross thought he heard Caleb whisper, *"Okay, Beth. Okay,"* before he spoke more loudly.

"Ross, I can't believe I'm about to do this, but meeting your friend has reminded me of something that Beth had been trying to arrange for months before…" He trailed off. When he spoke again, his voice was raspy from the tears he struggled to hold back. "She was relentless in trying to convince me to talk you into letting us set you up with someone. I told her over and over that it was something you wouldn't want to do, but she wanted you to meet our friend so badly. In Beth's defense, the woman she wanted you to meet really is a jewel. I've never met anyone that didn't like her. Once this weekend is over, will you meet up with her if I can get her to agree to it as well? For Beth?"

Ross suppressed a groan. He didn't feel like dating right now. In truth, he was quite certain that he never wanted to be in a romantic relationship with anyone again. It would be a waste of both his time and that of the unsuspecting woman who would also be guilt-tripped into meeting him, but how was he supposed to say no when Caleb made it about Beth?

He nodded, hesitantly. "If 'twas truly that important to her, then aye. Though I can assure ye 'twill not go as Beth hoped it would."

"Probably so, but at least I will have helped you two meet. I denied Beth the opportunity to arrange that while she was here, the least I can do is see it done now."

Seemingly annoyed by the lack of attention she was receiving, Tink chose that moment to make her presence known by letting out a high-pitched bark and pouncing on Caleb's feet.

Caleb looked down in surprise. "Did you get a dog, Ross?"

He ran a hand through his hair as he motioned to the couch to offer Caleb a seat. "Not exactly."

Caleb pointed to Sydney. "Is it yours?"

Sydney shook her head. "Nope."

"Then, whose is it?"

Caleb bent to pick Tink up, snuggling her close as he moved to sit down on the couch.

Ross sighed as he readied himself to give away Beth's secret. "'Tis yers."

Caleb raised his eyebrows as he looked suspiciously down at the dog in his arms. "Excuse me?"

"Beth gave her to me for safekeeping until Christmas. She intended to surprise yer girls. She thought that once ye saw how pleased they were, ye wouldna put up a fight about keeping her."

A slow, strange smile spread across Caleb's face. Much to Ross' surprise, Caleb began to laugh.

It unnerved him, and he watched on, unsure of how to respond.

After what seemed like forever, Caleb's laughter slowly turned into a soft sob. When he looked up at Ross, there were tears in his eyes.

"God, how I loved her. She tricked you, Ross. She never intended for this dog to be ours."

Ross argued with him. "Aye, she did. She told me so."

Caleb shook his head firmly. "I have no doubt she did, but she lied to you. Hannah is allergic to dogs. Has been since she was a baby. Otherwise, I would've gotten us one ages ago. She gave you that dog, knowing that in time you'd fall in love with it, and then you'd have a companion for this big, old apartment. Face it, Ross. This dog is yours."

CHAPTER 4

I arrived at Caleb's house early the morning of Beth's funeral so I could take care of Maggie while the rest of them readied for what would indisputably be one of the most difficult days of their lives. I watched her in the living room, bouncing her back and forth on my hip while she cried. She was still screaming when Caleb, his mother, Ellen, Beth's parents, sweet little Hannah, Ethan, and Ben left for the funeral. Four hours later she was still crying. No matter what I did to soothe her, she continued to wail in my arms. Eating, burping, changing her diapers, singing to her, rocking, nothing seemed to help.

Finally, at nearly two in the afternoon, her crying stopped and she settled down onto my chest to sleep. And I knew, without actually knowing, that it was now done. The service was over, and Beth had been laid to rest in the cemetery. Somehow, although she was too little to understand, Maggie knew, and she'd been crying right along with the rest of them until it was over.

As she slept, I moved to the rocking chair angled toward the bay window that looked out onto the street, sinking down to hold her as I tried to compose myself. The baby's crying had allowed me the space I needed to cry as well. Together, she and I had grieved the loss of her mother in our own special way.

Fatigued from the immense effort I'd put into trying to calm her all morning, I started to fall asleep but was suddenly awakened by the soft ding from my pocket—a text message from Gramps.

"The service was beautiful. Caleb insisted that he would drive you home, so I'm about to take your car back to my house rather than head your way to pick you up. I stayed with them until everything was done. They are all are headed your way now."

Taking every care not to wake the exhausted Maggie, I texted him back with one hand. *"Okay. I'll see you soon. Thank you for going. I know it meant a lot to Caleb. It would've meant a lot to Beth, too."*

While I doubted I would ever know the exact details of Gramps' conversation with Caleb the day after Beth's death, I knew it had somehow bonded the two of them together forever.

I ducked my head to kiss the top of Maggie's whisper thin hair. "You're going to be okay, sweet girl. You have so many people who love you. Everything is going to be okay."

I held her close to me and rocked her, falling asleep only to be awakened by a hand on my shoulder.

"Sue...we're back. Thank God she finally fell asleep for you."

I blinked a handful of times to wake myself and looked up to see Hannah held in her father's arms as she draped her head over his shoulder and slept. Caleb continued to talk as I stood from the chair, Maggie still in my arms.

"Hannah is exhausted too. She's cried herself out—fell asleep in the car on the way home. My mother is upstairs in the guest room. Everyone else has gone to pick us up some food. Why don't we carry the girls up to their room? Then I'll take you home, okay?"

I nodded, and with my free hand, I reached out to gently squeeze Caleb's arm. "Are you okay?"

His eyes were red, but his expression held steady. I suspect he'd shed as many tears as he was capable of crying today, too.

"Yes. We survived today. And we'll survive the next. And we will keep doing that until things don't feel quite as terrible as they do right now."

I nodded again, admiring his resolve as I followed him up the stairs to Hannah and Maggie's room. We settled them in and made our way downstairs and out the front door to Caleb's still-running car.

He didn't speak again until we were pulling out of his driveway. "Thank you for watching her."

"Of course."

"I'm starting marathon training with your grandfather on Tuesday."

Sensing that Caleb needed to talk about anything other than this day, I followed his lead. "Oh yeah?"

"Yeah. Also…we're going to make a quick stop before I take you home, okay?"

"That's fine. Where are we going?"

"The apartment building. You need a place to live, don't you? Laurel's apartment is still vacant since her move to Scotland. I knew that you and your grandfather didn't plan to live together forever, so I kept it vacant until you were ready to see it."

I eyed him skeptically as he turned in the opposite direction of Gramps' house. "How did you know I was looking right now?"

"Your grandfather told me."

I started to interrupt him. "He shouldn't have told you," but was quickly cut off by Caleb.

"No. He absolutely should have. I appreciate how he's not tip-toeing around me. He knows that for the sake of my girls I have to get back on my feet as quickly as possible. I know I'm going to be grieving Beth for the rest of my life, but their lives aren't going to stop, and I can't allow mine to stop either. It's good to deal with some work stuff, especially if it means helping you. You are interested in looking at it, aren't you?"

Slightly embarrassed, I nodded. "Yes. I was going to ask you if there were any vacancies in your building anyway. I just planned on waiting a little bit. Gramps wasn't kidding when he said he wanted me out soon."

"Her apartment is in great shape."

I glanced up at the old building as we pulled to a stop in one of the empty parallel parking spaces out front. I'd always admired its charm. It had character and a cozy feel to it that I loved—something so many of the newer complexes in the city didn't have.

"I know. I've seen it before, actually. When I was working with Kate after the fire that injured her so badly, we met at Laurel's apartment a few times."

Caleb paused outside the main door to fish for the right key. "Of course. Well, let's go see if you want it. If you do, it's yours."

———

The apartment was even more beautiful than I remembered—probably because during my previous visits my entire focus had been on helping Kate. Now, that I was looking at the space and imagining it as my own, I knew it would be perfect.

"Caleb, I absolutely want this apartment. I don't need to look anywhere else."

"You like it?"

"I love it. You know how hard it was for me to let go of my last place when Gramps got sick. I didn't think I would ever find another place I loved more, but this is so much nicer. When can I move in?"

He smiled and moved to one of the drawers in the kitchen. "Right away."

I watched as he reached into the drawer and retrieved the key before extending it in my direction.

"Here you go. You're not signing a lease. I don't want you stuck here if you decide it's not where you want to be. I know you'll pay. I'm not the least bit worried about that. This place is yours for as long or as short a time as you want it."

I moved toward him to pull him into a hug. "Thank you, Caleb. Gramps is going to be thrilled."

He laughed softly. "How about we order a pizza then go ahead and get some of your things from storage? We just have my car, so we can't get any furniture yet, but I can help you get a fcw boxes. It will make the place seem more like yours."

I was all for starting the moving process, but I didn't want to tire Caleb any more than necessary.

"Are you sure?"

He gave me one firm nod, and I knew there was no sense in arguing. "Yes. I need an hour or two of something normal. The girls are asleep. I'm sure my mother will call me if they wake up. Lately, my house is the last place on earth I want to be."

I could understand that.

"Okay, great. Let's go."

Three hours later, we'd moved all of my kitchen-related boxes from storage and had scattered them haphazardly around my new apartment. When that was done, exhausted and still hungry, Caleb and I sat on the floor with the box of now-cold pizza in between us as we munched away and sipped on the sodas we'd picked up on our way back to the apartment after getting our last load.

"The memorial was worthy of her. It wouldn't have been if I'd spoken like everyone wanted me to."

I was unaware that everyone had wanted him to, but I could certainly understand why he'd decided against it.

"Who spoke in your place?"

"You don't actually know him."

"Really?"

His answer surprised me. I thought I knew pretty much everyone Caleb and Beth did.

"It was one of our newer friends. He did a fantastic job. Touching and funny—he reminded me of just how easily Beth could push her way into someone's heart. I..." He hesitated and looked at me strangely. "I would like to talk to you about him, actually."

"About your friend?"

"Yes."

"Okay..." I had no idea where this was going.

"Beth wanted to set you up with him. She tried to talk me into speaking with Ross about it for ages, but I never did. He's agreed to the date. Will you?"

Confused, I stared at him for a long minute. Nothing in me ever suspected that our conversation was about to take this sort of turn. I talked to Beth all the time and she'd never mentioned anything about any new friend, let alone someone she wanted to set me up with.

"How was there someone Beth wanted me to date and I didn't know about it?"

Caleb gave a soft, sad chuckle and looked at me knowingly. "Ethan, Sue. Beth's the one who set you up with her brother, and that didn't end particularly well now, did it? She wanted to thoroughly vet this guy before saying anything to you about him."

I laughed thinking about how horribly Beth had felt when Ethan had ended things with me. She bore no responsibility, obviously, but it had been so hard for her to believe that she'd never realized her brother was gay.

"And after vetting this guy, she liked him?"

Caleb nodded, reaching for the last slice of old pizza. "She loved him. He's a good guy, Sue. It would've made her so happy for you to say yes."

I shrugged and lifted my palms up in resignation. "Then, I guess I really don't have a choice, do I?"

"You know Beth wouldn't have given you one."

"Fine. I'll go on one date. For Beth. But I'm not making you any promises beyond that."

"Of course. That's all I ask. You two just meet up and see how it goes. We'll see if Beth's instincts for matchmaking improved at all after her first shot at it."

CHAPTER 5

*R*oss could feel the banged-up spoon covered in various food gunk the moment he reached down into the sink. Mrs. Jenkins knew what plagued her disposal. She always knew precisely what was wrong with whatever problem she called him about. And despite the old woman's feigned weakness, Ross knew they were almost always things she could have easily fixed herself. Even so, Ross could never bring himself to point out that he knew Mrs. Jenkins only called with maintenance issues when she wanted the company of another human being, even if it was only for a few minutes at a time.

He couldn't blame her. He knew what loneliness was—understood it.

And so—even though it was the last day before Sydney returned to Scotland—he'd answered her call and taken time out of his day to indulge her, taking longer than he would on anyone else's apartment, pausing between each new task to visit about whatever was on the old woman's mind.

Today, all she wanted to talk about was his least favorite topic imaginable—him. With anyone else, he wouldn't have tolerated such invasive questioning, but his soft spot for the sweet, elderly woman grew each time he saw her.

"How old are you, Ross?"

"Now, Mrs. Jenkins, would ye like for me to ask ye about yer age? I am thirty-five."

The old woman leaned against the kitchen counter to look at him as he rinsed off the spoon and allowed water to run down the drain as he carefully tested the disposal to make sure the spoon was its only problem. As expected, no longer blocked by the piece of metal, it worked just fine.

"Hmm…I truly did reach down the drain before I called you, Ross. I couldn't feel anything."

He smiled gently at her and nodded. "I know ye did. Doona worry. 'Twas no trouble at all."

"If you have a moment more, I believe I've a bulb in my bedroom that is just about to go out. I can't reach it myself. It's been flickering on and off for days now."

"Sure, lass. Which bulb is it?"

Reaching into his bag for a spare bulb, he followed Marjorie into her bedroom, laughing silently to himself as he watched her try to decide which bulb looked like the most likely to be the first to go out.

When she finally pointed to one of the four in the ceiling fan, he turned off the lights, changed out the bulbs, and glanced down at his watch before she could create another task for him to complete.

It was nearly seven, and he desperately wanted to get back to enjoy one last meal with his friend.

"I'm worried I've a leak underneath by bathroom sink, as well."

Ross grinned and reached out to give Marjorie's arm a gentle squeeze. "I'm afraid I must go. I've plans that I canna miss. Why doona ye make a list for me—anything ye want me to look at or fix —and I'll come back in two days to see them right for ye?"

When he looked up to see Mrs. Jenkins smile, he knew he was free to leave.

"Yes, that will be just fine. Thank you. Let me grab the tin of cookies I made for you before you go."

Tool bag in hand, he waited by the door for the cookies he knew would be gone by this time tomorrow. It seemed to him that Mrs. Jenkins was determined to make him buy larger trousers.

When she returned, she eyed him suspiciously as she handed over the container of baked goods.

"Are your plans with someone special? A lady, perhaps?"

"She is a lady, but she is not special in the way ye are suggesting. She is only a friend. Now, I must go. Thank ye for the treats. Have a lovely evening and I shall see ye in a few days, aye?"

Mrs. Jenkins nodded and he stepped out into the hall to make his way back home.

<hr>

"*P*erfect timing. It's nearly ready."

Dropping his bag down inside the door to his apartment, he walked over to see if there was anything he could do to help.

"Sorry, lass. I truly intended to help ye more. Mrs. Jenkins never wants me to leave."

Sydney dismissed his apology with a wave of her hand. "Don't worry about it. It's better that you weren't here to help. People usually don't enjoy helping me when I'm in the kitchen. I can be a bit bossy. Or so I'm told."

Ross laughed. He didn't doubt that she was.

"I'm verra excited to finally taste yer cooking, lass."

"I hope it doesn't disappoint."

"'Tis not possible, I'm certain. May I at least set the table for us?"

Sydney nodded, and just as Ross reached for a couple of plates from the cabinet, the front door intercom buzzed.

"Sorry, lass. Give me just a moment. Someone is calling up from downstairs. It may be a delivery of some sort."

Leaving the plates on the shelf, he walked over to answer the incessant buzz. "Aye? Can I help ye?"

"Yes. I'm here to help my granddaughter, but it seems I've beaten her here from the store, and my cell phone has died so I can't call her to see how far away she is. I know where she leaves her spare key. Would you mind buzzing me in?"

Ross frowned and crossed his arms. All the building's tenants knew the rules. No one could enter without a key.

"Has yer granddaughter not given ye a key to her apartment?"

"No."

"I am sorry, but I canna buzz ye in. I've no way to verify ye are who ye say ye are. If yer granddaughter wants ye to have access to her home when she is not there, she should give ye a key."

Not waiting for the man to answer him, he left the intercom and went about the business of setting the table.

<hr>

*D*isappointed in myself for the amount of money I'd spent on apartment décor, I wobbled up to the front door of my building with my arms loaded down with bags.

"There you are. I was just about to give up on you and head home."

"Gramps?" I lowered my hands so the bags blocking my view of him cleared my line of sight. "Please tell me that we didn't have plans I forgot about?"

"No, not at all. It's just when you said you were going to buy some things for your new apartment, I thought it might be nice if I came over to help you set them up, but on the way over, the battery on my phone died, so I couldn't call you to see how far out you were."

"How long have you been sitting here? Was the manager not home? Did you try buzzing him to let you in?"

"That doesn't matter in the slightest. Now, hand me some of those bags and let's get inside."

"Gramps…" I frowned at him as I handed him a few of the bags.

"It wasn't all that long. An hour. Tops. I did call the manager, but he wouldn't buzz me in."

"What?" A sudden surge of anger coursed through me. "What do you mean he wouldn't let you in?"

Gramps reached for the keys I was struggling to manage and moved to unlock the door as he answered me.

"Now Allanah, don't go and get upset over nothing. The man had no way of knowing if what I said was true. I respect the fact that he wouldn't let me in. It means you live in a safe place."

I was shaking with anger by the time I stepped past my grandfather and into the building. Pushing the button of the elevator with my elbow, I turned to reassure him that it would never happen again.

"I'm so sorry, Gramps. I had a key made for you today. I'll give it to you as soon as we get upstairs."

I refrained from telling him what else I planned to do as we rode the elevator up to the tenth floor. I knew if I said anything, he would try to talk me out of it, and I was in no mood for that. I wanted to give the building manager a piece of my mind more than I'd ever wanted to do anything in my life.

As the elevator doors opened, I allowed my grandfather to step out first so he could unlock the door to the apartment. When he stepped inside, I brushed past him, dumped all of my bags onto the floor, and turned to leave.

"Make yourself at home, Gramps. I'll be right back."

I barely heard him call out to try to stop me as I allowed the door to slam shut between us.

On the same floor as my own, it was a short walk over to the manager's apartment.

The first time I knocked, there was no answer. The second time, I banged even more loudly as my frustration grew. I knew the man

I'd yet to meet was home. Gramps had spoken to him over the intercom.

Rather impatiently, I tapped my foot, counted to fifteen, then proceeded to bang on the door with the side of my fist as I called out to him.

"Look, I know you're there. You left my grandfather sitting out on the front steps of this place for God knows how long. Now open this door so I can talk to you."

I heard the moment he shifted inside and immediately began to rethink my knee-jerk decision to confront him. I had just moved in to this building. There was no reason on earth that the manager should've let anyone into the building on the sheer claim that they knew someone inside. I was just tired, sad, and overwhelmed, and when I'd found Gramps sitting outside, my desperate need to scream at someone boiled over. I had no real plan for what I would say after he opened the door, but it was far too late to back down now.

When the door did swing open, all I could do was stare.

Whatever I'd expected our manager to look like, it certainly wasn't the man standing before me. While there was no real reason for my assumption, I'd imagined someone much older, probably overweight, balding, and with Cheetos powder that lingered on a creepy, patchy mustache.

This man was none of those things. He couldn't have been but a handful of years older than me, and no one would ever describe him as overweight or balding. His head of hair was so beautiful it actually made me angry to look at him. And although he certainly wasn't smiling at me now, I had the nagging suspicion that if he did smile, that unfriendly look about him would disappear in an instant.

Stern eyes panned over my face, and he frowned before speaking. "Lass, unless ye've an emergency that canna wait until nine tomorrow morning, I am off duty for the night. Please respect my time and see yerself back to yer own apartment."

He reached to close the door in my face, but I quickly thrust a hand out to stop him and blocked the door with the palm of my hand.

"Oh…no way. Hang on just a second. You left my grandfather sitting out in the cold. Why didn't you buzz him in?"

The slightest hint of a smile teased at the corners of his mouth as he widened his eyes and lifted his chin to give me a nod.

"Ah. So the old man did really know someone in the building."

I screeched my reply to him. "Didn't he tell you that?"

The man crossed his arms and leaned into the doorway. "Aye, he did, but how was I to know if he was telling me the truth? I canna let strangers who have no right to access this building in just because they buzz my home and tell me to let them inside, lass. Surely ye can understand that. If ye wish for yer grandfather to have access to yer home, why doesna he have a key?"

"Because…" I was so angry that I was vibrating all over. "I just had one made for him today. I just moved in."

The asshole of a stranger didn't back down.

"Ah. So you're the lass whose moved into my old apartment. I'm sorry about yer grandfather, but I doona know him. If ye want yer grandfather to be able to come and go as he pleases, give him the key ye made for him today and know that ye are responsible for his behavior while he is here. Now, if ye'll excuse me, I am in the middle of enjoying my dinner and intend to return to it promptly. Goodnight, lass."

With that, he closed the door in my face as I stood shaking in the hallway.

CHAPTER 6

"Wow, she was not happy."

Ross sighed as he joined Sydney at the dinner table. He couldn't remember how long it had been since a woman had screamed at him that way.

"Did ye hear every word of that then?"

Sydney chuckled sympathetically. "Every word."

Ross raised his brows at her. "What is that look for, lass?"

"That's the friend that Caleb moved into Laurel's old apartment?"

He nodded. "Aye. Why?"

Sydney smiled as she raised another ravioli into her mouth. "Was she pretty?"

"Remarkably." He couldn't deny the truth of the fact. She was as beautiful a woman as he'd ever seen. With long dark hair, thick brows, and pretty green eyes, he found himself half glad she'd screamed at him. Otherwise, he wasn't sure he would've been able to gather his wits enough to speak to her at all.

"I wonder if that's who you're going out with tomorrow."

"No." The thought seemed impossible to him. "It canna be. She was terrible."

Sydney shook her head to disagree with him as Tink jumped up on his leg begging for a bite of food from the table.

"She wasn't terrible. I recognized the desperation in her tone. You weren't really the person she was mad at. You were just the person who got to bear the brunt of whatever was hurting her. She's Caleb's friend, yes? It goes to reason she was Beth's friend, as well. Good chance she's grieving just like you are."

If so, the woman's anger seemed entirely justified to him. For days, all he'd wanted to do was scream at someone.

"What makes you believe it might be her Caleb has set me up with?"

Sydney smiled as she unsuccessfully tried to sneak Tink a piece of dinner roll without him seeing. He frowned at her as she laughed.

"Think about it. She's pretty. Age appropriate. She just moved into the building, and she can clearly go toe-to-toe with you. If I was Caleb, that's exactly who I'd set you up with."

"Hmm…" He made the noise without realizing it as he crossed both arms across his chest. The possibility didn't upset him.

The date would go nowhere regardless. He was finished opening himself up to love, but at least she wouldn't be hard to look at over dinner.

On the day of the date I still couldn't believe I'd agreed to, I did my best to stay as busy as possible until I had to get ready. I spent the morning going over my patient schedule for Monday and continued to unpack and settle into my new home.

When it was finally time to prepare, dread and nerves began to settle in. I showered slowly as I tried to think of excuses I could use to get out of it. But every time I reached for my phone to call Caleb and cancel, I thought of Beth. I could sit through one dinner for her. And, if the stranger offered to pay, at least I would get a free meal at the best Indian restaurant in town.

A welcome distraction came when my phone rang and my sister's photo popped up on the screen.

"Georgie!" I smiled into the phone as I answered it. Georgie flitted about the world so often that phone calls were rare. "Where are you calling from?"

"New York, actually. About to board my plane to Boston."

"Boston? You're on your way here?"

"Yes, and I just got off the phone with Gramps. I called to see if I could stay with him, but he told me to give you a call. How long has it been since you moved out?"

I laughed, thinking of the freedom Gramps was so desperately clinging on to. Now that he had me out of his house, he wasn't about to let one of us move back in.

"Just a few days. What time are you supposed to land?"

"Five-thirty. Should be at your place by six-thirty at the latest, after I gather my luggage and everything."

"Oh, damn." I would already be on my date by then. "I won't be here when you arrive, but of course you're welcome to stay. Have the cab swing by Gramps' house so you can grab his spare key. Feel free to help yourself to anything in the kitchen. There's not much."

"Sure. No problem. Where are you going?"

"I…" I hesitated, dreading the squeal of delight I knew I was about to elicit from my older sister. "I have a date."

"A date! Then why are you sitting here talking to me? Go and get ready. You can tell me all about it tonight. Love you."

She hung up before I had a chance to respond.

If my suspicions were correct, there was going to be very little to tell her when I returned.

CHAPTER 7

With everything arranged by Caleb, I arrived at the Indian restaurant early. I wanted to get seated—preferably in a place where I could keep my eye on the door and watch for some man who looked as hesitant as I felt to enter.

When six-thirty came and went without anyone unaccompanied entering the restaurant, I began to worry that I'd been stood up. Just as I reached for my phone to text Caleb, I felt the light touch of someone's hand on my shoulder.

Dropping the phone back into my purse, I looked up to find my building manager standing beside my table.

"Sue?"

Thankful I was sitting, I groaned inwardly as my eyes grew wide. I'd not stopped screaming at this man long enough to tell him my name the last time we'd seen each other. If he knew it, there was only one reason.

"Please don't tell me you're Ross."

He nodded and removed his hand from my shoulder. "Aye. I'm sorry to disappoint ye. Would ye rather I leave?"

As the shock wore off, remorse flooded me, and I stood to attempt to correct my inexcusable rudeness.

"No. No, please stay." I extended my hand toward him. "Look. I owe you an apology anyway. It's been a tough week. Can we start again?"

Smiling, he took my hand. "Of course, lass. 'Tis a pleasure to meet ye."

Releasing my hand, he scooted into the opposite side of the booth as I returned to my seat. He looked even more handsome than he had the night before. He wore a light blue collared shirt that complimented his eyes, and the smell of his cologne was intoxicating. And God…how I loved his accent.

"Did you slip in through the back door or something? I didn't see you enter?"

"No. I've been here for some time. I was seated on the other side of the restaurant. 'Twas the waiter who suggested ye might be waiting for me over here."

"Did you know who I was?"

"No, though when I saw ye sitting here, I knew ye must be my date."

I nodded, as I glanced down at the menu to try and still my nerves. "Do you like Indian food?"

He shrugged. "In truth, I doona know. I've only had it once and 'twas a long time ago. I couldna tell ye a thing I ate."

"Would you like me to order a few dishes and some naan bread, and we can just share them?"

He nodded appreciatively. "Aye, thank ye."

As if called, the waiter suddenly made his way over to our table and I placed our order—garlic naan, Bhindi Masala, Butter Chicken, and some vegetables. As soon as the waiter left us, Ross continued our conversation.

"How do ye know Caleb? Were ye and Beth quite close?"

I didn't miss the sadness in his eyes as he mentioned Beth's name. The sudden emotion in his expression and the reminder that we had both lost a dear friend made me feel inexplicably close to him. All of the anger I'd felt toward him from our previous encounter vanished.

"Yes, we were. She and I were roommates in college, and we've stayed close ever since. I dated her brother for a long time."

He raised his brows in surprise and I knew what he was thinking.

"That was before Ethan came out. Back when we were all just doing our best to figure out how to express who we really were."

"Ah."

"And you? Caleb told me very little about you."

I listened in amazement as I realized what a small world we really live in. Not only did we share a connection from our friendship with Beth, but it had been Laurel who'd given Ross a place to live when he moved here from Scotland.

By the time he finished telling me about his friendship with Beth, our food arrived and we both dug right in. I delighted in watching him discover really excellent Indian food.

"So, you like it?"

"Aye. This willna be my last time here, though ye will have to remind me of everything ye ordered."

We visited and laughed about all kinds of things while we ate and for a long time after we were done. It wasn't until we looked up to notice the restaurant was nearly empty all around us that either of us moved to bring the date to an end.

"It seems we've nearly closed them down, lass. Shall we leave so they can close up for the night?"

I found myself reluctant to bring the evening to an end. Somehow, sharing stories about Beth had been cathartic and enjoyable rather than sad and gloomy. My heart felt lighter than it had in days as we made our way outside into the frigid air.

"I suppose we can walk back together since we're headed in the same direction."

He nodded and extended his arm. I gladly took it, not missing the firm muscles beneath his coat.

"Might I ask ye a question, lass?"

I looked over at him and smiled. "Of course."

"Is Sue yer real name?"

Surprised by the question, I stopped walking, forcing him to do the same as he faced me. "Why do you ask?"

He shrugged, a gesture I'd noticed he made frequently. It softened him a little. Made him look somehow less intimidating.

"I canna say for certain. 'Tis something about ye, I guess. Ye doona…ye doona look like a Sue to me."

I laughed. I'd never felt like one, either.

"Well no, actually. Sue isn't my real name, but everyone except my grandfather calls me that. My real name is Allanah."

He closed his eyes and smiled, and the gesture made my insides all swimmy.

"Allanah. The name suits ye far better. Would ye mind if I called ye that name instead?"

"Not at all."

He reached for my arm again and we continued our walk back to the building. When we reached the door, he turned to me. "I doona want ye to think that just because I know where ye live, I shall take advantage of it. Ye are under no obligation to see me again."

I'd already pulled out my phone. I wasn't worried about that in the least.

"What's your number? I'll text you mine."

He smiled and gave me a nod before giving me his number. "Perfect, lass. I shall call ye."

We made our way up the elevator together and once we stepped out onto our shared floor, he kissed my hand goodnight.

"I hope to see ye soon, Allanah."

Blushing, I let myself into my apartment, knowing I would be ambushed by Georgie the moment I stepped inside.

Sure enough, her arms came around me as she peppered me with questions.

"First of all, hello. Second, tell me everything. Was he cute? How was dinner? Was the conversation good?"

Every ounce of me had expected the date to go horribly. I was still so in shock that it hadn't, I scarcely knew where to begin.

"I honestly hate to admit it, but it was the most fun I've had with a man in years."

---

*W*hat had he done?

The question circled in his mind over and over as he collapsed down onto his couch.

That part of his life—the romantic part—was over. How could he have gone and let himself have such a good time?

His phone, not surprisingly, dinged inside his pocket.

Sydney.

He groaned as he read her text message. *"So...? Even though I'm exhausted from my flight, I haven't been able to sleep a wink. I HAVE to know how it went. Was it the girl from last night?"*

Quickly, he texted back. *"Aye. I believe I mayhap be in some trouble."*

Sydney only responded with one word—in all caps.

"WONDERFUL!"

CHAPTER 8

Georgie didn't let go of me for a long time, and I made no effort to push her away. It was good to feel her arms around me, good to know that even though we rarely saw each other, I did actually have family that existed in the world outside of Gramps.

Four years older than me, Georgie had always been too far ahead of me in everything for us to be all that close growing up. Just as I entered high school, she left for college. When I moved into my college dorm, she was packing up her bag to begin her worldwide travels.

We got along splendidly, but age and distance meant that we didn't visit nearly as much as I would like. When I thought back on my childhood, it always seemed strange to me that Gramps and I were the ones who'd remained in Boston. With my parents now enjoying their retirement in Washington State and Georgie in a different place almost every week, I often forgot just how isolated I was from those I loved the most until I had the opportunity to see them.

When Georgie finally pulled away from me, I looked her up and down and frowned. A year had passed since I'd last seen her. She looked different—and not in a good way. Her skin was pale, her eyes tired. She'd put on a few pounds. More than anything, she just didn't look like the unusually chipper Georgie I'd always known.

"What's going on with you? Are you feeling ill?"

Georgie shook her head. "No. Just exhausted, and if I'm honest, scared. I don't regret a minute of the last ten years, but I'm over it, sis. I'm done with the wandering. I want to settle down and make a home for myself somewhere, but I don't even know how to begin."

I looked at her sadly and reached to pull her into my arms once more, then walked her over to the couch on the other side of the room.

Somehow, after traveling more miles than I could count, my older sister had finally sewn all her wild oats and was ready to create some sense of normalcy for herself. I'm sure it was scary. Luckily for her, I'd pretty much skipped any wild oat sewing and had settled down into adulthood earlier than I probably should have. By now, I was a pro.

"It's all going to be okay. You may not know where to begin, but I do. For now, you're going to stay right here with me. Even though it's filled with packed boxes, I do have a spare bedroom, and it's yours for as long as you need it."

She pulled away from me and studied my expression as if trying to see if I'd made the offer out of obligation. I hurried to reassure her that that wasn't it.

"I want you to stay here, Georgie. I've missed you. I miss..." It surprised me to feel a lump rise up in my throat. "I miss having family around."

"I don't have any way to help you pay rent right now."

Georgie and I were technically half-sisters. While Georgie and I shared a mother, I'd not been lucky enough to share a gene pool with Georgie's absolutely loaded father who'd turned over a rather generous trust fund to her the moment she graduated college.

Georgie's admission that she couldn't help with rent meant that her decision to finally 'settle down' as she'd put it, probably had more to do with the fact that she'd finally spent all her money than any sheer desire to end her years-long adventure. Although, as I looked into her tired eyes, I had to admit to myself that it was probably a little of both.

"That's okay. It's not as if I was planning on having a roommate anyway. I'd be so happy to have you here. Just take some time to figure out what's next for you. Don't worry about rent."

She looked at me skeptically. "Are you sure? I have no idea what I really want to do with my life. My degree is useless."

That much was definitely true. Having a degree in fashion design and no eye for fashion wasn't going to do her a whole lot of good.

"Well, what are you good at?"

She shrugged. "I don't know, Sue. But I know that I'm not going to be able to just do nothing for very long. I'll start looking for a job soon. In the meantime, I'll clean your apartment, do your laundry, and help with meals to pull my weight. I know your weekdays are swamped with patients."

It had taken me a while after starting my physical therapy practice to get the hang of things—a long while—but after several years of trial and error, I'd nailed down a routine that somehow enabled me to balance work, groceries, and home care. I didn't need Georgie to clean my apartment. In fact, the very suggestion stressed me out. My routine was set. I was happy to have her live here, but it was just fine with me if she didn't mess that up.

As I was about to tell her just now much I *didn't* need her to clean my apartment, an idea popped into my head.

I didn't need her to clean for me, but I did know someone who was going to be in need of as much help as he could get once his world stopped spinning, and now that the funeral was over, that was bound to happen soon. It would only be a week or so before the casserole deliveries would slow, all the extended family would go home, and Caleb would be left to deal with more than he could handle. Having a clean house wouldn't solve everything, but it might at least take one thing off his plate.

"I think I've got my place covered, but would you be open to cleaning for someone else?"

She stared at me, and I could see as her expression changed that she'd realized where I was going. Gramps must've told her about Beth.

She reached out and gathered my hands in hers as she gently squeezed them.

"I'm so sorry about Beth, Sue. I should've said that the moment you walked in, but I just didn't want to upset you right after your date. It's hard, you know? You want people to know you care, but you don't want to say something that causes them to fall apart all over again if they've just gathered themselves up."

I nodded, swallowing another lump in my throat as I tried not to cry. "I know. It's okay."

Georgie continued. "I only met her that one time she spent Thanksgiving with us, but she was so incredibly sweet. And yes, if you're talking about me cleaning her home, I think that's a great idea."

"Great. I'll call Caleb later tonight and see if we can go visit with him sometime over the next few days. If he agrees—which I can't see any reason why he wouldn't—I'll pay you for it."

Standing, I grinned at her and bobbed my head toward the guest bedroom. "Now, let's go see what sort of progress we can make on that disaster of a room before it gets too late."

I didn't imagine we would make much. If my suspicions were correct, we'd spend more time talking than unboxing, and Georgie would be bunking with me, at least for tonight.

The morning after his date with Allanah, Ross woke up horny and irritated. He'd forgotten how much more pleasurable it was to be aroused by an interaction with an actual woman than the fantasies of his own mind. It wouldn't do. It wasn't good for him to start wanting again. His days of sharing his life with another had been put to rest with his marriage to Silva.

Knowing it was time for him to start his day, he moved to the bathroom and turned on the shower to allow the water to heat up. It was one of the many modern-day marvels that never ceased to amaze him—that one could create hot running water at will.

Just as steam began to escape from the top and sides of the shower curtain, his phone buzzed. Seeing that it was Caleb, he reached into the shower one more time to turn off the spray of water. He was undoubtedly calling to see how his date with Allanah had gone.

"Good morning to ye, Caleb."

Ross could hear Maggie screaming in the background as soon as he answered the phone. Caleb sounded stressed and tired as he answered him.

"I know I've been asking a whole lot of favors from you lately, Ross, but do you think I could ask one more?"

"O'course ye can. I want to help ye in any way I can. What do ye need?"

Walking across his apartment and over to his desk while he waited for Caleb to answer him, Ross glanced down at his calendar. It was Monday. For months now, Mondays meant a cooking lesson with Beth at their house followed by dinner with her family. It would be the first Monday without her. He knew it wasn't why Caleb had called him, but he made a mental note to tell Caleb his idea before letting him off the phone.

"Do you think you could walk Hannah to school on Tuesdays and Thursdays starting this week? And keep Maggie with you and watch her for maybe an hour after you drop Hannah off? I'm starting marathon training two days a week, and my trainer insists we do it early."

That was the last thing Ross could possibly imagine him asking. Him, take care of children? He didn't know the first thing about children. Sure, he'd been around Hannah and Maggie lots over the past year, but they'd never been left in his care.

He balked at the question. "Me? Do ye think...well, do ye think that best, Caleb? I doona know much about children, most especially babes."

Caleb interrupted him before he could continue. "There's no one else. I can't stand for my family to stay here another day. I'm getting them out of my house by tonight if it's the last thing I do, and all of my other friends have to be to work early. Your job is flexible. Besides, both of the girls adore you."

That pleased him. He adored them as well—even if they did scare him to death. Another question formed in his mind.

"Are ye sure wee Hannah is ready to return to school? Do ye not think 'twill be hard for her?"

There was a break in the conversation as Ross listened to Caleb hush and soothe Maggie. Slowly, the small child's wailing quieted.

"Oh, thank God. She's been crying since five this morning. I think she's picking up on the energy of everyone else in this house. As for Hannah, it wasn't my idea that she go back so soon. She wants to. She told me herself. And yes, I'm sure it will be hard for her, but it's hard just sitting around here, too. Everything is going to be hard for all of us for quite a long time, I expect. Will you do it?"

Ross couldn't argue with that. Of course, he couldn't say no. "Aye. I shall."

He thought he heard Caleb exhale in relief.

"Good. Now that I've got Maggie calmed for the moment, I'm going to go hint, not-so-subtly, to my mother and brother-in-law that it's time for them to return home. Thank you, Ross. I'll see you Thursday morning. If you can be here by seven, that would be great. That way I can get Maggie settled with you while I help Hannah get ready for school."

Ross hurried to tell Caleb his plan before he got off the phone.

"Aye, but ye will see me tonight, as well. 'Tis Monday, and I doona think Beth would like it if we stopped having our weekly dinners. I'll cook for ye and Hannah tonight. Surely Beth taught me enough that I can prepare one meal on my own."

Caleb sounded unsure as he answered him. "You really don't have to do that."

"I want to. And now, ye must get the rest of yer family gone, for I doona know if I wish to cook and clean for that many people."

"Deal. I'll see you tonight. You can tell me all about your date then."

Damn. Ross thought to himself, as he hung up the phone. He'd started to think that Caleb had forgotten all about it.

Of course, he wasn't so lucky.

$\mathscr{I}$t was wrong—he knew that much—but Ross had no idea how to go about fixing it. At least Caleb was busy with both girls. That way he wasn't in here to watch his total failure.

Frustrated at the coagulated sauce in front of him, he read through the recipe once more and threw up his hands in frustration. He'd followed it exactly. Still, it hadn't turned out. All of Beth's determination to make him a self-sufficient cook had been for naught.

Glancing at the clock, he did the calculations in his head. He'd started dinner early. Most likely, Sydney would still be awake in Scotland.

Silently admitting that he needed professional help, he pulled his phone from his pocket and tapped on the screen so that it would video-call Sydney. He could've wept with relief when she picked up after the second ring.

"Hey. What's up?"

Happy to see that she didn't appear to have just been awakened, he flipped the screen around so that the camera pointed into the pot of ruined pasta sauce.

"I followed the recipe, and still it has turned to complete rubbish. Can ye tell what I've done?"

"Ah. Yeah. That's um…That's not great."

He flipped the phone back around so that he could see Sydney's face. "Is it truly that bad, lass?"

Sydney nodded and laughed. "Yes. I'm not sure what you were trying to make, but you've curdled the sauce. You're going to have to start over."

As if she'd been able to smell his failure, Hannah walked into the kitchen at that precise moment, crawled onto one of the barstools around the kitchen island where the stove was, and peered into the pot. She looked up at him and crinkled her nose.

"I'm not sure it's supposed to look like that, Uncle Ross."

Knowing that Sydney would've heard the young girl and understood that she was being placed on hold, he set his phone down on the counter long enough to answer her.

"Aye. Ye are certainly right about that." He quickly pointed to the pan of frozen chicken strips he'd just heated for her. "Not to worry though, lass. Yer wretched chicken and absolutely terrible boxed cheesy pasta turned out just fine and are ready for ye to eat."

She smiled at him, and it made something inside Ross' chest ache. She was still so small, but when the young girl smiled, he could tell that she was going to look just like Beth when she was older.

"Is it the shaped macaroni and cheese?"

"Aye."

"Then, I promise you, it's not horrible."

He laughed and reached up in the cabinet for the young girl's favorite plate and bowl. He'd watched Beth reach for it enough times to know exactly where it was.

"I am pleased ye think so, Hannah, but I beg to differ with ye. Regardless, ye can go ahead and eat if ye are hungry. 'Twill be some time before I'm finished cooking for me and yer Da. I doona think he will mind."

She nodded enthusiastically. "Yes, please."

Quickly making her a plate, he handed it to her and waited until she headed toward the dining room with her food before returning to Sydney. The moment he lifted the phone to his face, Sydney spoke.

"Well, she sounds adorable. How's she doing?"

"The lass seems okay today, though her Da said that she cried herself to sleep last night. Poor thing. My heart is broken for her."

Sydney nodded sympathetically. "Mine too. Okay, let's see what we can do to salvage your dinner. What exactly is it that you're trying to make?"

"Vodka pasta. I ordered it from an Italian restaurant a few nights ago and quite liked it."

Sydney crinkled her nose at him and laughed once more. "Yeah, it's not supposed to look like that. Can you show me the recipe?"

Obeying her, he picked up the piece of paper and held it in front of the camera while he waited for her to read over it.

"This says to use half-and-half, and I think that was probably your problem. It curdles too easily when you mix it with heat. Look in the fridge and see if they have any heavy cream instead."

Thankfully, they did.

"Aye. They do."

"Not expired?"

He looked over the carton and smiled. "No."

"Good. Dump that sauce out and start again. Rather than half-and-half, use the cream. It'll substitute just fine, and it will be less likely to curdle. You can do it. I have faith in you."

Thanking her, he bid her farewell and moved to discard the ruined batch of sauce.

At least someone had faith in him. He had none whatsoever in himself.

*M*uch later than he originally intended, Ross served up a new batch of pasta for his friend.

"I'm sorry it took me so long."

Caleb dismissed him with a shake of his head. "Don't worry about it. It actually turned out for the best. It gave me time to get the girls down, which means I can enjoy my meal without trying so hard. It's exhausting trying to be strong for them."

Ross had no doubt of it. Caleb's strength over the past week astonished him.

"What do ye think of it?"

Ross watched nervously as Caleb went in for his first bite. When he smiled, Ross relaxed.

"It's delicious. And now that it's ready, you can't put it off anymore. How did your date go?"

Ross could see no reason to lie to him, even if he had no plans to ever see Allanah again.

"I enjoyed every minute. She is lovely."

Caleb's expression appeared way too delighted. Then just as quickly, so sad that it hurt Ross to look at him.

"Great. Then you two can go out again tomorrow night. There's a limo company in town that's doing Christmas light tours, and I booked Beth and me a private one a few weeks ago. I'd forgotten all about it until I got the reminder email from the tour company this morning. I broke down for the better part of the morning when I read it. Beth had really been looking forward to it."

Brushing past the fact that he knew he would feel odd going on a date intended for Beth and Caleb, Ross knew he would have to come clean about what he'd decided.

"That's a kind offer, Caleb, but I'll not be seeing the lass again."

"What? Why not?"

He shrugged. It wasn't something he could easily explain to anyone. "I dinna expect the date to go well, so I dinna think 'twould be a problem, but I simply doona wish to date."

Ross could tell by Caleb's confused expression that he was about to pry further, but Ross was momentarily saved by the sound of Caleb's phone ringing from across the room.

Ross continued eating as Caleb got up from the table to grab his phone.

"Speak of the devil. It's Sue."

Ross cringed at the name. How anyone thought the name suited her baffled him.

"Doona say anything, Caleb."

"Yeah." Caleb laughed as he carried the ringing phone back over to the table. "Do you really think I'm going to listen to that?"

Dread settled into Ross' stomach as Caleb answer the phone.

"Hey, Sue."

Closing his eyes, Ross ran a hand through his hair as his nerves doubled. Only able to hear Caleb's end of the conversation, he listened in.

"Oh, really? Look, the house is already starting to fall into disarray. You don't even need to bring her here for an interview; I'll happily let her clean whatever she wants to. Thank you, Sue. I appreciate the thoughtfulness more than you know."

Silence filled the room, and Caleb listened to whatever Allanah was saying. Eventually, when Caleb spoke again, Ross knew he was in trouble.

"That sounds great. Hey, listen. Ross is here with me right now, and he was just telling me how much he enjoyed your date. He wants to talk to you, actually. I think he has a pretty cool idea about something you two could do tomorrow. Do you mind if I hand him the phone?"

His friend's grief was the only thing that kept Ross from sending something hard and heavy flying toward Caleb's head in that moment. Knowing he was now trapped into asking Allanah out on another date, Ross took the phone from Caleb's hand.

"Good evening, lass. How are ye?"

The sound of her voice when she answered him was warm. He could envision her smiling on the other end of the call.

"I'm well. I didn't mean to interrupt you two. I was just reaching out to Caleb about a possible job for my sister."

"Ah." He could think of no reason to delay the inevitable. "Are ye free tomorrow night, Allanah? Would ye like to accompany me on a Christmas light tour?"

"I'd love to."

"Perfect. I'll text ye with the details. I'm handing the phone back to Caleb now."

Furious, he watched as Caleb tried to keep from laughing.

"That sounds great, Sue. I'll be here at two o'clock tomorrow afternoon to meet your sister. Thanks again."

The moment Caleb hung up the phone, he burst out laughing.

"Get that look off your face, Ross. Trust me. You'll thank me for this later."

While a lovely idea in theory, the idea of looking at Christmas lights from the heavily-tinted windows of a limo just didn't work. Fifteen minutes into our two-hour ride, we still could see nothing out the windows.

"Do you think we're on a street with lots of lights, right now?"

Ross, who I could see was growing angrier by the second, nodded as he reached to roll down the window to his left.

"Aye. Look."

Sure enough, the street we were on was draped in lights, with nearly every house more decorated than the last. The only way we could see anything that was worth looking at was by keeping that one window down, which we couldn't do; the freezing snow and sleet were coming down too hard to keep the window cracked for more than a second.

I laughed and leaned back into my seat. "It's really a big con, isn't it?"

Rolling up the window, Ross turned to look at me. "Aye, and the company that offers these tours know it. 'Tis infuriating."

I pointed to the speaker above my head. "And do you think they have the Christmas music on so loudly so they can't hear us bitching about it throughout the whole tour?"

His eye widened as if the thought hadn't occurred to him. "Aye."

Sensing Ross' anger, I attempted to salvage the date with a little distraction. I patted the seat next to me so he would move closer as I spoke to him. "Let's just forget about what we're supposed to be seeing, and just get to know one another a little better."

Ross took a big, long breath, smiled at me, and scooted closer.

"Aye. Ye are right. Tell me what ye do, lass. We spent so much time speaking of Beth during our first date, we truly learned little about each other."

"I'm a physical therapist, and I specialize in helping people who have been injured due to accidents or illnesses. I own my own practice."

"Oh, that's right. I'd forgotten Caleb mentioned yer profession to me. From what he says, ye're the best in Boston."

I cringed. I hated talking about myself, especially my work. While I was proud of what I did, the work drained me. Giving my all to patients every day always left me exhausted when I closed up to go home. It had become increasingly important over recent years to really separate my work and home life. Real breaks from my work allowed me to be more fully present when I was with my patients.

Not that my work didn't sometimes seep into my personal life. I had several patients who, once discharged from being my patient, had become cherished friends.

"And what about you? I know you manage the building now, but what did you do before? And what brought you to the States because, if I'm guessing correctly, you're from Scotland, yes?"

He hesitated and ran a hand through his thick, dark hair, and I couldn't help but wonder what about my question made him uncomfortable. Was it my question about his past work history or the mention of his homeland? Regardless, based on the guarded expression in his gaze, I didn't think he was about to give me enough information to figure it out.

"Aye, Scotland. I've done many things, none of them worth speaking about."

"Hm." I made the noise as I narrowed my eyes at him, hoping he would open up a little more if I let the silence between us sit for a moment. He didn't, and knowing that he didn't really owe me any information this early on, I decided to let it pass.

"Your accent is incredible, by the way. I love it."

He laughed and shook his head. "Ye wouldna have thought so if ye'd met me when I first came to the States. My…" He paused, and my suspicion that he was trying to hide something rose again. "Those that knew me then often said they could barely understand me. I've worked to lessen it, just a bit."

"Oh, don't do that." I protested. "It's quite sexy." I blushed, hardly believing my admission. I glanced at the half-empty glass of champagne sitting next to me. I hadn't had nearly enough to blame my loose lips on that. I just felt comfortable around him. Too comfortable, really, especially considering how guarded he seemed to be.

"Thank ye for that. Doona worry, I'm certain that no amount of work will change my accent from what 'tis today. I fear I am stuck with what I have now."

Needing to recover from my embarrassment, I continued to try to draw something more out of him. "What about your family? Do any of them live here?"

He gave his head one small shake. "No. I doona have much family left. My Da died when I was verra young. I have no siblings, and my mother…" He paused and glanced away. That small gesture was enough to let me know that this too was a painful subject for him. Ross—it shocked me to realize that I didn't actually know his last name—was turning out to be far more complicated than he first seemed.

"You don't have to tell me about anything you don't want to."

He turned back to me and gave me a sad smile. "There is no reason for me not to tell ye, lass. 'Tis only that thinking of her makes me rather sad. I havena seen her in years. She had me later in life, and now she has—I believe the term for it now is Alzheimer's. She doesna know me anymore, and 'twould only upset her to see me. I write often, and she is well cared for. She is the only reason I would ever return to Scotland. Since 'twould do neither of us any good for me to see her, I shall likely only return to see her buried."

That was a lot to unpack. If his mother was the only thing that would ever bring him back to the country he grew up in, there was clearly more hurt lying beneath the surface. And what on earth did he mean by, *the term for it now is Alzheimer's?* That made him sound like he'd been around way before the disease had a label. I didn't imagine he was that many years older than me. But there was only one response that could be deemed appropriate to what he'd just shared with me, and it wasn't more questions.

"I'm so sorry, Ross."

He shook his head and gave me his signature shrug. "'Tis life. We all carry wounds. Now...I believe 'tis my duty to discuss a way for me to make amends to ye for this rather abysmal date. Will ye allow me to think up another Christmas activity for us to do tomorrow?"

It delighted me that before this date was already over he was thinking about the next. Despite the fact that I'd gone into our first date certain it would be a bust, I was now just as certain that I wanted to spend more time with my new acquaintance.

"Sure. Although, if this snow keeps up, we're not going to be able to leave the building tomorrow. Maybe we should do something at one of our places? Do you have a favorite Christmas movie?"

He shrugged again. Why was his shrug so freaking sexy?

"I couldna say. I havena seen verra many."

"Have you seen *It's A Wonderful Life?*"

He shook his head and my eyes widened in horror. What sort of sad, senseless world had this man grown up in?

"Then, it's decided. That is a film you cannot go one day longer without seeing. I would invite you over to my place, but my sister has just moved in and the place is a disaster. I'm still not fully unpacked."

"No worries, lass. Ye can come over to my apartment, and I shall cook ye dinner. All ye need to bring is yerself and this film ye seem so keen on me seeing."

"Done."

Approximately one hour later, the driver pulled up in front of our apartment building. Ross stepped out first and immediately gave the poor guy a piece of his mind.

"Do ye have the name of yer boss, sir? For I've need to contact him straight away. While yer driving was satisfactory, this wee tour is a scam, and ye all well know it. Ye should be ashamed of yerself."

The college-aged kid sighed and reached into the front of his coat to pull out a business card. Clearly it wasn't the first time he'd had to deal with unhappy customers.

"Look, dude. I'm just trying to earn a little extra money while I'm home during Christmas break. I'm sorry you didn't have a good time."

Ross took the card from the young man, and without saying another word, reached his hand inside the car to help me out into the snow.

He leaned in to whisper into my ear as I stood up out of the car. The warmth of his breath caused shivers to rush down my spine.

"Let's get ye inside before I decide to toss this fool into that pile of fresh snow over yonder."

Laughing, we ran hand-in-hand to the door, not stopping until we were safely inside and stomping off the excess snow from our boots inside the doorway.

Ross reached to call the elevator while I continued to stomp around on the mat. The doors to the lift opened quickly, and he held them open for me as I hurried inside. The moment the doors closed, he pulled me close.

"May I kiss ye, lass?"

I nodded, but then my brain seized up with nerves, which immediately caused me to grow nauseous. I didn't know if it was because it had been so long since my last kiss, or if the proximity of him was just too much for me to bear in that moment, but I panicked as his lips came toward me and threw my head to the left so that his lips landed hard on my cheek.

Mortified, I stumbled out of the doors the moment they opened on our floor and mumbled a goodbye to him over my shoulder.

"Thanks for a great time. I'll see you tomorrow."

I wasn't for sure, but I thought I heard him laughing as I all but ran away from him.

I barely made it to my bathroom toilet before I vomited up my champagne.

---

*R*oss stood at the end of the hallway, allowing Allanah time to make her way inside her apartment. His laughter at the awkward moment quickly grew to frustration as he made his way down the hall.

A date that should've gone terribly had been even better than the first. He'd even set himself up for another. And he couldn't blame that date on Caleb's meddling.

The moment his key made contact with the lock, he could hear Tink begin to lose her mind with excitement. Opening the door, he quickly reached for her leash and bent down to scoop up the wee pup that was more fur than body.

The squirmy dog licked his face up and down as he glanced around his apartment for any puddles of pee. Unable to help himself, he snuggled the dog close and kissed the side of her face.

"Thank ye, lassie, for going along with the housebreaking so splendidly. Ye truly are a bright pup. I'll give ye that."

Hooking the leash to her collar, he made his way back to the elevator to take Tink outside before the storm got even worse.

The elevator still smelled like Allanah as he and Tink stepped inside. It sent memories of her warm cheek hitting his lips as he moved in to kiss her, and he laughed once more.

It had been without a doubt, the worst kiss of his life.

Why then, did he suspect that it just might end up being the one that he cherished the most?

CHAPTER 11

*A*t a quarter to six the next evening, I looked myself over in the mirror and did my best to swallow my rising nausea.

"Sue, I think you need to take a breath. Your shoulders are pulled up far too close to your ears. You're tense." She pushed herself up from the floor where she sat helping me unbox stuff and moved over to grab my shoulders as she massaged them gently. "Why do you seem so much more nervous today than you did yesterday?"

Taking her suggestion, I drew in a shaky breath and tried to relax.

"I don't know. I think it's because despite my best efforts not to, I quite like him. And I've gotten in my head about kissing him. If I repeat last night's fiasco, I'm done for; I know it."

She raised her brows at me, and I had the sudden urge to hug her, though I was kept from doing so by the tight grip she had on me. Perhaps it was because I was missing Beth and just needed the comfort of family around me, but time and time again over the past few days, I would look at my sister and be overcome by the realization that I'd missed her far more than I'd let myself feel. I

81

hoped that all she said was true, and that finally, she was here for good.

She grimaced, which did nothing to help my nerves.

"Yeah, well, giving him your cheek, and then running off to vomit isn't great. But you've got to shake it off."

"I'm going to do my best."

I pulled away from her and moved over to the box labeled 'TV cabinet,' and began to rummage through it for my copy of *It's a Wonderful Life.*

"Georgie, can you go into the kitchen and grab the bottle of wine that's sitting on the counter?"

It didn't take me long to find my copy of the film. By the time I turned around, Georgie was standing beside me with the bottle I planned to take over to Ross' apartment with me.

"Okay. I guess it's time for me to go."

Georgie nodded. "Have fun. And remember, don't panic. It's just a kiss."

That was easy for her to say. She'd never laid eyes on Ross. She had no idea how intimidating his good looks were.

"Flip the camera around and show me the apartment. The food's set. Now we need to make sure you aren't about to frighten her off by inviting her over to a disaster of an apartment."

Ross rolled his eyes and did as Sydney bid.

"I did clean, lass. I'm not a fool."

"I didn't say you were, but you are a guy, and sometimes things that you would never think of will be glaringly obvious to a woman."

He panned the length of his living room with the camera so Sydney could look things over.

"Do ye approve?"

"I'm impressed. Now, turn me back around so I can tell you goodbye."

Laughing, he flipped the camera back to his face.

"Ye are the bossiest lass I've ever known."

Sydney shrugged. "Probably true. Okay, I better let you go so you can take Tink outside before she gets here. That way maybe she will be good for the duration of your date. Text me tomorrow?"

He nodded. "O'course. Goodnight."

As if Tink had understood every word Sydney had just said to him, the pup jumped up on his leg in anticipation of being led out into the snow.

"Alright, alright, lass. But ye canna roll around in the snow as ye usually do, and we canna stay out verra long. 'Tis nearly a blizzard outside. I doona want ye freezing to death."

Tink yipped in response. Reaching for the dog's leash, he headed to the front door.

He and Tink made it just past Allanah's door before she stepped out into the hallway. He called out to her to get her attention, and she turned and smiled at him. It took only a second for Tink to steal the show as her attention shifted toward the pup.

"And who is this?"

She crouched down in the hall as the pup bounded toward her.

"Her name is Tink. 'Twas a trick of Beth's."

Allanah looked up at him as she continued to pet Tink's head.

"A trick?"

"Aye. She asked me to watch the pup. She said 'twas a gift for the girls, though 'twas truly just for me."

Allanah laughed, and Ross loved the sound of it.

"That's the best sort of trick I can think of. Sounds like you came out on the winning end."

"Mayhap so. I dinna think so at first, though I canna deny that the wee beastie is growing on me." He paused and bobbed his head toward his apartment. "Go ahead and make yerself at home, lass. I'll just be a moment. I need to take Tink out before it gets too dark."

Giving Tink one last pat, Allanah stood and moved to the side so he could pass her.

"Oh no, it's okay. Let me just set this inside really fast, and I'll go with you."

He frowned at her. "Are ye sure?"

"Yeah. Absolutely."

It took no time for her to set her wine and movie inside his apartment. Together, the three of them made their way to the elevator. As the door opened and they stepped inside, he couldn't help but wonder if she was also thinking about their kiss the night before. By the slight red tint to her cheeks, he imagined that she probably was.

* * *

*D*inner was incredible—rigatoni with vodka sauce accompanied by a salad and some of the best garlic bread I'd ever had in my life. By the time we sat down to watch the movie, I was full, happy, and—for the moment—no longer nauseous.

"You're a very good cook, Ross."

He smiled and shook his head as I dug in for another bite.

"Doona be fooled, lass. 'Tis the only thing I can properly make on my own, and 'tis only because I've had plenty of practice making it this past week."

"Ah. That explains your lack of appetite."

He laughed. "Aye, though I canna tell ye how pleased I am that ye enjoyed it." He gave the fire one last poke and faced me. "Shall we watch it?"

"Yes, I think we should. You'll love it."

He shrugged—his favorite gesture—and moved to flip off the lights for the movie.

"We shall see."

I braced for the inevitable awkwardness. That part of the earliest stages of dating when you sit in a darkened room with someone for the first time, and neither party knows whether to reach for the other's hand or how close you should sit. It was a ritualistic, fumbly half-hour that I knew well, which was part of the reason it astonished me when Ross reached for me the moment he sat down on the couch, shattering my expectation that he would be like all the others.

"Come here, lass. The only reason I would ever wish to sit through a Christmas movie is to hold someone as beautiful as ye close to me."

You'd think I would be too old to swoon at a line like that, but my insides ran hot as the compliment swept through me. As eager to be inside his arms as he was to get me there, I leaned against him, my head resting on the front of his chest as he wrapped his arms around my shoulders.

"Do you not like Christmas?"

I felt him shrug behind me.

"There was a time when I did."

"But not anymore?"

There was a small gap before he answered me, and I knew that I wasn't going to get an explanation.

"Mayhap this year will be different."

Without another word, he pressed play on the remote. All through the movie, he held me close as he trailed his fingertips up and down the length of my arms while Tink slept in my lap.

Far too much time had passed since I'd been held in this way, and I reveled in it. When the movie finally came to an end, I glanced up at him to see tears in the corners of his eyes.

"You did like it, didn't you?"

He nodded. "Aye, lass, and I liked the company even more."

I saw him glance at my lips and my heart began to pound against my ribs in the familiar, frantic panic of the night before.

In an effort not to repeat my previous freak-out, I sought to go in for the kiss first, but I moved too quickly, and instead, basically head-butted him so hard we both cried out in pain.

He recovered quickly, laughing as I reared back in horror.

"Come here, Allanah. Let's try that again."

He moved to reach for me, but I bolted away from him as my stomach surged, and I pushed myself off the couch as I hurried to the door.

"Another time, perhaps. I better be going. Thanks for a lovely evening. Goodnight, Ross."

As soon as I closed the door to his apartment, I full-on sprinted back to my own. Shoving my keys into the door as quickly as possible, I unlocked the bolt, hurried inside and collapsed against the door as Georgie looked at me from the living room couch in confusion.

"Do I need to grab a trash can?"

I nodded. "It's official. I'll never hear from him again."

---

*H*ow was it that a hard whack to the head had given him such an unbearable erection? This second attempt at a kiss had been even more disastrous than their first, but somehow it had him even more worked up.

God, she'd felt so good in his arms. She was soft, and sweet, and too likable to be someone he only shared one night with.

Allanah was the sort of woman any man would want in his life, which made everything about the situation even worse.

He would only hurt her if things continued. She wasn't the sort of woman who might be interested in anything casual. If she were, the thought of a single kiss wouldn't make her so nervous. She was the sort of woman who would always want more. And he had nothing more to give.

Her quick retreat from his apartment would make it easy for him to let things just fizzle out naturally. Allanah would surely be busy with family for Christmas. He would simply keep his distance. Over time, she would stop expecting him to call her again.

He'd done what Caleb had asked him to. He'd gone out with the lass for Beth's sake not only once, but three times.

That was enough. It would have to be.

hree Months Later

"Okay, Danny. You did great today. I truly believe you'll be walking without the walker within the next few weeks."

The old man smiled as I heard the doors to our right swing open. His wife, on time as usual, was here to pick him up. Her entry was followed quickly by Gramps, who was here to take me to dinner.

I watched as he looked at me still standing near my patient, and he gave me a quick wink before taking a seat near the door to wait on me.

"Same time Monday, yes?"

I nodded, and turned to speak to Danny's wife, Charla. "I can tell that you're making him work at home. I appreciate it. He's healing more quickly than some patients half his age."

She beamed with pride as she looped her arm with her husband's. "He puts up a fight, but I always win. He's going to be ready to go on vacation with our grandkids by summer if it's the last thing I do."

I laughed as I walked with them to the door. "It won't be the last thing either of you do, and we will make sure he's ready to keep up with the grandkids by then."

They both thanked me, and I watched them make it safely to their car through the window before turning to address Gramps.

"Thanks for waiting. Is Georgie meeting us there?"

"No. She bailed. Said she already had plans. Looks like it's just you and me."

"Hmm." I frowned as I thought about Georgie. Not that I minded it just being the two of us for dinner. It was only that Georgie seemed to have plans with alarming frequency lately, and I could never get her to share what those plans were. I could only assume that years of being away and having no one to report to had made her dead set on maintaining her privacy.

Gramps nodded as if he read my thoughts. "I know. She's a bit of a mystery, isn't she? If you question her too much, she just pulls away more." Gramps gave both of his thighs a quick pat before pushing himself up from his seat and dismissing the subject all together. "So...how does deli food sound? I'm craving a pastrami on rye."

"Sounds great. You can just drop me off here before you head home."

There was a fantastic deli place close to my office. Even though it was now March, winter still held a tight grip on Boston, and I wasn't about to have Gramps walking in below-freezing weather.

The moment I made it to Gramps' car and opened the passenger door, I was met by the overwhelming smell of floral perfume.

"Good God, Gramps. Maybe you should tell Gladys to take it easy on the perfume. I'm not sure you'll ever get that smell out of your car."

Gramps scrunched up his nose in agreement as he reached to

buckle his belt. "If that was Gladys' perfume, I would gladly tell her. It isn't. It's her mother's."

I still hadn't actually met Gladys. Although her name made me believe that she was most likely close to my grandfather's age, the mention of Gladys' mother brought horrifying images to mind of Gramps dating someone closer to my mother's age.

"Gramps, just how old is Gladys exactly?"

Please be at least seventy. Please be at least seventy. I played the mantra in my mind like a prayer as I awaited his response.

He laughed as he turned on the engine. "Relax, Allanah. She's eighty-five."

My eyes widened in response as I tried to calculate the youngest possible age for Gladys' mother.

"That's older than you, Gramps. That would mean, her mother would have to be..."

"One hundred and one. The old crone is one hundred and one and as sharp as a tack."

"Wow." The smell really was overwhelming. "Maybe you should have Gladys tell her to take it easy on the perfume?"

Gramps' laughed. "Gladys is terrified of her mother. So am I. If Merle wanted to pour the entire bottle of perfume all over my leather seats, I'd let her."

I chuckled, as he pulled out of the parking spot, but I didn't have a chance to respond, before Gramps spoke again.

"I don't want to talk about Gladys, Allanah. I'm taking you out to dinner because I want to talk about you."

"Oh, is that right? Fantastic. What exactly is it that you're concerned about?"

I crossed my arms as I sighed in preparation. Why was it that all of my family members seemed so intent on maintaining privacy in their own lives but saw absolutely no reason to extend me the same courtesy?

"I think you need to start dating again, and quickly. You've let all of that mess with Caleb's friend throw you off. Time to get back on the horse."

It had taken most of my effort over the past three months to keep Ross off of my mind. After that dreadful night where I'd head-butted him, nearly vomited, and then fled his apartment, I'd not heard a word from him. Worse, I'd passed him in the hallway numerous times and all I would get from him is a polite nod and sheepish smile before we would each keep moving in our intended directions.

Of course the whole mess had thrown me off. I was mortified, disappointed, and hurt. I knew that I didn't know Ross well—not at all, really. But I just wouldn't have expected someone that Beth wanted me to be with, and someone that Caleb recommended so highly, to ghost me so ruthlessly.

Not that I blamed him. I'd made a fool of myself on both dates, but a huge part of me had hoped he would just be a little more patient. He wasn't. And the radio silence that had followed our *It's A Wonderful Life* date had embarrassed me to the point where I was just as likely to join a convent as I was to date over the course of the next year.

And if anything happened to go wrong in my apartment for the duration of my life there, I would just have to live with it because there was no way I was ever going to resort to calling Ross for help.

"We're not discussing this, Gramps."

He persisted as he activated the blinker and turned into the small parking lot of the deli. "But Allanah, I'm…"

I cut him off, keeping my voice firm. "Gramps, I'm serious. You don't ever talk to me about Gladys. Georgie doesn't talk to me about anything lately. I'm under no obligation to discuss my dating life, or lack thereof, with you. If that's the only reason you wanted to eat with me, turn around and take me back to my car."

Parking, he let out a loud, sad, sigh and turned frustrated eyes on me.

He stared at me hard another minute before giving in. "Fine.

Let's just spend our evening gossiping about what your parents are up to in Washington."

That I could do.

"Done. Now, let's go inside. I'm starving."

"She's gotten quite used to you. Look at how she settles into your chest."

Ross nodded, the corner of his mouth pulling up in the slightest hint of a smile despite himself.

It pleased him that both Maggie and Hannah felt comfortable with him. And the fact that Maggie now tended to fall asleep within minutes of being strapped to his chest on the mornings he walked Hannah to school only made the whole ordeal that much easier.

"Aye. I'll admit I've gotten quite used to the wee lass, as well. Hannah, too. I'm not sure I'm looking forward to the day yer marathon training comes to an end and I no longer have these mornings with them."

"Same."

Hannah's voice came from the doorway, and both men turned in unison. Dressed in matching clothes with both of her Velcro shoes on the right feet, her hair brushed, and her backpack on, she was ready to go.

Ross watched as Caleb beamed at her and moved across the room to scoop her up into his arms. "You're too good to me, Hannah. You're such a big girl the way you get ready almost entirely on your own."

Ross resisted a laugh, as he looked at Hannah roll her eyes over his shoulder as she tried to squirm out of his arms.

"I'm in kindergarten, Dad. What do you expect? Now, we better go. If I don't get there early, Brandon will try to take my cubby. And I have the best one in the whole class."

Caleb set Hannah on her feet and turned to look at Ross.

"You heard the girl. Sounds like the three of you better get going. There are clean bottles on the kitchen counter for Maggie when you get back. I'll see you in a few hours."

Ross reached for Hannah's hand as Caleb gave them a brief wave before jogging toward the front door.

As usual, it took Hannah all of three seconds for her to start talking his ear off. "How old do you have to be to have boyfriend or girlfriend?"

Ross' eyes grew wide as he glanced down at the young girl in horror. "At least twenty years older than ye, lass."

Hannah pulled her nose up in disgust as she laughed at him. "No, silly! I don't mean for me. I meant for you. Are you older or younger than my Dad?"

Ross shrugged. He honestly wasn't sure. "I doona know, but I imagine we are close to the same age."

She nodded, as if she'd suspected as much. "Then, why don't you have a girlfriend or boyfriend, Ross? I mean..." She paused. "I know why Daddy doesn't. But I can't think of any good reason that you don't."

Ross shook his head. The things that came out of the small child's mouth never ceased to amaze him.

"Some just doona wish to have a girlfriend or boyfriend, lass. Mayhap I am one of those."

Hannah's face scrunched up as she shook her head. "No. You're not one of those, Uncle Ross."

Of course the wee lass didn't believe him. He didn't believe himself.

Not a day had gone by since that December evening that he hadn't kicked himself for deciding to step away from Allanah.

"Mayhap, I doona have a girlfriend because I am a fool who canna seem to keep one."

Hannah nodded. "Now that I can believe."

*H*annah had ruined his day. Her small mention of a girlfriend had brought the one person he worked so diligently to keep from his mind right to the forefront. All morning, thoughts of Allanah plagued him.

He'd not behaved well toward her, he knew. For a short time, he'd been able to convince himself that he was retreating from the situation for her sake, but really he'd taken the coward's way out.

His phone buzzed in his pocket, stirring him from his thoughts.

Mrs. Jenkins. A surprising amount of time had passed since he'd heard from the woman.

He answered it, thankful for something to stop his self-defeating thoughts.

"Mrs. Jenkins, how are ye, lass?"

"Good afternoon, Ross. I'm fine. Just fine. But there is a hole in the back stairwell window. It's causing a terrible draft."

Ross glanced at the clock. Five on a Friday. He wasn't going to be able to get anyone out there to fix it.

"Thank ye for calling me. 'Twill most likely be Monday before 'tis fixed, but I'll go and tape it up to keep the wind out straight away."

"I just thought you should know about it, dear. You know me. I can't ever take the elevator. Those contraptions are death machines, I tell you."

Ross laughed. "If ye say so, Mrs. Jenkins."

"Yes. I do say so. Now, go and get that taped up, and when you're done, stop by my apartment, and I'll have a warm loaf of banana bread for you."

"I'll see ye shortly, lass."

*P*erplexed, Ross leaned back to try to see the entirety of the damage to the window. What could have caused such a perfect hole? Nothing lay on the ground at the bottom of the stairwell. No bird or rock had come through the window. Whatever it was, had hit with a lot of force.

The window sat high above him. Setting up his ladder so he could reach, he then placed tape onto his work belt so he would have everything he needed right at hand.

Once up the ladder and eye level with the busted window, he began his work, all the while thinking of Allanah. Of her beautiful eyes, and her thick head of hair that had smelled so wonderful as she'd leaned into him during the movie.

What had been his reason for stepping away? Why was he so set against ever loving again? Now, after months of missing her, he couldn't remember.

Everything happened quickly then. The door to the stairwell swung suddenly open and a giant yellow lab bounded up the stairs and toward the ladder.

He heard the ladder shift before he realized what was happening, but it only took half a second for him to feel it give way beneath him. His right foot slipped beneath the ladder step, keeping his leg trapped in the metal as it crashed to the ground.

He fell with the ladder, his leg caught and twisted. He heard his bones crack, heard the awful popping, as the stairwell swirled around him. He glanced down to see his thigh bone exposed to the wintery air.

The last thing he heard before passing out was the panicked sound of the young resident whose dog had just tried to kill him.

"Ah, shit. Hang on, man. I'm calling an ambulance."

CHAPTER 13

"You're not Ross."

Disappointed that Hannah wasn't at least a little bit more excited to see me, I nodded and smiled as I stepped into the house.

"You're right, I'm not. I'm going to be walking you to school in place of Ross for the next few months."

Hannah looked shocked. "Months? I know Dad said he had some broken bones, but I was really hoping they'd be better by today."

From all that Caleb had told me on the phone, chances were good Ross wouldn't be walking them anymore for the rest of the school year. Not only had he broken his thigh bone in two places, but his knee was entirely busted, as well. His surgery had been extensive, and his recovery would be long.

Karma. It had to be karma. I was fine with it—even if that did mean I wasn't quite as good a person as I thought I was.

"Bones take a really long time to heal, but I promise to try to be as good of a walking companion as Ross was."

Hannah ducked her head. "Not possible."

Ouch.

"Hannah, we already talked about this. Sue doesn't have to be doing this for us. She's helping us out. You are not to be rude to her, do you understand me?"

I tried to wave Caleb off. I didn't want him scolding Hannah, but it was already done.

Hannah looked up at me remorsefully. "I didn't mean to be rude to you, Sue. I'm sorry. I like you too. It's just that I *really* like Uncle Ross."

I smiled and reached out to tussle the top of her hair. "It's okay. I get it. We all have our favorites."

Caleb reached for Hannah's backpack and held it out for her so she could slip it on.

"Will you grab Maggie's carrier from my bedroom?"

Hannah nodded and hurried out of the room.

"Thank you for doing this, Sue. It really would've been okay for me to miss some training."

I laughed. "Are you kidding? No, it wouldn't have been. Gramps would've never let you hear the end of it. You guys are so close. I don't mind, truly. I've just bumped my mornings back. It's really not a big deal. One of the perks of running my own practice—I'm the boss."

"I…" Caleb started to say something and then stopped.

"What?"

He hesitated. "It's nothing. I know you'll say no, and I wouldn't blame you one bit, anyway."

Now I had to know what he was talking about.

"What? What is it?"

"It's Ross. He's going to need physical therapy, Sue, and there's no one else in Boston he should go to when we all know you're the best."

I shook my head in protest.

"No. That's not true, Caleb. There are lots of great physical therapists. I'd be happy to give some recommendations."

Caleb continued. It seemed that now that he'd started, he was determined to see this conversation through. "You're right. There are some excellent therapists, but they're not the best. That's you. And frankly, Sue, I need Ross back at work as soon as possible. I'm having to take over his maintenance jobs while he's out of commission, and that's a whole lot harder for me to do now that Beth's gone and it's just me and the girls. I know he was a jerk to you. But you're the most professional person I know. Do you think you could set that aside and help him? For my sake?"

God, Caleb was good at saying just the thing that made it impossible to turn him down. But he was right about one thing. I *was* a professional. Surely, I could separate my own feelings from the job in front of me if I took Ross on as a patient.

"Fine. I'll work him in on the mornings after I walk the girls to school. Tell him to be at my office by ten a.m. sharp."

Caleb grimaced and I could already sense where he was going to go.

"He can't travel there by himself, Sue, and I can't take him then either. He doesn't really have anyone else here. Can you just work with him in his apartment? Wouldn't that be easier on everyone?"

All I would see every time I stepped foot in Ross' apartment would be memories of me ramming my skull into his, but I couldn't very well tell Caleb that.

"Fine, Caleb. I'll head over there right after you get back from running. You owe me. I hope you know that."

He leaned forward and pulled me into a tight hug before kissing the side of my cheek.

"You're the best. And yes, I know I do."

---

*E*very part of him hurt. Never in his life had he felt so helpless. He hated it. And he hated the look of absolute pity on Sydney's face as she stared at him from his phone.

"Your color is a little bit better today. That's good."

He grunted, unsure of how to respond.

"I'm so sorry I wasn't there for your surgery. I wish I could travel over there to you right now, but I'm just too swamped with work."

He hurried to reassure her. He was not Sydney's responsibility, no matter how much his friend seemed to have taken that job on.

"Nonsense, lass. I doona want ye here. I'm fine on my own. Mrs. Jenkins has delivered more food to my apartment than I'll ever be able to eat. She's also taken to doing my laundry and making sure I have what I need. Tink is keeping me fine company, and Caleb is somehow finding the time to come over and walk the pup for me. I'm as well as I could be right now. Truly."

A sudden knock on his door surprised him. The only people to stop by since his surgery were Caleb or Mrs. Jenkins, and they both always just walked right in without knocking.

Sydney furrowed her brows at him. "Are you able to get up to answer the door?"

He shook his head. "Aye, I could, but I willna do so. 'Tis unlocked. Hold on just a moment."

"Okay."

Leaning slightly toward the door so his voice would carry, he called out to whoever was on the other side. "'Tis unlocked. Ye may come in."

When a brief moment passed in silence, he called out again, louder this time. "Did ye hear me? Come in. The door is unlocked."

The door handle turned and to his surprise, Allanah stepped into his apartment. "I heard you."

Ross quickly directed his attention to Sydney. "I must go. I'll text ye later."

He hung up on her without another word and twisted toward Allanah.

"Allanah. What are ye doing here?"

Her face was tight and expressionless. Not that he could blame her. He could hardly expect a warm greeting after the way he'd simply disappeared without explanation.

She pointed to his elevated leg. "You're injured. Caleb asked me if I would work with you."

"Ah." His leg was currently cast from hip to ankle. He couldn't imagine what they could work on.

As if reading his mind, she continued. "Today, we will just make sure you're moving the rest of your body. Stretching, twisting. Being limber and keeping your blood circulating will help later."

He stared at her. How could she come in and get right to business without demanding an explanation for his horrid behavior?

When the silence stretched on too long, he decided to try to clear the air first. "Allanah, lass, I believe I..."

She interrupted him, giving her head one quick, firm, shake. "No. When I am in this apartment, it is in a professional capacity. Is that understood? If not, I'll be happy to refer you to some other really great therapists in the city. What happened was months ago. There's no need for us to talk about it. Not now. Not ever. Okay?"

There was a glimpse of the woman who'd screamed at him after keeping her grandfather locked out in the cold. He knew he shouldn't be smiling at her, but he couldn't help it. The contradiction between the two sides of Allanah—the flirty, soft lass who'd ridden with him in the limo, and the tough, sassy, professional, intrigued him.

Rather than quip back with what was on his mind, he replied in the only way that would get her to stay.

"Aye, lass. I understand perfectly."

"Good."

She turned just long enough to set her bag down by the front door and remove her shoes.

Then, she slowly walked toward him, moving to stand behind the couch.

"Let me see your hands and we will begin."

By the time Allanah left him, he was sore, happy, and God help him, his cock was hard.

Allanah could choose to keep her interactions professional if she wished it.

He knew without a doubt that he would be unable to do so.

CHAPTER 14

 *ne Month Later*

"*I*'m really not sure this is a good idea, Ross. You'll be so sore afterwards, and it won't be good if we exhaust you."

Staying angry with Ross was the only way I knew to keep things strictly professional with him. Despite my best efforts, I'd not been able to stay angry with him for long. I understood why Hannah and Caleb adored him so much. I could see why Beth had, as well. Ross simply had a way of getting under your skin.

While he'd done as I had asked him the morning of our first session and never mentioned our previous time together, somehow, over the next few weeks, his warm demeanor and charm had lessened the hurt I'd felt over all of that mess.

And so...against my better judgment, I was standing in the doorway of Ross' apartment at six in the morning, helping him get dressed and ready with his crutches so he could accompany me on my bi-weekly walk with the girls to school.

"'Tis the best idea I've ever had, lass. I need out of this

apartment. I need to rebuild my strength, and I miss the girls. I've strong arms, and I'm steady with the crutches. I willna fall."

I sighed, knowing there was no talking him out of it.

"Fine. Maggie and Hannah will be delighted to see you."

⁂

And they were. Hannah squealed and nearly knocked him down when she opened the door to find him standing there. I had to hurry to step in between them, reminding her that he was still healing and couldn't pick her up.

When we made it inside so I could ready the girls, Maggie squirmed in my arms as she reached for Ross.

"Let me sit down and hold her a minute, lass. We are early. We doona need to leave just yet."

Seeing Ross so eager to hold the baby made something flutter uncomfortably inside my chest. I bobbed my head in the direction of the rocking chair in the living room in resignation.

The moment he was seated, Maggie reached as if the only thing she wanted in the whole world was to be held by him.

"I haven't grown on you at all, have I, little one? Not after a whole month of these morning walks together."

Hannah laughed and ran over to reach for my hand. "You've grown on me a little bit, if it makes you feel any better."

I smiled down at her. "It most definitely does."

We all glanced toward the sound of steps on the stairway and turned to see Caleb jog down in his running clothes.

He beamed when he saw Ross. "Ross! It's so good to see you out of the house." He paused and mouthed the words *thank you* to me before moving over to shake Ross' hand.

Then he turned to face me once more. "I gotta tell you, Sue. Your grandfather is a taskmaster. I can hardly keep up with him."

"He's surprisingly spry for his age, and I'm glad to hear that the chemo doesn't seem to have slowed him down."

Caleb twisted and lifted his arms up to stretch as he talked. "If it has slowed him down, there's no way I would've wanted to run with him before chemo. He's going to dominate the race."

He probably wouldn't dominate the entire race, but he most certainly would win his age division—of that, I had no doubt.

"I bet you're going to surprise yourself with how well you do, as well."

Caleb stopped bouncing around and stretching and moved to tell his girls goodbye before answering me. "I'll just be thrilled with myself if I finish the damn thing. That's my only goal. Thanks for everything, guys. I'll see you two in a few hours."

The old grandfather clock in the corner of the living room chimed once to indicate the half hour, and I walked across the room to reach for Maggie.

"Time for us to go."

*T*he walk, while good for the morale of Ross and the girls, had done exactly what I'd expected it to do. It exhausted him. By the time we said goodbye to Hannah at school, I noticed that his hands were shaking and insisted that Maggie and I see him back to his apartment before I returned to Caleb's house.

"Thank you for letting me go today, lass."

I laughed and opened the door to his apartment for him, taking care not to disrupt Maggie who was sleeping against my chest.

"I didn't let you do anything. You were going to go no matter what I said."

He did his signature shrug as best as he could while leaning on crutches. "Mayhap so. Still...thank ye."

He was pale, and I knew he needed to lie down.

"Drink lots of water this morning, and take a good long nap. Let's work in an extra session tomorrow evening, okay? I think you need it after today. I'll come by after I finish my appointments, if that's good for you."

He nodded then laughed. "O'course. What fun could I possibly be having in this condition?"

"I'm sure you could find some sort of trouble if you really put your mind to it."

Laughing, he winked and closed the door as Maggie and I made our way back to the elevator.

By the time I made it back to Caleb's, Georgie was already there, wiping down the kitchen counters.

She extended a bottle filled with Maggie's formula as she began to stir in her carrier.

"How did that go? I know you were nervous about it this morning."

"About as well as I expected it to. It wore him out, but he loved it. So did the girls, so I guess that's what matters."

Unhooking the carrier, I lifted Maggie into my arms, shifted her into a position where I could feed her, and moved to sit on one of the barstools so I could visit with Georgie while she cleaned.

"What is it about handsome men and babies, Georgie? It did something strange to my insides to watch Ross with the two of them."

Georgie laughed and paused her wiping to come and sit down next to me.

"I think it's just in our DNA. Makes us want to breed."

"Not that I'm interested in Ross in that way anymore. I'm just no longer angry and embarrassed over the whole situation, is all. And it's not like anyone could deny that he's attractive."

Her brows were arched so high they looked like they were about to rise off the top of her head. "Uh-huh. Tell yourself whatever you need to."

I protested. "I'm not telling myself anything. It's the truth."

"Uh-huh. Look. I don't actually care. You let me have my private life. I'll let you have yours. Do you think I can ask you a favor though?"

"Of course."

"I've been seeing this guy for a little while now, and we're both getting a little tired of having to do everything at his place. Do you think you could maybe make yourself scarce tomorrow night—at least until ten, or so? If you can't or don't want to, I understand. I know it's your place, and I'm not even paying rent. I just thought it would be nice if the two of us had a change of scenery."

"Sure. I'll find something to do. It's not a problem. Can I ask the name of the man you're seeing?"

She smiled, and I knew right then I was getting nothing.

"No, you may not. It doesn't matter in the least."

Laughing, I stood to go and rock Maggie until Caleb made it back from his run.

"Fair enough, sis. Fair enough."

CHAPTER 15

"Can you rotate to the right a little bit more? Don't overextend, but if you can stretch slightly farther, I want you to try it."

Ross did as I asked without argument. Surprisingly, he was a pretty good patient. I knew that if he continued to work as hard as he had to date, he would heal far faster than most.

"Okay, release it."

As he twisted back to his original position, the front door of his apartment swung open and an elderly woman with pink hair and overalls strode into the living room. She had oven mitts on her hands and held a casserole dish as she strode into the kitchen without giving me a second glance.

"Good evening, Ross. How are you feeling today?"

Giving me a wink to let me know that he wanted a minute, he pushed himself up from the couch, reached for his crutches, and hobbled off after the woman.

"Feeling better all the time, Mrs. Jenkins. Ye do know that ye doona have to cook for me every night, aye? I still have far too much food left over in the fridge."

I moved to stand at the edge of the kitchen, as I watched in fascination.

Mrs. Jenkins dismissed him with a huff. "Then freeze it if it's about to go bad. I like having someone to tend to again. Who is this?"

She surprised me by pointing at me, and I realized that she'd been so focused on walking to the kitchen that she hadn't seen me when she first came in.

I extended my hand as Ross spoke.

"This is, Sue. She's my physical therapist. She lives in the building, as well."

It surprised me to hear him call me Sue, as he never called me that, but I blew past it as I shook Mrs. Jenkins' hand.

"It's nice to meet you."

"You too. It's always nice to get to know those that live in the building."

She released my hand and pointed back at her casserole.

"It's hot now, so dig in soon and then freeze the rest. Now, I'm going to go before your little dog decides to attack me."

I frowned at her and looked at Tink in confusion. The puppy would never attack anyone, though I said nothing until the door closed behind Mrs. Jenkins on her way out.

When she was gone, I scooped Tink up and rubbed her reassuringly.

"What was that about? Why is she worried about Tink attacking her?"

Ross shrugged as he made his way back over to the couch.

"I couldna begin to tell ye. She's been terrified of the wee pup since she first laid eyes on her."

"Why did you introduce me as Sue? You never call me that."

The question slipped out of me before I had a chance to stop it.

"Ah." He pursed his lips as if he wasn't quite sure himself. "I suppose I quite like that I am one of the few that call ye by yer real name."

It was an honest admission, and somehow seemed an intimate one. My skin grew hot, and I felt my cheeks blush. I hurried to change the subject.

"Okay, I think we've done enough for tonight. I suppose I'll be on my way."

"Back down the hall, aye?"

His question reminded me of the promise I'd made to Georgie, for that was, in fact, where I was about to go.

"Crap." I covered my face with my palms. "Well, no, actually. That's not where I'll be heading right now. Georgie has a date over. I told her I would stay gone until ten."

"Where will ye go, then?"

I really needed to work on adding more friends to my social circle. I could think of nowhere to go.

"I would go over to Gramps' place, but if I remember correctly, he's having his girlfriend over tonight. The last thing I want to do is walk in on anything that might throw me into a catatonic state, so I'm actually not quite sure."

He responded immediately. "Stay here, lass. We can watch television, and ye can help me eat some of Mrs. Jenkins latest casserole. 'Tis only a few hours until ten. It makes far more sense for ye to stay here for a while than to go out somewhere else. We can open a bottle of wine."

His last statement triggered an automatic response that kept me from getting really awkward about the whole situation.

I shook my head firmly. "No way. Not with the pain meds that you're on. No alcohol until you're off all of them."

He frowned playfully. "Ye're no fun at all, lass."

Resigning myself to the fact that I was about to have to relax my strict rule of professionalism for just a little while, I headed toward the kitchen to get us two plates.

"You're absolutely wrong about that. I'm a ton of fun." I lifted the foil on the casserole. I couldn't tell what it was, only that it was covered—absolutely smothered—in cheese. "Do you have any bagged salad or anything in the fridge? I'm afraid if we only eat this, we both might end up with a clogged artery."

His voice carried from his place on the couch. "No, lass. All the food in my kitchen right now is courtesy of Mrs. Jenkins, and she is not much of one for anything of the green variety."

Grimacing, I made a mental note to bring him some salad and green juice the next time I came over as I prepped two plates of the greasy, delicious-smelling dish.

<hr>

*H*e was such a fool. What had made him ask her to stay? The pressure inside of him to tell her the truth had built for days. How was he supposed to suppress it when she was sitting next to him on the couch, laughing at the stupid jokes on an old sitcom?

Every few minutes, he glanced at the clock, wishing the minutes away so that ten o'clock would come and she would leave him. How could he both want her there and want her gone so much at the same time?

"Are you okay?" Her voice pulled him from his thoughts as he registered her confused expression. "You look like you're in pain. Do you need me to get you some more ibuprofen? You've had all you can have of the other stuff today."

He had to tell her. He couldn't stand it a minute more. Each and every time she left after one of their sessions, he spent the rest of the day and night dreaming about her. All of his nonsense about never wanting a relationship again seemed unimportant to him now.

"I am in pain, lass, but not because of my leg."

Her brows furrowed further. "Then what? What's up?"

He twisted and reached out to grab her arm, pulling her toward him before he could talk himself out of it—before she had time to react.

"I know ye said we could never speak of it, but I canna stand it a minute longer, Allanah. I owe ye an apology for how I treated ye. I know ye must be angry, or at the verra least, confused. 'Twas not that I dinna care for ye. 'Twas that I did." He paused and corrected himself. "I do. And by God, lass, all I've thought of doing for the past three months since ye ran out my door is this…"

Without another thought, he pulled her against him, crushing her lips into a kiss so deep and quick that she didn't have time to panic and pull away from him.

Instead, she melted into it, moaning into his mouth as her lips moved against his.

My body responded to the pressure of Ross' lips against my own long before my brain did. By the time my brain registered what was happening and began to shoot off alarm bells that I needed to pull away from him, my body was already all in.

Ross pulled away from my lips just long enough to trail his across my jawline and to my ear. Once there, he whispered huskily, sending shivers down my spine. "Ach, lass. That is more like it. I knew ye could kiss if only ye would allow yerself to stop thinking so much for a moment."

I couldn't afford to stop thinking. Not with Ross. It had been difficult enough to do when we were just dating. Now, it was impossible—now, he was my patient.

"Ross…" My breath was ragged as I moved to place my palm on his chest so I could push him away. "I can't…I can't do this."

Obediently, he stopped and pulled back from me just enough to measure my expression.

"Do ye truly want me to stop, lass, or do ye just think that ye should ask me to?"

I didn't want him to stop. What I truly wanted to do was to pull down his sweatpants right here on the couch and ride him until we both came.

I realized as he narrowed his eyes at me that I still hadn't answered. My mind had drifted way too far into the fantasy of me straddling him.

"Lass?"

Taking a ragged breath, I closed my eyes and tried to find some sort of measured calm.

"First of all, you're my patient now, Ross. This is impossible because of that. Second, I'm not sure that I *do* want you anymore. I know you've apologized, but that doesn't make what you did go away. I know that I freaked out on both dates, and that behavior couldn't have been attractive, but I thought we'd gotten along quite well. Then I just never heard from you again."

He frowned, looking sad. I crossed my arms as I awaited his rebuttal.

"Let me begin with yer first point of contention. I havena paid ye a dime for yer services, lass. Nor have I ever been to yer office. I know that no doctor referred me to ye, and I doona suspect that ye have any sort of patient file on me. In every true sense, I am not yer patient. I am simply a man ye have been kind enough to help at Caleb's request. So, that point is moot."

He paused to give me a wicked smile, clearly pleased with himself.

"As to yer second point, I canna say I'd blame ye one bit if ye truly doona want anything to do with me. I behaved horribly, and not a day has passed that I havena berated myself for it. Nothing I say can excuse how I handled things. But I would like to explain the best I can, if ye will allow it."

He gave me no time to actually tell him whether or not I would *allow* it before continuing on.

"I am frightened of how taken I am with ye when I know ye so little. Romance doesna come easily to me. Such potent feelings of wanting have only occurred one other time in my life, and that dinna end well for either of us, lass. My history with caring for those that I love most is poor. I often disappoint those who never disappoint me. I doona wish to do that to ye.

"I was happy to meet with ye to satisfy Caleb. And though I know 'tis not kind, I would have happily continued to see ye if I knew I could do so without truly falling for ye. But the moment I knew I couldna—the moment I knew that my heart would inevitably be yers if I spent any more time around ye, I knew 'twould be best for ye if I stepped away. Yer quick retreat from my apartment the night we watched the movie simply gave me a good opportunity to do so."

He paused long enough to take a deep breath before leaning in a little closer to me.

"And lass…there was nothing unattractive about yer nervousness each time I tried to kiss ye. In truth, each time ye fled me, I was left hard and yearning for ye."

He stopped then and leaned back on the couch, crossing both arms over his chest in a gesture that mimicked my own.

Flabbergasted, I let the silence hang between us as I processed all that he'd said. It was a damn good explanation. One that had my insides all fluttery and my cheeks flushed. All of my clothes felt too tight, and despite the thickness of my sweater, my nipples had tightened to tiny points at his admission that I'd left him with an untended erection more than once.

Finally, I decided to ask the one question at the front of my mind. "So, what's changed, Ross? Are you suddenly so sure that you won't hurt me? Why kiss me now if you were so certain that you had to stay away before?"

"Do ye want the truth, lass?"

I nodded. "Always."

"I am certain of nothing, Allanah. I've no confidence that I am capable of not hurting those that I care for. And if we return to seeing each other, I know that it willna take long before I care for ye as much as I care for anyone else in my life. All I can promise ye is that I will do all that I can to make better decisions going forward than I have in the past. 'Tis up to ye whether or not ye are willing to risk the damage I may do."

I frowned at him. "Are you asking me to risk it? All you did was kiss me, Ross. I haven't actually heard you ask me to do anything."

He smiled, gave me a shrug, and scooted closer to me on the couch. I was pretty sure that sometimes I just baited him with comments or questions that I knew would make him shrug just so I could watch him do it.

He reached for my hand and I allowed him to take it.

"Aye, lass. Allow me to take ye out again. Allow me the chance to win ye over. Will ye do so?"

While probably unwise, I wanted him. I'd wanted him for months, despite the fact that he'd behaved so horrendously. But I wasn't the sort of person to give anyone third or fourth chances. He needed to know that one more chance was all he was going to get. I didn't care for baseball. Three strikes was far too many.

"Fine. I'll let you take me out again, but we need to be clear about something before we start this up again, understand?"

He nodded, a small smile beginning at the corner of his mouth.

"I like my life, Ross. I've worked really hard to create it. I like my job. I like my family. And while I don't have a lot of friends, I'm close to the ones I do have. I've been single for a long time, and I've been happy for every minute of it. Do I want someone in my life? Yes. But, I don't *need* you. And I don't need unnecessary drama or heartache in my life. I'm not going to play wishy-washy games. You decide one more time that you don't want this—I'm out. You screw this up once more—you won't hear from me again. Got it?"

He hesitated, and as I watched that hint of a smile disappear and his expression change, my hard-ass resolve softened. He didn't want to screw this up, I could tell, but he'd been truthful before—he truly didn't believe that he would be able to prevent it.

Overcome by empathy, I reached out to grab his hand.

"Just be honest with me always, and I'm sure we'll be okay. I'm willing to try my best, if you are. Okay?"

That seemed to relax him, and he lifted my hand to his mouth as he kissed my knuckles.

"Aye, lass. I assure ye, I shall try harder at this than I have anything in my life."

CHAPTER 17

*O*nce I'd agreed to give him another chance, and he'd agreed to try his best not to be a total moron, we spent the next few hours making out like teenagers.

It was wonderful.

Happy, and tired—I was rarely up past ten-thirty—I unlocked the door to my apartment and stepped inside just after midnight.

Not surprisingly, my night owl of a sister was still up, watching an old *Seinfeld* episode on the television. Her head popped up from the other side of the couch as soon as she heard me.

She gave me one hard look up and down and smiled. "Somebody just broke her code of ethics."

I frowned. How could she possibly know that? "I have no idea what you're talking about."

She cocked her head to the side and shook her head. "You're kidding me, right? Your makeup is smeared to hell, sis. And clearly, this Ross guy has some sort of beard or stubble situation going on because your upper lip and nose are red and chafed from making out."

Horrified, I threw my bag down and hurried over to the small mirror I had hanging near the front door.

She was right. Any trace of lipstick was gone, and my nose was bright red and rough. While Ross didn't normally have a beard, being so homebound, he'd allowed his facial hair to grow. I'd hardly noticed it while kissing him.

Eager to justify my behavior, I faced her. "He's not really a patient. Not officially. I've never seen him in my office, and I've not billed him."

Georgie laughed, waved a dismissive hand, and then waved me toward her. "Sue, I honestly wouldn't care even if he was 'officially' your patient. I've always been one to see things much more gray than black and white. There are exceptions to every rule."

I was exactly the opposite.

"Well, there shouldn't be. And this isn't an exception. He's not really my patient." Feeling rather guilty, I tried to direct the conversation away from me. "Enough about this. How did your evening go? Any chance you're ready to give me any more info on this mysterious guy you're seeing?"

She smiled and then shook her head. "The night was great, but no, there's nothing to tell you. You know me, Sue. I don't like to talk about my personal life. And I'm a little hesitant to throw myself into anything after my last relationship."

That seemed to be the ongoing theme of the night.

"Okay. Fine. But you had a good time? He seems like a good guy?"

She leaned into me and rested her head on my shoulder as she yawned. "I had an amazing time. And yes, I know for a fact that he's a really good guy. Don't worry, Sue. I'm not trying to keep you out of the loop. I'm just being cautious. When I think there's anything worth telling you, you'll be the first to know."

"Before Gramps?"

She laughed and reached for the remote to turn off the television. "Yes. Before Gramps."

*H*e woke early, restless and frustrated with himself after a fitful night of sleep. After Allanah left him, his mind churned with worry and regret. She'd felt good in his arms—her lips soft and warm and welcoming, just like he'd known they would be if only she would just allow herself to relax.

He wanted to be with her, wanted to try to not repeat the same selfish and self-defeating mistakes of his past, but those memories haunted him. The pain he'd caused, the friends he'd abandoned, the mother he hadn't seen in years—he didn't deserve happiness even if he could find it.

Reaching for his crutches, he got out of bed, phone in hand, and hobbled toward his desk in the other room. The corner of his left crutch caught on the doorway and nearly sent him flying onto the floor.

Cursing, he caught himself as he threw the crutch to the ground, spooking Tink. She yelped and leapt back to keep from being hit by the falling crutch.

Regret filled him. He loved the wee pup, despite himself. The last thing he ever wanted to do was scare her.

Damn his lack of magic. Not so long ago, an injury like this would've been healed in an hour. Such magic would've exhausted him for days, but a week in bed compared to months of this madness was nothing.

How did regular mortals stand their weakness? He would never get used to it.

Lowering himself to the floor in the hallway outside his bedroom, he reached out toward Tink and called to her.

"Come here, lass. I'm sorry I scared ye. Ye know that I wouldna hurt ye, aye?"

Quick to forgive him, Tink bounded toward him, leaping into his arms as if nothing had happened only moments before. She licked the side of his face as he held her close, and tears began to fill his eyes.

He couldn't do this. This place—this mindset—was a dark, familiar thing to him, and it never did him any good.

He needed advice. Someone to keep him from spiraling into a whirlpool of self-hatred that would cause him to ruin a second chance with Allanah before it even truly began.

Five-thirty was far too early in the morning to call Caleb, but it would be mid-morning in Scotland. Sydney always gave the best advice anyway.

She didn't answer.

He tried again.

Still nothing.

With a young baby, and a castle kitchen to run, he didn't suppose he should be too surprised.

"Ach, Tink. What would ye tell me if ye could speak?"

The small pup stopped licking him and looked at him hard, love in her eyes, as another idea occurred to him. There was one other in Scotland known for her advice, and thanks to Sydney, he now had the number to reach her in his phone.

The old witch had disappointed him the first time he'd sought her help, though now he could see that while she'd not given him what he wanted, her refusal to help him had been necessary. He'd been meaning to speak with her anyway—to try and reassure her that she need harbor no guilt over Beth's death.

He scrolled through the short list of contacts in his phone, stopping at the letter 'M.'

Morna.

Tapping her name so that the phone would dial, he crossed his fingers in the hope she would answer.

"Hello."

Startled by the fact that the phone never actually rang before he heard Morna's voice, Ross fumbled over his response. "Ach, aye, uh, good morning. This is Ross. We have met twice…"

She interrupted him, laughing. "Aye, lad. I know who ye are. I've been waiting for ye to call all morning."

That surprised him. "Ye have?"

"Aye. I still have my magic, remember? I woke with my shoulder bone tingling, and I knew I would hear from ye today."

Not having the slightest idea how to interpret the oddity of that, he decided to brush past it.

"Morna, lass, I feel I should've reached out to ye before now. When Sydney came to visit me a few months back, she mentioned that ye felt some guilt over Beth's death. As someone who used to have magic, please let me assure ye that ye bear no responsibility for what happened to her. Deep down ye know that 'twould have been wrong for ye to intervene, aye?"

There was a brief silence, and he thought he could hear the slightest hint of a sob on the other end of the phone. When Morna spoke, her voice was broken.

"Aye. I do. Though I thank ye for saying so. 'Tis only that I often wonder what good 'tis to have the power to change such fates, if 'tis wrong to do so. And I have ignored fate before and saved the life of one whose time 'twas to go, and this lass dinna have wee bairns who depended on her. How can I justify making an exception for her and not Beth?"

Ross didn't know that Morna had prevented the fated death of another before, and he couldn't deny that her admission made him wonder the same thing. While he didn't know the woman of whom Morna spoke, surely Beth had been just as deserving of life.

But how could he say such a thing? It would do neither of them any good now. The witch needed comfort as much as he did. The least he could do was give it to her.

"It does us no good to berate ourselves for past mistakes, lass. Mayhap the fate of the woman ye saved was not to die, but to be saved from death by yer magic. If we believe that fate is as powerful as we say 'tis, then that must be so. And if so, Beth's fate was to truly die, not to be saved by ye. Ye did nothing wrong. Either way, we canna ever know for sure, and we canna change the past. We can only move forward the best we know how to."

He listened to Morna sniffle, and he could imagine her brushing away tears before she spoke.

"Thank ye, Ross. It means much that ye've reached out like this." She hesitated, and then continued. "But surely that is not all that caused ye to reach for the phone this morn."

Guilt swirled in his gut. Perhaps, it should've been the only thing he reached out to her for. It would certainly have made his words of comfort seem more sincere. To approach her with his problems now made him feel as if he only offered his comfort in the hopes she would do the same to him.

"No, lass. I just wanted to tell ye that. I hope ye have a lovely day."

Rather than the goodbye he expected, Morna laughed and called his bluff. "Nonsense, lad. Talk to me about the girl. 'Tis my specialty."

He should've known she would know if he lied. Sighing, he decided to speak plainly. "My past clings to me like the heaviest of cloaks. I feel ruined. Unworthy. Certain to repeat what I've done before."

"Ach, lad. Ye doona need advice from me. Ye need only to listen to the words ye told me. Be kind to yerself. Give yerself the same grace ye offered me. As ye said, ye canna change the past—only do yer best going forward, aye?"

Morna was right. He would never be as hard on another person as he always was on himself.

"Aye. I suppose so."

"Ye are not the same man ye were before. Ye willna make the same mistakes as that man. Ye will make new ones." She laughed gently, before continuing. "Doona fear the mistakes, they are inevitable. Just listen to the lass. From what I've seen, she is wise. She knows her own mind. Be honest with her. Doona hide who ye are."

It unnerved him to know that Morna watched them, but in truth, it came as no real surprise.

"I shall try."

"Good. And Ross, ye might wish to make a trip down to yer mailbox this morning. There's been a package sitting in it for weeks now."

"Aye?"

"Aye. A package ye'll be angry with yerself for not opening sooner. Saving someone from a fated death might be against nature, but healing someone from a few wounds certainly is not."

Lifting Tink off his lap, he thanked the witch and hung up in a hurry to stumble down to the mailbox.

He couldn't get to the witch's package soon enough.

CHAPTER 18

When I woke Saturday morning to see the clock at straight up ten o'clock, I leapt out of my bed in a panic before remembering I didn't have to go to work. It was the first weekend in recent memory that I'd been able to sleep a wink past my normal wake up time of six.

Smiling, I allowed myself to fall leisurely back onto my bed as I reached for my phone.

I already had two text messages from Ross.

The first:

"Good morning, Allanah. I'm afraid I've come down with something. I'm not feeling too well this morning. I think it best that I spend the weekend recovering."

And then:

"Allow me to accompany you on Tuesday morning when you walk the girls to school again, and are you free Tuesday evening for our date?"

I looked at the time stamp on the messages. He'd sent them at seven. By now, I was certain he was growing nervous that I hadn't yet replied—I would've been.

I typed out my response and hit send.

"I'm so sorry you're not feeling well. Let me know if you need me to bring anything by for you. And while Tuesday works great for a date, I'm not sure you should come with me to walk the girls. It exhausted you last time. I'm worried if you do that, you'll be too tired to take me out. ;)"

Seconds after the message showed delivered, I could see him typing a response. His reply popped up shortly after.

"I assure you, I'll have plenty of energy for our date. I'll meet you by the elevators at six-thirty Tuesday morning. I'm counting the hours until then. Have a wonderful weekend, lass."

Setting my phone down, I stretched my arms high above my head as I smiled.

I would be counting them, too.

I spent my weekend with Gramps and Georgie as we worked to help him pare down his wardrobe to make some space in his closet. Things with Gladys seemed to be getting pretty serious. As she was staying with him more often, he thought it would be nice to make some room for her to leave a few things.

At least he thought so until he actually set about the task of cleaning out his closet. Then, the three of us all realized what a clothes hoarder Gramps really was.

Between all weekend wading through piles of jackets and vibrant ties at his place, followed by an incredibly busy Monday with patients, the wait between Ross' text Saturday and our plans for me to meet him at the elevator on Tuesday morning seemed remarkably short.

I left my apartment early, intending to arrive at the elevator a few minutes before our planned time just in case he wasn't there at six-thirty and I needed to go down the hall to his apartment to see if he needed help. He didn't. To my astonishment, he was already standing by the elevator doors—sans crutches—shaved, and as put together as I'd ever seen him.

Confused—and concerned—I frowned as I approached him.

"What the hell is going on, Ross? Why aren't you using your crutches? You need to get your weight off that leg right this second."

He smiled and bent to lift his pants leg as he explained. "I'm all healed."

My mind reeled. It was impossible. He was progressing more quickly than most to be sure, but his injuries had been extensive. There was no way in hell he was healed.

"No, you are not." Dropping my bag to the floor, I bent down to examine him.

His leg looked entirely normal. I reached for the hem of his jeans and pulled them up as far as they would go, all the while expecting him to scream out in pain at any given second.

There was no scar from the surgery, and his muscles didn't look the slightest bit atrophied from being in a cast for weeks.

"It doesn't make sense, Ross."

Feeling like I'd stepped into *The Twilight Zone*, I released my grip on his jeans and rose from the floor, still frowning.

He shrugged. "I doona know, lass. I woke Saturday morning feeling dreadful. My whole body ached. I thought I had the flu. By Monday morning, I felt much better. When I went for my appointment with my surgeon, he was as astonished as ye are. It seems I've had some sort of miraculous healing."

While part of my brain knew I should be relieved that he was no longer injured, the most dominant part of my mind was growing bewildered and angrier by the second.

"That doesn't happen, Ross. I...I don't understand."

I reached up to rub my forehead—a headache coming on quickly.

He stepped forward to grab my wrists as he gently pulled me toward him and kissed my cheek.

"Take a breath, lass. I know 'tis strange, but 'tis what's happened. Doona distress over it."

He moved the back of my hand and laid his fingers on my forehead.

"Ye feel clammy, lass. As ye can see, I'm well. I'll walk the girls to school on my own. Go and rest until ye have to go to work. I'll pick ye up tonight at six."

I was sure I did feel clammy. My brain was having the most difficult time processing what I'd seen. I'd never witnessed or heard anything like this in my life.

Confused as I was, I was a little worried my wide eyes and pale cheeks might frighten the girls anyway.

"Okay. Maybe that's best. You're sure...you're sure you're totally well now?"

He picked up his leg, putting all of his weight on the one that was still dreadfully injured four days ago and began to hop up and down on it.

"Aye, lass. I'm fine."

My eyes wide with shock, I said goodbye and made my way back to my apartment.

Nothing about it made sense.

Despite the impossibility of it all, I couldn't deny what my eyes had just seen.

At least it meant he wasn't my patient officially, or unofficially, anymore.

I could go on my date tonight guilt-free.

CHAPTER 19

"Iknew this was going to happen."

Hannah looked up at him as he stepped into the house, as if she weren't the least bit surprised to see him without his crutches.

"Ye mean my leg?"

The young girl nodded as Ross turned toward the sound of Caleb descending the stairs, little Maggie in his arms.

"Ross? How? What?" Caleb continued to fumble over his words. "Where are your crutches?"

"I doona need them. Seems I've healed."

Ross didn't miss the fact that Caleb's bewildered expression bore a remarkable resemblance to the one on Allanah's face earlier.

"You've what? Ross, I saw what you looked like last week when you decided to walk the girls with Sue. How is that possible?"

He couldn't very well tell anyone, save perhaps Sydney, the truth of his miraculous recovery. If he mentioned that a Scottish witch mailed him a potion, he imagined it wouldn't take long before both Allanah and Caleb started looking for ways to have him committed.

Instead, he decided to go with the easiest explanation—none at all. As far as they were concerned, he was as in the dark to what could've caused such rapid healing as they were. He could deal with the incredulity for a time. He could deal with just about anything if it meant having the full use of his legs and body. He was ready to get back to work.

"I doona know. 'Tis as much a surprise to me as 'tis to ye, I imagine, but I see no sense in dwelling on it. I'd rather just be thankful that I'm well and get back to work. I've told Allanah that she needn't continue to fill in for me with the girls. As ye can see, I'm well enough to walk them on my own."

Caleb continued to frown, but slowly began to nod his head in resignation. "Okay. Well, I suppose we are all due a bit of a miracle after the past few months. I'm just glad you're better. It will help me a ton to have you back at work." He hesitated, shifting Maggie in his arms before continuing. "Not that I minded, of course. I truly wanted you to take all the time you needed."

Ross gave him a quick nod and extended his arms toward Maggie. "I know. Now, let me see her. Ye best be on yer way. 'Tis yer last week of training before the big day, aye?"

Caleb groaned and closed his eyes as he answered him. "Yes, and I'm so nervous that I'm barely sleeping."

"You don't need to be nervous, Daddy. It's going to be great."

Ross looked down at Hannah and gave her a wink of approval at her effort to reassure her father.

"Thank you, sweet girl. You have a good day at school today, okay?"

Taking Maggie from Caleb's extended arms, Ross watched as Caleb bent to give Hannah a quick kiss on her forehead before standing to leave.

"And, I'm off. Wish me luck. That old man is relentless."

Quickly strapping Maggie to his chest, Ross helped Hannah with her backpack then reached for her hand as they headed out the door behind Caleb, both of them wishing him luck in unison as they turned and walked off in separate directions.

Hannah wasted no time to dig in with her usual questions. "Why didn't Sue come with you this morning? She didn't want to see us?"

That was the last thing Ross ever wanted Hannah to think.

"O'course she wanted to see ye, lass. 'Tis only that it took her by surprise to see me feeling so well. She needed a moment to herself before work."

"I wasn't surprised."

He smiled, bouncing a little bit to soothe Maggie.

"Aye, why is that, lass?"

The little girl looked up at him and shrugged. "I've been asking Mommy to help you get better so we could see you more again. She never really answers me back, but I still knew she would help."

Ross stopped short as Hannah's words caused his eyes to grow blurry with tears and a lump rose in his throat. He didn't want the girl to see him cry. If she could talk about her own mother without getting emotional, surely he could do the same.

"Ye talk to her?"

Hannah returned her gaze to the sidewalk in front of them as she spoke. "Yes. Dad said that not having our Mom around means that we have an angel assigned just to us. While I don't know much about angels, you've got to be able to talk to them, or what's the point really?"

He didn't trust his voice not to break when he spoke. He coughed to try to push away his need to cry. "I doona know much about angels either, lass, but I imagine ye are right."

Hannah looked up at him, her expression knowing. "You miss her, too, don't you?"

"Aye, Hannah." His voice did break then, but he continued on. "Every day."

***

I spent most of my morning distracted by the impossibility of Ross' recovery. It just didn't make sense. There was no scenario, no explanation that I knew of, that made it possible. In the end, however, I decided that Ross was right. It was a good thing that he was healed. There was no sense in me dwelling on it beyond that.

It was easier once I got to work. With patients to pour myself into, I was able to forget about Ross' leg and our upcoming date. I hadn't the slightest idea what we were doing. He'd never told me, and I'd been so dumbfounded by the way I'd found him this morning, that it hadn't crossed my mind to ask.

I shot him a quick text message as soon as I got home from work.

"What's the dress code for tonight?"

It took him twenty minutes to reply, which made me hope that it was nothing I needed to dress up for. His delayed reply had me running behind.

"Casual. Bring socks. We're going bowling."

Bowling? I stared down at my phone and frowned. I was a terrible bowler, and it had been years since I'd done so.

Determined to put on a good face—it didn't really matter whether I was good or not—I dressed in jeans, knee-high boots, and a v-neck sweater that paired really nicely with my favorite scarf.

I'd just finished applying a little bit of blush to keep me from looking so washed out when I heard him knock on my door.

He looked as handsome as he had on our first blind date, when he'd walked up to me sitting in the booth at the Indian restaurant.

"Are ye ready to get yer arse whooped?"

"What?" I looked at him, confused.

"Bowling, lass. I plan to beat ye in bowling."

"Oh." I sighed, then laughed. Of course he'd meant bowling. Having my brain muffled so early in the morning had thrown me off all day. "You probably will beat me. Are you good?"

He shrugged. "I've truly never bowled."

Laughing, I reached for my purse and stepped out into the hall with him to close the door. Georgie wasn't home. I wondered if perhaps she was out with her new beau. It seemed we were increasingly becoming passing ships in the night.

"If you've never bowled, then why are you so sure you'll beat me? Admittedly, I'm a terrible bowler, but at least I've done it before."

I turned toward him after locking the door to see him extending his hand toward mine. I gladly took it. His hand was warm and large around my ever-cold fingers.

"'Tis a feeling, I suppose. I hope ye doona expect me to take it easy on ye just because I like ye so much."

"If you do that, it will make me like you quite a bit less."

I destroyed him. My score for each of the three games we played was abysmally low, but Ross must've been close to winning the world-record for the most gutter balls in an hour. If I'd had any mercy at all, I would've insisted we put up the bumper rails.

I didn't.

He pouted all the way to the pizza place around the corner from the bowling alley.

"I canna understand it. I'm usually quite good at games."

"It's karma, Ross. You talked a big game, and it came back to bite you in your 'arse.'"

He gave me a playful little shove with his shoulder as we approached the small pizza dive.

"Are ye making fun of my accent, lass? Ye've a bit of one yerself."

He clearly had no idea how hard I'd worked to minimize my Boston accent. Offended, I whirled on him.

"I do not!"

He laughed as we found an open booth in the corner by the door.

"Aye, lass. Ye do. I like it."

"Well…" At least someone did. "Thank you."

The waitress showed up shortly and we ordered a bottle of the house wine and a supreme pizza—their specialty—for us to split.

As she walked away from the table with our order, Ross leaned across the table and spoke to me, his voice low and soft. "I think ye are the most beautiful woman I've ever seen."

Our table's location caused the cold air from the door to linger, but despite the frigid air, warm heat flooded my body at his words. I knew I was blushing and tried to look down so he wouldn't notice, but he stopped me by reaching forward and gently lifting my chin so I looked at him.

"Doona look down, lass. Ye doona believe that about yerself, do ye? Ye should."

I wasn't used to such attention, and I felt uncomfortable and exposed beneath his gaze. Rather than accept his compliment, I hurried to deflect.

"Are you going to the race on Saturday?"

He tilted his head and narrowed his eyes, and I knew he was silently reprimanding me for brushing past his kind words, but he didn't push the subject further and instead answered my question. "Aye. O'course. I'm waiting at the finish line with Hannah and Maggie. Do ye want to go together, lass?"

That truly wasn't why I'd asked the question. It had only been my desire to change the subject to anything that didn't have to do with me. If we went together that meant Ross would surely meet

Gramps and Georgie. I would have to introduce him. How would I do that? What was this? It was still so new. Regardless, I had known he would go to the race, so whether we went together or not, he was bound to meet them anyway.

"Sure. It will last hours. It would probably be good if you had some help with the girls. Do you mind if my sister joins us?"

"Not at all."

At that moment, our waitress returned with the bottle of wine and two glasses. Just as she began to pour them, my phone went off —Georgie.

I looked at Ross guiltily.

"I'm sorry. I thought I had it on silent. It's my sister. Do you mind if I answer it?"

He waved me on. "O'course not."

Nodding, I stood from the table and walked a few steps away to an empty corner of the restaurant before answering the phone.

"Georgie? Is everything okay?"

"Hey. Yeah, yeah, it's all good."

She sounded drunk.

"Have you been drinking? Do I need to pick you up somewhere?"

She laughed, knowing she'd been caught. She was definitely drunk.

"Just a little bit, sis. You don't need to pick me up. I'm home, but my..." She hesitated, and I suspected she was in the same predicament I'd just been going over in my mind. She wasn't sure how to refer to the man she'd been seeing, either. "My friend and I went to a whiskey tasting downtown. He's fine, but it got the better of me. I really want him to stay until I get to feeling better. Do you think you could stay at Gramps' house tonight? I already called him and he said it was fine."

I knew she wasn't lying. Georgie was the lightest of lightweights. Had she told me her plans for the evening, I would've advised against it.

"You hate whiskey."

Georgie lowered her voice, seemingly so her man-friend wouldn't hear her. "Yes, well, it wasn't really about the whiskey, obviously, Sue. More the company, ya know?"

Groaning, I leaned against the wall. I no longer had any of my stuff at Gramps' house. If I stayed over there, I would have to sleep in my clothes and go to bed without brushing my teeth.

"I really don't see why there's any need for me to avoid my apartment, Georgie. You two will be in your room, won't you? My bathroom is attached to my room. Once I get home, I'll just lock myself in there."

I'd not minded staying away for a little bit on Friday, but Georgie's behavior now had me worried this was about to become a regular occurrence. If so, it wouldn't be long before she would have to find her own place.

"Please, Sue." She sounded exasperated and tired. I could tell she was putting a lot of effort into not slurring her words.

I didn't want to drive all the way over to my grandfather's house, especially after my date, but I also didn't have any desire to be the one holding her hair back while she vomited.

"Fine. But we can't make this a habit, okay?"

"Of course. Love you."

She hung up the phone before I could say anything else.

The pizza was being delivered to our table by the time I made it back. Ross looked at me with concern.

"Has something happened?"

I shook my head, and reached for a slice of pizza. "No. Nothing bad. My sister got a little carried away at a whiskey tasting she went to with the guy she's seeing. He's staying over at my apartment, and she asked me if I would mind staying at my grandfather's tonight."

He furrowed his brow, and reached for his wine glass before he spoke hesitantly.

"I...I doona wish ye to think me inappropriate. I know 'tis early still, but ye may stay at my apartment if ye wish it. I've a spare room. Ye doona need to sleep in my room if ye doona wish to."

Oh, I wished to. I knew that I didn't know him nearly as well as anyone I'd ever slept with in my past, but it had been far too long since I'd enjoyed that part of my life. I liked Ross. I trusted him. And whether it was inappropriate or not, regardless of whether or not it might be too soon, I knew that I was ready and willing to find myself in his bed.

"You sure?"

He nodded, a mischievous grin spreading across his face. "Aye, lass. I'd love to have ye there."

"Okay." I took a sip of my wine for courage. "I'll stay. But I can't see any reason why we should go messing up your guest room."

His brows inched up his forehead in surprise, and I thought I saw the slightest hint of a blush spread across his cheeks.

"Me neither, lass. Shall we ask for a to-go box?"

CHAPTER 20

*I*t had been too long since he'd buried himself in a woman. His cock throbbed inside his jeans—a result of the kiss they'd shared in the elevator. The surprise pressure of Allanah's lips against his own and the way she'd leaned into him until his back hit the back wall of the elevator, her chest pressing into him, made him hard in an instant.

He couldn't get to the apartment fast enough. He fumbled with the key as he struggled to get it in the lock, groaning as the sound of Tink's excited whining reached his ears. He would have to take the pup outside straight away.

Closing his eyes, he tried to think of anything that would reduce his erection. He didn't want Allanah to take notice of it yet, let alone any of the apartment residents that might see him on his way outside.

Turning the key, he reached for the handle and opened the door for them to step inside. He extended the pizza box to Allanah and sighed in relief as the pressure inside his jeans released just a little.

He wasn't an animal. He could control himself until the appropriate time. Just because she was staying in his apartment—in his bed—didn't mean she was ready to have sex with him.

"Lass, will ye take this to the kitchen? I must take Tink outside. Make yerself comfortable."

Not bothering with Tink's leash, Ross grabbed it on the way out the door as he scooped up the squirmy pup, whispering in her ear on the way to the elevator.

"Hello, lass. Ye'd think I was gone for a week, the way yer tail is wagging. Will ye do me a favor? Pee quickly so I can get back to the apartment."

The pup let out a shrill bark the second the elevator opened before leaping from his arms.

What could possibly be taking them so long?

The thought turned itself over and over in my mind as I checked my watch. Thirty minutes. While I'd never had a dog of my own, I couldn't imagine that it should take half an hour for the puppy to go about her business.

In the time since Ross and Tink left, I'd gone to the bathroom to make sure that my hair wasn't doing anything crazy, started a fire, and arranged a picnic of sorts with our barely-eaten pizza in front of the roaring flames.

Five more minutes. I'm giving them five more minutes before I go downstairs to see what's up.

I made the promise under my breath, all the while staring at the hands of my watch, unease growing.

With ten seconds remaining, I pushed myself off of the blanket I'd spread out in front of the fire and moved to grab my coat, just as the door to Ross' apartment flew open.

Ross held a trembling Tink tight to his chest, and both of them were soaked through.

"What happened?"

Dropping my own jacket, I hurried over to pick the pizza up off the blanket and yanked it off the floor before hurrying toward him with it. Reaching for Tink, I grabbed her, wrapping her up in the blanket and holding her tightly as Ross stomped his feet and pulled off his wet coat.

"'Tis my fault. I dinna put her leash on her in time, and she jumped from my arms when we reached the ground level of the building just as a resident walked through the front door. She ran for it. I doona think she meant to run away. I think she thought it a game of sorts, but she frightened me to death. I just knew she would be hit by a car before I could reach her."

Tink whimpered, but I could feel her muscles begin to relax as I sat close to the fire and continued to rub her.

"Why are the two of you wet? It wasn't raining, was it?"

"No. She leapt into a fountain and dinna take to swimming at all. I had to jump in to save the poor thing from drowning."

I looked down at Tink and then back at Ross. He was pale, and I knew it had a lot more to do with how frightened he'd been than how cold he was.

"It's okay, Ross. You saved her. She's all right."

He nodded as he stepped on the heel of his left boot with his right foot so he could step out of it.

"Aye. I doona think I realized until tonight just how much I care for her."

I squeezed Tink a little closer and bent to kiss the top of her head.

"How could you not? She's a sweetheart. Look. I've got her. I'll get her warm and dry. Why don't you get out of those wet clothes and take a quick shower? Then we can put something funny on the television to decompress for a bit."

"Thank ye, Allanah. I'm glad ye are here."

He turned and moved in the direction of his bedroom. As soon as he was out of sight, I reached for a piece of the leftover pizza now precariously balanced on a plate on the fireplace mantle and tore off a bit of the crust to give to Tink.

"You've had a rough night. Just don't tell your dad, okay?"

Tink yipped and lifted her head up to give the underside of my chin a quick lick.

———

$\mathcal{T}$ears fell freely the moment the hot water began to pour over his shoulders. He wouldn't have been able to forgive himself if something had happened to Tink. She was the companion he hadn't known he needed.

He stood underneath the hot spray of water longer than usual as he allowed his emotions to subside and his adrenaline to slow.

He could hear the television going when he stepped from his bathroom into his bedroom, and he dressed quickly so he could make his way back to Allanah.

Tink must've heard him exit the shower, for the pup trotted into his bedroom—dry and looking no worse for wear after her great adventure.

"Ye canna do that to me again, lass. Ye gave me a terrible scare."

Tink tilted her head from side to side, her eyes intent on him as she tried to figure out what he was saying to her.

Dressed in sweats, t-shirt, and socks, with his hair still wet, he made his way back into the living room.

"What are ye…"

He stopped as he neared the couch and noticed that Allanah's eyes were closed. She was already asleep.

He bent down to whisper to Tink. "I think I shall bunk in here tonight, lassie. Yer wee little set of stairs is set up beside my bed if ye decide ye'd rather sleep in there."

Tink answered him by leaping up onto the couch and curling up at Allanah's feet.

Following her lead, Ross moved over to the couch and lifted the corner of the blanket as he gently scooted in beside Allanah.

"Do ye mind if I join ye, lass?" He whispered the question softly, hoping he wouldn't fully wake her.

She responded by shifting herself over and lifting her head so that as he wrapped his arm around her, she settled easily into the crook of his arm.

The scent of her hair wafted up to him, and she sighed as he reached over to brush back the hair that had fallen over her face.

Whispering under his breath, he resigned himself to a night of torture.

"I hope ye two lassies find sweet dreams, for I know I willna sleep a wink."

CHAPTER 21

I woke just after dawn snuggled into Ross' chest with Tink curled up between my legs. Ross' right arm hung awkwardly off the side of the couch, and I wondered how long it had taken him to fall asleep. He couldn't have slept well. I smiled. I couldn't remember the last time I'd been held like that all through the night.

If I were honest with myself, the answer was most likely never. Not like that anyway. Not where someone held me all night long, sacrificing his own comfort while I slept like a rock.

It eased my guilt a little to know that at least he was asleep, snoring quite loudly, now.

As gently as I could, I scooted out of my little nook on the couch and carefully lifted myself over him so that he would keep sleeping.

"Come on, Tink."

Still dressed in my clothes from the night before, I grabbed my coat, attached Tink's leash to her, and led her downstairs for what would hopefully be a much more boring potty trip than what the small puppy had experienced the night before.

Thankfully, she peed quickly and without incident. When we returned to Ross' apartment he was still sleeping. I refreshed Tink's water bowl and set about looking for something to make for breakfast.

While his fridge was full, my choices were limited. The only thing that wasn't one of Mrs. Jenkins' casseroles was a carton of eggs and the leftover pizza from last night.

Eggs would have to do. After searching for a pan, I managed to get the eggs scrambled and coffee made without waking Ross.

When breakfast was ready, I grabbed the small tray from his coffee table and loaded it with the contents of our breakfast before returning it to its place beside Ross.

"Good morning." I leaned in close and gently kissed his cheek. "I thought you might be hungry since you didn't really eat anything last night."

Slowly, his eyes flickered open.

"I made some eggs and some coffee. I assumed since you had a coffee maker, you drink it."

He reached for the coffee cup first.

"Aye. I never drank it in Scotland, but it has become a daily ritual since I moved to the United States. Thank ye, lass."

He took a long sip of the hot brew then reached for my hand, encouraging me to scoot closer to him.

"I hope ye doona mind that I joined ye on the couch as ye slept. The opportunity to hold ye was too tempting."

"Do you think I would've made you breakfast if I minded?"

"I hope not. Have ye heard from yer sister, this morning? She is likely to feel dreadful."

"I'm sure she does. Georgie has an incredibly low alcohol tolerance. I can't imagine what got into her last night. I've always known her to be someone who likes her drinks to be way more sugar than anything else. And a whiskey tasting? Who even likes whiskey?"

Ross laughed and rose to gather our plates. "I do. Mayhap more than I should. Caleb does, as well. Have ye never noticed his collection of whiskey?"

I definitely hadn't.

"No, I never have."

"Lass?"

I glanced up from my seat on the couch to see Ross standing—now free of the dishes he'd just taken to the kitchen—at the end of the couch, his hair messy from sleep, the slightest hint of stubble lining his jaw. He looked incredibly sexy, and there was a dark glint in his eyes that made me nervous in the most thrilling way.

"Yes?"

"For my own well-being, I need some clarification."

Curious, I urged him on. "Okay. Shoot."

"Did ye fall asleep on my couch so ye wouldna feel pressured to sleep in my bed?"

"No." I stood and moved over to him, stepping close and leaning in to give him a short kiss. I didn't linger. I was certain that my breath was terrible after falling asleep basically mid pizza slice and without brushing my teeth. "Not at all. I was holding Tink and, as she got warm, so did I. The fire was going, and before I knew it, I was asleep. I promise you, I was actually quite looking forward to being in your bed."

He groaned and wrapped his arms around me, holding me tight as he went in for a deeper kiss and pushed himself up against me. He was hard against my stomach.

Melting into the kiss for just a moment, I quickly put a hand in between us and pushed him away.

"I have to go, Ross. I only have an hour before I need to leave for work."

Reluctantly, he stepped back.

"Ye are killing me, lass."

I smirked at the prominent erection on display beneath the thin fabric of his sweatpants.

"I'm sorry. Look, I've got a really busy week, but I'll see you the morning of the marathon, yes? Maybe we can do something that night?"

He walked me over to the door, his breathing still heavy.

"Aye. 'Twill be the longest three days of my life."

I leaned in to kiss his cheek.

"You'll live."

As I walked out the door and back toward my apartment, I heard him call out to me.

"'Tis yer fault if I doona, Allanah.

CHAPTER 22

"I honestly can't believe that you're up. I thought for sure you would change your mind and just meet us at the race."

Unlike Georgie, I was accustomed to waking early. Regardless, the pre-dawn alarm had been rough. Although I was now showered and dressed, I still felt sluggish as I stepped into the living room to find Georgie waiting on me, two coffee cups in hand.

"Are you kidding? I'm not about to miss the chance to meet Ross and Gladys in one chaotic morning!"

I widened my eyes at her as I drew in a calming breath. Everything was about to get hectic for sure. Since Caleb and Gramps were running together, and Georgie didn't want to go to the race by herself, everyone was set to convene at Caleb's house at the crack of dawn. Caleb and Gramps would leave for the race together, and the rest of us—Ross, Georgie, Gladys, Hannah, Maggie, and myself—would go together.

Awkward introductions and interactions were bound to occur. Georgie was beside herself with excitement.

Taking one of the coffees, I headed toward the door. "Just

promise me you're not going to say anything mortifying to him, okay?"

She frowned, and then smiled mischievously. "I'm offended that you think I would ever do such a thing."

I laughed as I waited for her to step into the hallway so I could close and lock the door. "Yeah, right. You live for whatever drama you can cause."

"We'll see."

Together, we speculated about what Gladys would be like and what it meant that Gramps was finally allowing us to meet her. It was the first time we'd been offered the chance to meet one of his ladies, and I found myself pressured to like her.

It was a quiet morning and the walk to Caleb's took even less time than usual. Georgie and I approached Caleb's door just as Gramps pulled up in his car.

I poked Georgie in the ribs and motioned to the car with my head. "There they are. We should wait, right? Meet her before we enter the house?"

She nodded in agreement. Retreating, we stepped back down the steps leading to Caleb's front door and waited for Gramps and Gladys to exit his car.

"Good morning, girls. Are you two ready to watch me kick some ass today?"

I laughed as Gramps walked toward us, his arms stretched wide as he readied to pull us both into a hug.

I had no doubt that he would do just that—especially in his age category.

"Of course."

I could see Gladys over his shoulder as she stood back shyly waiting for an introduction. She was just as cute as my grandfather.

Petite with long, dark hair and even darker eyes, she too looked much younger than her age. I smiled at her, hoping it would encourage her to approach.

When she didn't, I pulled away enough to whisper in Gramps' ear. "I think you better introduce us."

"Ah." He stepped back, smiling. "Yes, of course. Girls..." He paused and twisted long enough to wave Gladys forward. "This is Gladys. My...my..." He faltered, and Georgie stepped in to finish for him.

"She's your girlfriend, Gramps."

He visibly blushed and reached for her hand.

"Yes, yes, of course. It's only that I feel too old to have a girlfriend."

Gladys smiled and leaned into him gently. "You're not. Trust me."

I extended my hand toward her. "I'm so happy to meet you. I've heard so many wonderful things."

That wasn't true, exactly. Gramps had been extremely tightlipped about Gladys, but I could see she was nervous. I figured it was always nice to be nice.

The door to Caleb's house opened behind us, as Caleb called out to the group.

"What are you guys doing out here? It's cold, and you're all going to be standing out in the weather plenty today. Get inside."

Obliging him, we made our way in. I hung back, intentionally going in last so I could talk to Caleb.

"Where's Ross? Is he here yet?"

Part of me had worried all weekend that he would get cold feet about getting thrown in to meet my family so early and all at once.

Caleb nodded. "Oh yeah. He's been here for a while. He's feeding Maggie upstairs in the nursery. He should be down in a bit."

Relieved, I joined the others in the living room just as Hannah ran toward Georgie and threw her arms around my sister's legs. I watched in shock.

"Georgie, I've missed you!"

Saddened that I never got a greeting like that from Hannah, and astonished that my sister was getting one now, I stared in confusion. I thought Georgie had been doing most of her cleaning while Hannah was at school.

"You've missed her?"

"Yes. I haven't seen Georgie in weeks." Pausing, Hannah redirected her attention toward Georgie. "And you know what? The new housekeeper isn't nearly as good as you are. And she's not nearly as nice either."

Georgie spun toward me, still holding Hannah, her expression frazzled and guilty. "Umm…I've been meaning to tell you."

I glared at Georgie as I waited for her to elaborate, but as she opened her mouth to speak, Caleb stepped forward to intercede.

"It's all my doing, Sue. I should've told you. I've a friend who needed a housekeeper who was more full-time. I know you've been paying her, but this guy was offering her way more money. I just couldn't deny her the opportunity. So I fired her."

I continued to stare at Georgie as I scowled at her. I couldn't make a scene in front of everyone. Instead, I took a measured breath before speaking. "What exact date did you stop working here?"

She bowed her head in what I could only assume was shame. "A month ago yesterday."

Shaking my head, I thought of the four checks I'd given her during the past month that she'd already cashed. "You owe me a thousand dollars."

She looked up. "I know, I know. I haven't spent it. I'll get it back to you."

She was saved by the sound of footsteps descending the staircase behind us, and I turned to grab Ross to keep him from being peppered with questions.

Maggie was already strapped to him in her carrier, sleeping.

"Good morning, lass."

He leaned in to kiss my cheek as I greeted him at the bottom of the stairs. "Good morning."

I turned to introduce him to Georgie, Gladys, and Gramps, but Caleb held up a hand to stop me.

"Hang on. Your grandfather and I have to leave in just a minute. You all can do introductions on our way out the door. Let's just make certain everyone is on the same page."

In unison, we all nodded, awaiting his instructions.

"You guys will wait at whatever spot you can find near the finish line, yes?"

Again, we all nodded.

"Great. Let's all go get lunch after we are both finished racing."

He turned toward me. "After lunch, I'm driving the girls up north an hour to my mother's house for the weekend. I've got a massage scheduled for this evening, and I plan on spending the weekend doing absolutely nothing. I've already packed Maggie. Hannah insisted on packing herself. Do you mind helping her finish then make sure both bags get loaded into my car? Your grandfather and I will take his vehicle to the race. You guys can go in mine since the car seat for Maggie and the booster seat for Hannah are already set up. The keys are hanging on a hook next to the garage door. Sound good?"

I smiled at him. It wasn't as if any of us had any choice. "Of course. Good luck. We'll be cheering you guys on the whole time."

Clearly calmed by my assurance that we had it under control, Caleb moved to grab Hannah from Georgie's arms, leaving me to quickly introduce Ross.

I didn't need to do anything. Before I could move, Ross brushed past me and walked right over to my grandfather, his hand extended.

"Hello. 'Tis a pleasure to meet ye, sir. I'm Ross, Allanah's boyfriend."

I could see Georgie balk at him in surprise as I felt my own jaw drop. To see him so confidently introduce himself as my boyfriend —something we hadn't even discussed yet—after watching my grandfather falter over the same introduction with someone he'd been dating for much longer, was incredibly hot.

I stood back, allowing him to continue down the line, next introducing himself to Gladys and then to my sister.

As soon as he was done, Caleb began to hurry Gramps out of the house, and the rest of us were left to get ready for the marathon.

Hannah spoke first as soon as Gramps and her father were gone. "Is it okay if Georgie helps me finish packing?"

Quickly resigning that I was just never going to be Hannah's favorite, I nodded. "Of course it is."

As they took off for her room, Gladys reached for Maggie who had stirred and was now fussing.

"Let me take her for a little bit. I'm good with babies."

Ross quickly lifted Maggie from the carrier and allowed Gladys to move to the rocking chair in the living room with her, leaving Ross and me alone in the entryway.

I pushed him back a step so we were hidden from Gladys' view and leaned in to give him an enthusiastic kiss before trailing my lips up toward his ear to whisper.

"You are so getting laid tonight."

He groaned and leaned forward to nibble my ear before trailing my jawline to pull me in for another kiss.

CHAPTER 23

"I heard what you said at my house."

Ross stirred at the touch of Hannah's fingers pulling on his own to get his attention. Careful not to elbow anyone in the crowd around him, he squatted down low to listen to her.

"What, lass?"

Hannah tilted her head to one side and looked up at him, knowingly. "You heard what I said, Uncle Ross. I said, 'I heard what you said.' Sue is your girlfriend. I knew you didn't really want to be alone."

The little girl crossed her arms smugly against her chest.

Ross smiled and shrugged. "Aye, I suppose ye did know better than I. Can ye see a thing, lass? Do ye want me to pick ye up?"

Hannah nodded, and he quickly lifted her above his head and onto his shoulders.

"Whoa! Be careful, Uncle Ross. Don't let me fall."

He held tight to her ankles. "Doona worry about that, lass. I promise I've got ye."

Allanah stepped up beside him with Maggie snuggled into her.

"Did you see any extra blankets in Caleb's car? I think Maggie is cold. It's going to be hours before this race is finished. Maybe one of us should've stayed at the house with the girls for a while and brought them later?"

Casting his eyes upward, he looked up at Hannah. "Are ye cold, lass?"

She called down to him. "Yeah. Very."

Turning to look past the crowd, he spotted a diner not far down the street.

"Why doona I take them to get some breakfast at the diner down the way? The three of us can keep warm for a while. Ye can call me if ye think Caleb or yer grandfather are close to finishing and we will return."

Relief flooded Allanah's expression.

"Are you sure you don't mind? I would, but I feel like I should be here the whole time."

Ross reached out to squeeze her hand. "O'course, lass. 'Tis yer grandfather."

He reached up to lift Hannah off of his shoulders and lowered her to the ground.

"What do ye say we go grab a bite to eat? I'll have ye back before yer father is done running."

"I say that's great."

He returned his gaze to Allanah.

"'Tis settled then. Place Maggie in her stroller. We will see ye in a bit."

There was no way the small child was going to finish all the food she'd ordered. Ross watched with amusement as the waitress set three chocolate chip pancakes twice the size of her head down in front of her, followed by a large glass of orange juice, two scrambled eggs, and some bacon.

"Whoa."

He'd never seen Hannah look so intimidated.

"Doona worry. Let's get ye a plate, and ye can move over whatever ye think ye can actually eat. I'll take care of the rest."

Unlike Hannah, he'd not had anything to eat today.

"Okay. Deal. This is more food than I eat all day."

Laughing, the waitress winked at Hannah. "It's too much, really. I don't know why we serve such big portions. I'll be right back with another plate and a set of silverware for you."

With Maggie now sleeping happily in her stroller, Ross jumped to answer his phone the moment it began to ring in an effort to keep from waking the baby.

It was Sydney.

"Good morning, lass. How are ye?"

The usual happy tone of Sydney's voice was missing as she answered him, and it caused unease to work its way up his spine.

"Hey, Ross. I'm doing well. Do you have a minute to talk?"

The waitress appeared beside their table again. Seeing him rock Maggie's stroller gently back and forth with one hand while holding onto his phone with the other, she gave him a little smile and leaned forward to help Hannah put some of the food onto another plate. He whispered a thank you to the woman before returning his attention to Sydney.

"'Tis the Saturday of the marathon I told ye about. The race is going now, but I've escaped to a diner with Caleb's girls for a bit of breakfast and to get out of the cold. I've some time. Is everything okay?"

The sound of Sydney sighing on the other end did nothing to calm him.

"Yes and no. It's not an emergency, and I've debated all day whether or not I should even call you. I know what you've said to me about this before, but in the end, I decided that it wasn't up to me to make this decision for you."

It had to be about his mother. He could feel it in his gut.

"She's worse, aye?"

"Yes. Callum received a letter from Griffith while in the past today. He brought it back through as soon as he opened it. The healer in Griffith's territory doesn't believe she has more than a few months left."

His hunger vanished as an uncomfortable knot settled in his stomach. This news was inevitable. In truth, he was surprised that she'd lasted this long. The degenerative disease had plagued her for years. His only solace was knowing that she'd long since said her goodbye to him. She wouldn't be missing his presence now. And all of the arrangements for her care had been attended to years ago.

"Thank ye for telling me, lass. If Griffith sends other news, ye will tell me, aye? When she…she goes, I will return long enough to see her buried."

"Ross…" Sydney hesitated. "I didn't call because she doesn't have much time left. I called because she's asking for you."

Surprise coursed through him. She'd not asked for him in years. He'd hoped that by some miracle, she wouldn't forget that she'd already lost him once. If so, it would make everything so much easier for them both.

"What?" He knew it was possible. He knew that those with the disease often reverted back to earlier times. He'd just hoped that in this one instance he would remain inaccessible to her. It was difficult enough at a distance, but he wasn't sure he would be able to stand seeing her in person after all these years.

"Griffith writes that for weeks now she's been slipping in and out of the same time period in her life." She hesitated, and he could sense where she was heading. "Ross, she doesn't remember your supposed death. Each time she lands there, you're all she talks about. She's become quite agitated."

He would have to go back. The promises he'd made to himself to never return to Scotland meant nothing now. If his mother remembered him—if she needed him—he had to go.

Ross knew that the healer's suspicion of months meant nothing. She could go quickly or linger much longer. He would have to leave soon. And worse, he had no idea how long he would have to stay away. Most likely, it wouldn't be a short trip.

Arranging things with Caleb would be difficult enough, but what about Allanah? He'd promised her he wasn't going to run again, but now he had no other choice.

He would have to say goodbye.

CHAPTER 24

Something was up. I suspected it from Ross' tone when I called to tell him that it was time for them to meet back up with us at the race, but I knew for certain when I saw the expression on his face.

His jaw was tight, his eyes red, and his shoulders were stiff and pulled up uncomfortably as if it was taking all the strength he had to keep whatever he was feeling—whatever was upsetting him—in.

"Is everything okay?"

He gave me one curt nod as he began to pat Maggie's back as she stirred.

"I'll tell ye later. Would ye mind if we doona go out tonight, lass? Could we just order in and spend the evening curled up on the couch with Tink?"

He didn't know me well enough yet to realize that an evening in was pretty much always going to be preferable to me than just about anything else. Regardless, I expected that the change of plans had much more to do with whatever had happened during the last few hours than him sharing the same enthusiasm for being a hermit as me.

I frowned at him, trying to show concern. "Sure, but are you sure..."

He interrupted me, gently reaching out to place his hand on my arm. "I canna talk about it here, lass—I doona wish to upset either of the girls. Later, aye?"

Obliging him, I nodded and turned back to look at the finish line just in time.

To my surprise—I'd honestly expected Gramps to beat Caleb by a mile—Caleb and Gramps had stayed together, and they were just rounding the last corner toward the finish line.

Together, we screamed and cheered for them, and it didn't take long for Maggie's screams at being awakened by such noise to join in with our chorus.

Among the crowd of runners and the hoards of people looking on, it took some time for Gramps and Caleb to find their way to us once they were done. While they both looked unquestionably exhausted, I'd also never seen either of them look so proud.

"I cannot believe I did that." Caleb beamed as he turned to pull Gramps into a big, sweaty hug. "Thank you for pushing me to do this, and for helping me train, and for..." Caleb choked on his words as tears filled his eyes. "For all of your wisdom. It's helped me break out of the darkness of these past few months."

Now blubbering with almost as much enthusiasm as little Maggie, we collectively carpooled over to Gramps' favorite Italian restaurant and indulged in a carb-heavy lunch to reward our favorite runners.

After several enjoyable hours of food, conversation, and laughter, we all scattered. With Caleb and his girls in his car, and Gramps and Gladys in his, Georgie, Ross, and I were left to walk the short distance back to our apartment complex.

"What are your plans tonight, Georgie? Are you seeing your *friend* tonight?" I emphasized the word for good measure. She'd remained so tightlipped about the situation that I still had no idea what to call the man she'd been seeing.

"Yes, but not until late. He's out of town until this evening. I was planning on being in the apartment until eight or so. After that, I won't be back until tomorrow night sometime."

Ross increased his pace, walking ahead so Georgie and I could talk in private.

"Okay. How are things going?"

She blushed and smiled at me. "Really, really good."

"And that's all I'm getting, isn't it?"

She laughed and nodded enthusiastically. "Yep."

Our plans to order dinner went out the window the moment we sat down on Ross' couch after taking Tink for a much-needed potty break and short walk outside.

"If you're hungry, Ross, please feel free to order something for yourself, but I honestly don't think I can eat another bite. I'm pretty sure lunch is going to have me feeling stuffed until morning at least—maybe longer than that."

He laughed, and scooted in closer. "I couldna agree with ye more, lass. The only thing I'm hungry for is ye."

His lips found mine quickly, and it only took a second of us kissing for Tink to jump off my lap and give us one quick, annoyed bark of disapproval.

"I don't think she likes watching us kiss."

He bobbed his head toward his bedroom. "Then I suppose 'tis good I've a door that separates this room from my bedroom. Will ye join me?"

I looked at him, examining his expression for any sign of the distress from earlier. Whether it was the enjoyable company at lunch or his desire to get me into his bed, I didn't know, but whatever had been bothering him so much earlier was no longer visible in his eyes or furrowed brow. While I wanted to know what had happened, I also had no desire to remind him of whatever it was. Surely it could wait until morning.

"Tink will be okay out here by herself?"

He laughed and stood, offering me his hand. "Aye. I'll let her into the room when we truly intend to sleep." He winked at me and slowly led me toward the bedroom.

CHAPTER 25

*A*llanah's passion matched his own. The moment he closed the door to his bedroom, gently backing her into it so he could press himself up against her as he kissed her, she moaned and wrapped her arms around him, her fingernails digging deliciously into the back of his head.

"Can I undress ye, lass?"

She pulled back long enough to give him a nod before she started to fumble with the buttons on his shirt.

Ross laughed, allowing her to work her way down the front of his shirt before pushing her hands away.

"I canna pull yer sweater off when ye've got hands on me. I wanna see ye, Allanah."

She nodded again, saying nothing as she lifted her arms high for him to pull the sweater up and off her body.

She was as beautiful as he'd known she would be. He groaned at the sight of her black bra and leaned forward to kiss the mound of her breast before reaching behind to undo her bra.

Just as he reached for the clasp, an awful knowing slammed into his gut.

He couldn't do this.

Not now.

He wanted it as badly as he'd wanted anything, but it wouldn't be right for him to use her in this way now, not when he'd yet to tell her that he would have to leave.

If he slept with her now—if he went ahead with what they both wanted—she would be angry with him come morning.

He'd already done wrong by her before. She'd never forgive him if he did it again.

"Lass…" He whispered against her breast before reluctantly pulling away from her and bending to reach for her sweater so he could hand it back to her. "I canna do this."

She frowned at him as she fumbled to cover herself with her sweater. The expression in her eyes was one of hurt and confusion, and he hurried to reassure her.

"'Tis not that I doona want to, Allanah. I want it as much as I've ever wanted anything, but I fear ye would be angry with me if I did."

Her cheeks still rosy from desire, she breathlessly tried to argue with him.

"No. I promise you. I'm not going to be mad. I…I want this, too, Ross."

He closed his eyes as he ran his hands over his face and through his hair in frustration.

Could he not have just a few months of easy? Just a brief moment of time where everything didn't seem quite so hard was all he wanted.

"I have to leave the states as soon as possible, Allanah. I doona know when I'll be back. It could be many months. Mayhap half a year."

"What?"

She balked at him, the color draining from her face as she slowly walked to sit down on the edge of his bed.

"You're going to have to give me more of an explanation than that, Ross."

Sighing, he moved to sit next to her, his heart heavy as the thoughts of his mother came crashing back down on him.

"Do ye remember what I told ye about my mother the night we tried to look at Christmas lights?"

When she only answered him with a solemn nod, he continued. "Sydney, my friend and contact in Scotland, called me while I was at the diner with the girls. Mother hasna spoken of me in ages, but she is now. And she's verra distressed by my absence. The healer who cares for her believes that she is nearing the end of her life. If she needs me now, I canna stay away."

Her expression softened, and Ross had to choke back tears as she reached for his hands.

"Ross, I could never be angry with you for leaving to take care of your mother. Of course you have to go."

Hesitating, she swallowed hard, and he could see that her eyes were starting to grow wet with tears, as well.

"But you're probably right. It would only complicate things if we were to sleep together. And long-distance relationships never really work, do they?"

He sighed and nodded. She had no idea just how "long-distance" their relationship would be if they didn't end things now. In the seventeenth century, there would be no video calls or texting to maintain some sort of connection. Once he left, there would be no communication with her at all.

"No, lass. Though it breaks my heart to say so, I doona think that it would."

She stood, still holding on to one of his hands, pulling him up until he was on both feet, also. Once he stood before her, she wrapped her arms around him in a hug, burying her head into his chest.

"So what does that mean for us?"

He couldn't stand the thought of being alone tonight—he wanted her with him until the very last minute when he was forced to say goodbye.

"I doona know, but will ye please stay, Allanah? I willna try anything, I swear to ye. Let me hold ye while I sleep. We can speak of everything in the morning."

She pulled back to look up at him, and it broke his heart to see tears falling freely down her face.

"Okay, Ross. I'm all for delaying this for one more night."

I woke much later than usual. I could tell by the angle of the sun streaming in through the large window in Ross' bedroom. Sleep had come easily, despite the cloud of sadness that had hung over us through the night.

As promised, Ross tried nothing. Instead, he held me close as I slept with my head against his chest, the two of us saying nothing more after my agreement that we could talk about everything later.

I'd felt him shift me hours earlier, and I feigned a deep sleep as he slipped from the bed at dawn. We both needed some time alone to think things over.

He worried that I'd be angry at him, but the opposite was true. His desire to be there for his mother only made me like him more.

I didn't want to say goodbye to him. Every part of me dreaded sitting down to eat the breakfast I could smell him making in the kitchen, but I couldn't see any other way for this to go.

Perhaps it would be different if this weren't so new; if things were more established between us. If all of this had happened a year into our relationship, it would've been a no-brainer to hang on to things while he went to care for his ailing mother. But we weren't there yet. The months of laying that sort of foundation hadn't happened. A handful of dates and his declaration that he was my boyfriend didn't immediately make this something more than it was. I still knew very little about him and vice versa.

It wouldn't take long for both of us to begin to resent the difficulty that would inevitably arise in conversation, and things would end quickly—most likely with both of us disliking the other. That was the last thing on earth that I wanted.

I lay there for a long while after waking, staring up at Ross' ceiling. I was still in the same clothes I'd had on last night, with Tink curled up at my feet as the sadness of all of it swirled over and over in my mind.

The past year had been so hard on both of us. And if the little tidbits of information I'd managed to squeeze out of him were any indication, it wasn't just Beth's death that had been difficult for him in recent years.

I already cared about him so much. I didn't want to agree to something that would make me dislike him. That's all a long-distance relationship would do.

There was a soft knock on his bedroom door, and I quickly sat up in the bed. "Come in. I'm awake."

He looked so sexy. In a t-shirt and sweats with messy morning hair, it took all of my restraint to keep from launching myself at him.

"Breakfast is ready, lass, and I made far more than the two of us can eat. How about we take some of this over to Caleb before we return here to talk? Mayhap it could be a congratulatory breakfast for completing his marathon? Mayhap it will allow me to get on his good side before I have to tell him that I'm leaving."

I smiled at him, knowing that he was only doing what he'd done the night before—delaying the inevitable conversation about what this would mean for us.

I didn't mind. I was as keen to delay all of this as he was.

"Sure. Let me just run my fingers through my hair and clean the smudged mascara off my face. I'll be right out."

He gave me a wink and closed the door between us. Giving Tink a quick pat, I stood and made my way to the bathroom.

My hair looked awful. At least Caleb wasn't anyone I was trying to impress. Hurrying so the food he'd prepared wouldn't get cold, I freshened up with a few splashes of water and used my finger as a toothbrush before joining Ross in the living room.

By the time I was ready, he was dressed and had the food all packed up.

For the first bit of the walk to Caleb's, we remained silent, but as we rounded the last corner to his townhome, I couldn't stand it anymore.

"When are you leaving?"

He sighed and looked over at me, sadness in his eyes.

"Tomorrow."

That answer was enough to silence me the rest of the way to Caleb's house. Even though he'd said he was leaving, I'd just never imagined that it was going to be quite so soon.

Hoping that Caleb wouldn't want us to stay and visit, I rang the doorbell and waited for him to answer.

After about thirty seconds, I tried it again. Still nothing.

"He's probably still sleeping. Should we just let ourselves in and leave the cinnamon rolls on the kitchen counter with a little note?"

Ross eyed me nervously. "Do ye not think he will mind the intrusion?"

I shook my head and reached into my pocket for my keys. "We're bringing him food. He most definitely will not."

Laughing, Ross nodded and stepped into Caleb's house first as I pushed open the door.

The moment we stepped inside I could hear noises coming from the kitchen.

Ross looked back over his shoulder at me as we walked together in the direction of the strange sounds.

"Maybe he's already cooking."

I laughed, never for a moment suspecting what awaited us around the corner.

"It doesn't sound like cooking. It sounds like two people..."

I trailed off as we stepped into the entryway, and my mind

seized up in its effort to process the sight that was on full display before us.

Georgie sat butt naked on the kitchen island, her hands splayed back behind her to keep herself steady, her breasts thrust outward on display as Caleb—also naked—thrust himself into her.

CHAPTER 26

It took a long time—too long, really—for any of us to respond.

Caleb and Georgie froze mid act, their faces flushed red in embarrassment, their eyes slowly glazing over in horror as they took in the sight of us standing in the room with them.

I had to reach out to grip the doorway, and Ross fumbled the cinnamon rolls, nearly dropping them on the floor in shock before recovering.

To his credit, he was the first to move, setting the baked goods down on the island next to them before slowly backtracking toward the doorway.

"We uh…we dinna mean to interrupt. There's some cinnamon rolls if ye are…if ye are hungry. We will just be on our way."

He attempted to reach for my hand, but I quickly evaded his reach as anger flared up in me.

"Georgie." I stared daggers at her, as I watched the color in her cheeks drain until she looked like she might faint. "What the hell is going on?"

She didn't answer me, just shifted enough to cover up her bare breasts as Caleb pulled out of her and hurried to cover himself as he spoke.

"It's not what you think, Sue. We've been wanting to tell you both about this for a while."

I shook my head and held out my hand to stop him. "A while? You two have been doing this for *a while*? Georgie." I pointed at her. "Meet me at the apartment."

I turned to leave, but Ross blocked my path.

"I think ye should pause a moment, lass. 'Tis not as if they were doing anything wrong. We were the ones who entered without warning."

My shock and sadness came together in a flurry of rage as I pushed him out of the way and screamed at him. "They weren't doing anything wrong? Ross, look at them!" I threw my hand back behind me toward them. "What about Beth? She's only been gone a few months. How could…"

Ross surprised me by firmly gripping my arm and pulling me out into the hallway so quickly that I stopped talking mid-sentence. Frustration flaring in his expression, he pushed me against the wall and gently covered my mouth with his hand.

"Ye are going to regret anything else that ye say, lass. This is not about Caleb and Georgie. Ye are upset about what I've told ye. I'm upset about it, too, Allanah, but doona take out what we're going through on Caleb or yer sister. Ye are not being fair, and if ye stop to think on it for thirty seconds, ye shall realize it. We know nothing about this yet, lass. Regardless, 'tis Caleb's prerogative to do whatever he wants."

He continued with his hand still against my mouth. "If 'twas just sex, that's fine. Yer sister is grown enough to make her own decisions, and ye know Caleb must be in need of some comfort however he chooses to find it. And if 'tis more, lass, that is fine, as well. Ye know Beth would've wanted him to move on. Either way, I willna let ye attack him for betraying Beth when I've no doubt he's tormented himself over it as much or more than ye intend to, and 'tis not true anyway. Why doona ye go back to yer apartment and talk to Georgie about all of this? I will stay and talk to Caleb."

He released his grip on my mouth and stepped away.

"I dinna mean to be harsh with ye. I just urge ye to practice some calm here, lass."

I was quite certain the only person to ever put me in my place in such a way was Gramps. Part of me wanted to rage against him, but as I stood there against the wall listening to my sister crying in the kitchen, I knew he was right.

"Fine. I'll listen."

Georgie burst into the apartment still crying hysterically a few minutes after I made it back myself.

Luckily for my sister, I'd taken Ross' advice and used the few minutes of solitude on the walk back to calm myself down considerably. I reached for her hand as she blubbered and collapsed down onto the couch next to me.

"I'm sorry, Sue. I should've told you. Please. Please don't be angry with me. I know Beth was your friend. I don't want you to think that I'm disrespecting her in some way."

I pulled my hand away and held it out to stop her. I needed to hear everything from the beginning.

"Take a breath, Georgie. I'm not angry with you. I just need to understand what's going on. How did this all start?"

She let out a shaky breath, and I could see the relief spread over her face as she realized that I didn't believe she'd committed some unforgivable offense.

"We started out just talking, truly. He was there a lot when I cleaned, and I could tell he needed someone to talk to—someone who didn't know her as well as everyone else, ya know? I think it helped that he could talk to me about Beth without me breaking down into tears right there with him. But over time, an attraction formed. He fought it. I did too. But, Sue." She paused and let out a small sob. "This isn't some fling. We're...we're in love, Sue. This is real."

I'd been expecting an explanation that ended up somewhere in the realm of friends with benefits. I'd never expected her to tell me that they were in love.

Tears filled my eyes as I thought of Beth. Part of me wanted to be angry for her, to find some fault in the fact that Caleb had found love again so soon after her death, but as I sat silently before my sister, I simply couldn't. It was exactly what Beth would've wanted for him, and it was unquestionably what she would've wanted for her girls. I could feel it just as surely as if she were sitting next to me telling me so herself.

Crying, I reached for Georgie's hand. "You're not ever going to find a better guy, sis."

She let out a loud sob once more and leaned in to hug me. "I know."

"Does Hannah know?"

She leaned back and looked at me uncomfortably. "No. We're both trying to be really cautious with the girls. We need to make sure this is something that's going to last before we let them in on anything."

"I think that's probably the best thing you guys could do. They don't need to get attached and then lose anyone else."

Georgie nodded in agreement. "I think so too." She paused, and then continued. "You promise you're not mad?"

I shook my head as I sighed and leaned back into the couch. "Of course not. I won't pretend that it wasn't one of the greatest shocks of my life to walk in on you two like that, but no, I'm not mad. I'm upset about something else, and I just unleashed it all on you two. I'm sorry."

She reached out and squeezed my hand sympathetically. "There's nothing for you to be sorry for. No one needed to see what was going on in that kitchen. I'm sure I would've had a similar reaction to seeing your tits flailing about."

I laughed, the sad knot in my chest relaxing for a moment.

"I have much smaller tits to flail about than you, so it probably wouldn't have been quite as traumatic."

I winked in jest and reached for the television remote, intending to veg out for a bit to try to alleviate my sadness until Ross texted that he was back at his apartment. Instead, Georgie grabbed the remote out of my hand before I could actually turn the distraction mechanism on.

"You're really going to mention that you were upset about something else and then not tell me what that something else is? I don't think so. Spill."

I frowned at her as I crossed my arms. "Why is it that I'm the only person in this family that isn't entitled to keep things to myself?"

She shrugged nonchalantly. "I don't know, but the precedent is already set, so it's not like you can start hiding things from us now. What's up?"

I sighed and shifted as I reached for a blanket to drape over myself as I spoke. "Ross' mother is dying, and she's in Scotland. He told me last night that he's leaving. He's going to be gone for months. While we haven't officially decided anything, it pretty much means that it's the end of whatever this is, and I'm just rather sad about it, okay?"

She frowned and shook her head in what appeared to be frustration. "I'm sorry, but why is that your obvious conclusion? Why would his leaving to take care of his mother mean that things have to end?"

I raised my brows as the absurdity of her asking such a question rose in my mind.

"Oh, come on, Georgie. You know as well as I do that long distance rarely works even when you've been with someone for a long time. Just think about the boyfriend you had when you decided to set off on your years' long travels. You guys had been together for three years and it ended within three months. This is still new. It would fizzle out with frustration and anger in three weeks, if we tried to keep things going, and neither one of us wants that."

She crossed her arms, mimicking my position. "Then go with him, stupid."

"What?" My voice climbed to an uncomfortable pitch.

"You heard me. Go with him. You work for yourself, Sue. You told me just the other day that this is the easiest work has been for you in a while. Most of your patients have almost completed their therapy regimens, and your new patient needs only minor rehabilitation. You might not be able to leave with him in the next few days, but you could follow him in a week or two."

I started to protest, a thousand excuses of why that wasn't possible popping up in my mind, but she held out a hand to stop me before I was able to utter a word.

"I can argue any excuse you throw up. The apartment? I'll continue to stay here and tend to it. Work? I'll reiterate the fact that you are your own boss and can rearrange your schedule and either finish with your current patients or refer them to another doctor for the remainder of their therapy. You did it once when you were taking care of Gramps during his treatments. I guarantee that you can do it again. Money? Don't try to pretend that it's an issue. I know how frugal you are, and I saw your last bank statement lying on the kitchen counter last week. You're more than covered for the amount of time you would need to be in Scotland. You know you want to go. Just do it."

I did want to go. Of course I did. But my desire to go didn't mean that Ross would want me to. The few times he'd mentioned Scotland had clued me in on the fact that returning to his homeland was going to be difficult for him. Add to it the fact that he was going there to say goodbye to his mother made it even more so." Ross was private. There was no reason why he would want to share his grief and pain with me there to watch him go through it.

"What if he doesn't want me to go?"

"Then things end like you thought they were going to five minutes ago. You really don't have anything to lose by making the offer. If the last few months have taught you anything, surely you've learned that we need to hold on to the people we love while we have them."

I startled at her words, embarrassment flooding my cheeks with color.

"I don't…I don't love him, Georgie."

She ducked her chin and looked up at me, knowingly. "Whatever. Of course you do. You're picky, but once you're in a relationship, you fall easily. It's just that soft, open heart of yours. Should you tell him that yet? Probably not. But you don't have to pretend with me. You love him. That's great. Just don't let him leave without you when there's no reason for it."

My phone pinged in my pocket and I glanced down at to see a message from Ross:

"I'm driving out of the city with Caleb to pick up the girls. Should be back for dinner. Want to meet me at my apartment at six for Chinese take-out and that talk we should've had this morning?"

Nerves churned in my stomach as the truth of everything Georgie had just told me settled in. She was right. I shot back my response as the decision cemented in my mind.

"Sounds good. See you tonight."

If Beth were here now, she would've been sitting right next to Georgie urging me to do the exact same thing. At dinner, I would ask him. And if he wanted me, I would go to Scotland, too.

CHAPTER 27

"All right. We're out of the bulk of the traffic now. Time for you to tell me the real reason you wanted to ride with me to pick up Hannah and Maggie. I know you don't really care about whatever Georgie and I are doing, so that's not what you want to talk about."

Ross ran both hands through his hair with a sigh. The entire day was already shit, surely it would be better to tell his news to Caleb now when his mood couldn't really get any worse.

"I have to leave, Caleb. My mother is verra sick. She has been for some time. I received news yesterday that she's asking for me. She doesna have much time left, and I have to go to her."

"Ah, man." Caleb shook his head, his eyes remaining on the road. "I'm so sorry. Of course you have to go. Don't worry about a thing in regard to work. Things are a little easier now. I have my feet underneath me more than I thought I would at this point. I can manage while you're away. I know a handyman I can keep on call to help with maintenance issues. How long do you think you'll be gone?"

He frowned, dreading the answer he knew he must give.

"Mayhap months. I feel I must stay until the end, and I doona know how long that will be."

Caleb hurried to reassure him. "It's not a problem, Ross. You stay gone as long as you need to. The marathon is over, so I'll be able to get back to walking Hannah to school on the days you and Sue were doing it for me. Your job is not in danger at all."

"Thank ye. I also thought I should come so that I can say goodbye to Hannah. I'm leaving tomorrow."

"Good call. She would've been furious if you'd left without saying anything to her. She will miss you. We all will. But we will be fine. What about Sue? Have you told her yet?"

He nodded. "Aye."

"And? What does that mean for you guys?"

Ross shrugged. All day he'd tried to find a way to not do what he knew he must. He'd come up with nothing.

"It means that we are over before we've truly had a chance to begin. 'Twould never work long distance. My mother lives in a verra remote part of Scotland. Any means of communication will be difficult to find."

"Do you want things to be over?"

"O'course not. She has been a bright spot in many months of darkness."

Caleb surprised him by slowly pulling the car over to the side of the road and shifting into park before turning to look at him. "Then don't be a moron, Ross. Don't let her go if you don't want to. Ask her to come with you!"

He laughed, dismissing the notion without question. Of course he wanted her to come with him, but that wasn't possible. Far too many of his secrets lay buried in Scotland, and that was precisely where he intended to keep them.

"'Tis not possible."

"Why?"

"I have a full and varied past in Scotland, Caleb. Much of it I doona wish to revisit. I have done unforgivable things. I couldna bring Allanah there without her finding out about all of it. She would then truly despise me. I would rather it end now, while she still cares for me, than for it to end with her despising the man I once was."

Caleb stared at him hard for a long moment before speaking again. "I think you're glazing over the most important thing you just said there, Ross. The man you once were is not the man you are today. None of us can do anything about our past. Sue knows that. And while I don't know what supposedly horrible actions you're referring to, if you explained it to her—if you were honest—I know she wouldn't think any less of you at all."

If only Caleb knew how deeply he'd hurt the last woman he loved, perhaps he would understand. How could any woman trust him with her heart after what he'd done with the last one that was placed in his care?

"No. She would. Now place the car back in drive. I doona wish to talk about this a moment more."

Without a word, Caleb did as he bid, and together they sped down the road.

To even order take-out with Allanah would be a mistake. Best to rip off the bandage quickly.

He would end things as soon as she arrived at his apartment.

CHAPTER 28

I arrived at Ross' apartment at two minutes before six, my nerves so high that I had to keep bending to put my head between my legs so I wouldn't vomit right in his doorway. I didn't want to feel the embarrassment that I knew would flood its way through my whole system if he turned me down. I knew it was forward for me to ask him, but I also knew that I wasn't ready to say goodbye.

Keeping my left hand against my stomach, I took a breath and reached to knock on the door. It flew open, and the expression on Ross' face did nothing to ease my nerves. His mouth was tight, and he didn't smile at me or reach to pull me into a hug as I stepped inside.

The only warm welcome I received was from Tink who began to yap at my heels as she jumped excitedly up on my leg. I bent to pet her, her happy excitement helping to calm my nerves. As I rose, I steeled myself to speak before I had a chance to talk myself out of asking.

"Ross, you and I both know that the entire purpose of this dinner is to somehow politely end things, but I really don't want to do that. What if..." I hesitated, the absurdity of my suggestion giving me pause. But then I thought of Beth, and how I would do just about anything to have more time with her, and I knew that I had to—at the very least—ask him if he wanted me while I still had the opportunity to do so. "What if I came with you to Scotland?"

His brows rose as his tight mouth parted just a little, and it pleased me to see that his expression softened as my question sank in. When he finally spoke, his voice was unsure.

"Do ye wish to do that, lass?"

I nodded. "Yes. I couldn't leave with you tomorrow, but I could probably make it there within the next two weeks. I would have to do some rearranging with my work schedule, but yes, I could go with you."

He smiled then and I audibly exhaled as my nausea subsided.

"Aye. I would love for ye to come. Now, come here and let me kiss ye."

I found myself in his arms, our lips meeting with a familiarity that shouldn't have been possible with our limited time together.

I moved my lips to his ear as he slowly backed me toward the bedroom. "Promise me you're not going to stop this as soon as I get halfway undressed this time."

He laughed and gave my earlobe a quick nibble before huskily answering me. He pushed his erection into my stomach to emphasize his answer. "I doona think I'm physically capable of it this time, lass. I've denied myself of ye too many times now."

Tingles rushed down my spine as his warm breath tickled my neck and I grew slick in anticipation as his erection pressed into me.

He closed the door quickly behind us, stepping away to remove his shirt while he quickly bobbed his head in a silent plea for me to do the same.

There would be no foreplay—not this time. I could tell by the urgency of his movements, his ragged breath. The intensity of his gaze caused my own breath to hitch uncomfortably.

I hurried to pull my sweater up over my head, pausing on the way to quickly undo my bra. Together I removed the two pieces of clothing, my nipples hardening in response to the sudden rush of cool air on my skin.

He groaned as his eyes raked over my breasts, and his hands moved to his belt as he pulled and tugged to undo his buckle. He pulled the belt off in one swift motion, his fingers deftly unbuttoning his jeans as he kicked off his shoes and lowered his pants. As he rose, his cock sprang free, rising in all its glory, causing me to blush as I took in the sight of him naked.

It had been so long since I'd been touched by a man. My lovemaking drought aside, I was certain I'd never wanted anyone inside me so badly. I ached in anticipation of the delicious stretching I knew I would feel the moment he pushed himself inside me. The muscles in my stomach tightened as I waited for him to enter me.

"Take me, Ross. Please...." I gasped and my lower lip began to shake as I spoke. "Please take me."

He groaned again, stepping forward to undo the button of my jeans as his lips lowered to my right nipple, biting as I cried out in so much pleasurable that I grew embarrassingly close to climaxing right then and there. I threw my head back at the delight of feeling his lips on my breast, his fingertips causing my stomach and thighs to break out into goosebumps as he pulled my jeans to the floor.

"Get on the bed, Allanah, and for God's sake, open yer legs."

I scrambled to the bed, climbing on top and then lying back on the propped up pillows, obeying him without question.

I'd dreamt of this moment for months, each time imagining how shy and embarrassed I would feel in front of someone so exquisite. But none of that anticipated self-consciousness existed as I brazenly opened myself to him, grinning as I watched him swallow and his breath catch.

"No one should be so beautiful, lass."

I snorted. The heat of the moment dissipating a little as the hilarity of what he'd just said hit me.

"Ross, have you ever actually looked in a mirror? You are in no position to give such a compliment."

He laughed. It was a dark, raspy, almost threatening sound. Slowly—his manhood still hard and protruding out so far from his body my legs nearly closed themselves together in reflex—he crawled on top of me.

"Allanah." He whispered my name against my ear, goosebumps spreading across my neck as I squirmed underneath him. "Kiss me."

I obliged him, rising up to meet his lips as he leaned away from my ear. As I rose he moved his right hand behind my head, combing his fingers through my hair, until he got a handful of my long locks and pulled ever so gently.

I gasped and grinned into his mouth.

"Do ye wish me to let go, lass? I doona want to hurt ye."

"No." I gave my answer with a little too much enthusiasm, and he laughed in response.

"Ye are a little more adventurous than ye let on, aye, lass?"

I shrugged, trying my best to mimic his trademark gesture. "Maybe. Why don't you find out?"

He groaned again, giving my hair a harder tug this time, my head falling back as his mouth dipped to my breasts again. He quickly plunged himself inside me.

I'd expected my body to put up some slight resistance to the unaccustomed intrusion. Instead, I was wet and ready for him. He slid in all the way to the hilt as we both cried out in pleasure.

I squeezed him, and he groaned so loudly that his lips pulled away from my nipple in ecstasy. I smiled at watching something I'd done elicit such a reaction from him.

"Ach, lass." His lips were shaking as he drew in a breath. "Ye are...ye are so tight."

I squeezed him again, causing him to jerk and moan.

"Have mercy on me, lass. I doona wish to finish until I've made ye do so."

I smiled and reached for him, digging my nails into the back of his head as I pulled his mouth back to mine.

After kissing him, I trailed my lips to his ear and whispered. "Then make me come."

A low, almost growling noise escaped him, and he began to move in and out so slowly and deeply that the feel of him began to swirl up from my stomach, radiating through my body until I was writhing underneath him, my hips bucking up with each plunge. I moaned and gasped as the sensation grew.

Sensing I was close, he shifted his weight to his left palm, and moved his right fingers to touch my sensitive center. His fingers easily found just the right place, and with a few strokes, I was overcome. I cried out as I orgasmed and lay shaking beneath him.

He removed his hand, but continued his slow pumping motion, ducking to kiss me as he picked up speed. Before I even had time to cool down, the sensation built again, and as he neared his own climax, I found myself on the precipice once again.

"I don't think I can do it again, Ross."

He laughed against my mouth and began to move his hips with even more intensity.

"Aye, ye can. And ye shall."

As if his words had drawn it from me, I spiraled up once again, and together we found release.

CHAPTER 29

It had taken no time for sleep to find Allanah, but worry and regret plagued Ross as he held her.

How could he have allowed himself to be so easily swayed? The moment she asked him if she could come with him to Scotland, all his previous worries had vanished. In that moment, it was as if his past hadn't existed and all he felt was the joy of knowing she wanted him. The joy of knowing that someone didn't believe him to be the selfish, life destroyer he believed himself to be.

There was no backing out of it now. He'd already said she could come, and the truth was, he wanted her to. But she couldn't find out about his past. Allanah was too good, too kind and pure to understand the mistakes he'd made. Knowing would ruin all that she felt for him, and he wasn't sure he could survive having his heart broken again in such a way.

Surely there was a way to keep the worst of it from her. She would have to learn to accept that people truly could—and in his experience regularly do—travel through time. But the rest of it— namely Silva—he would have to find a way to keep that part of his life a secret. He simply couldn't lose another person he loved.

Loved.

The realization occurred to him in a whisper, the thought entering so easily it surprised him. It made everything more concrete in his mind. Whatever he had to do to keep Allanah protected from the person he'd once been, he would do it. He loved her. He suspected he would always love her. And he'd lost too much love in his life to let another person go.

He could bear the guilt of omission if it kept her in his life. If it meant keeping her, it would unquestionably be worth it.

Sighing, she stirred against his chest. As her eyes slowly flickered open, she gazed up at him in the lamp light.

"What time is it?"

He glanced over at the clock. "'Tis only eight o'clock, lass. I believe I wore ye out."

She smiled at him and squeezed him in a hug. "Yeah, you did. I don't know about you, but that Chinese food take-out we'd planned sounds even better now than it did before."

His stomach growled in answer, and they laughed together. "Aye, lass, it does. I need to take Tink out anyway. If ye will call while I take her out, I'll pay for everything when they get here."

She nodded, pushing herself up from his chest. Her hair was tangled and wild around her face, and the sight of her bed head was enough to make him ready for another round. Carefully, he pushed that thought away and focused on the task at hand.

"Sure. What do you want?"

"I am not a picky eater. Get whatever ye want."

Rising from the bed before his desire to take her once more overtook him, he dressed quickly and went in search of his dog. Perhaps some cool, fresh air would help to clear his troubled mind.

*W*ho knew sex made me so completely ravenous? As I looked over the take-out menu while Ross readied Tink for her walk, there wasn't a single thing on the menu that didn't look appetizing.

"I'm thinking Kung Pau Chicken, some noodles, egg rolls, and shrimp fried rice?"

"Sounds perfect, lass. We won't be long."

With that, Ross and Tink left. Rather than call for the food right away, I hurried to the bathroom to properly look myself over. I looked—and there was simply no other way to put it—sexed up. My hair was in utter disarray. My lipstick was smudged all over my mouth, and my mascara had started to flake off in an incredibly unattractive way.

I kind of loved it. I was well past due for a good toss in the hay. And my God, had it been good! I'd not known sex could feel quite like that—so wholly satisfying and dirty but oddly healing, as well. I was still slightly shaky and weak, but I felt relaxed and peaceful.

Freshening up took longer than I'd anticipated. By the time I got off the phone with the restaurant, Ross and Tink were walking back in the door.

"Did ye get it ordered?"

"Yes. Should be here in half an hour. You want to make a plan?"

He smiled at me before bending to unhook Tink's leash from her collar. "Ye do like a plan, doona ye, lass?"

Most of the time I truly did try to suppress my desire for organization, but it usually didn't take people very long to figure out just how Type A I really was.

"I do. You got a problem with that?" I winked at him.

"No. Not at all. We should talk, and since I'm leaving tomorrow afternoon, I doona have much time."

The dread of knowing he was leaving tomorrow weighed on me so much less now that I knew I'd be joining him. Still, it surprised me that he'd been able to put together everything so quickly.

"What did Caleb say? I assume you've talked to him."

Removing his boots and giving Tink a treat, he moved to sit by me on the couch.

"He was incredibly gracious, as I'd known he would be. Hannah was none too pleased with me though. I had to promise to bring her back something *Scottish*."

I smiled. "That shouldn't be too hard."

As soon as she finished her treat, Tink set off at a full run and leapt up between us on the couch. I reached to pull her close in a snuggle.

"What about Tink? Is it difficult to travel internationally with her?"

"'Tis slightly more complicated, but I have a friend who I'm quite certain will be willing to help me with the last-minute arrangements."

"A friend?"

He nodded, and I knew that once again, that was all the information I was going to receive. I often found the subjects he was so tight-lipped about strange, but I suppose he had his reasons.

He reached out to grab my hand. "I will spend the first night I arrive in Scotland with friends at Cagair Castle."

I interrupted him, too intrigued by the mention of a castle to stop myself. "You have friends at a castle?"

He smiled and nodded. "Aye, but ye shouldna get too excited by that. Ye canna throw a rock in any direction without hitting a castle in Scotland."

I laughed. "Really?"

"Aye. They're everywhere. Have ye never been?"

I wrinkled my nose, slightly embarrassed, although I had no reason to be. My sister was the exception, I knew. Most people didn't regularly get to go gallivanting all over the world the way she did.

"No. I've never really been out of the United States. I have a passport, but that's only because I got one for a cruise Georgie and I went on five years ago. But I got so sick the first day that I never actually made it off the boat at any of the stops."

"Ye will love it. 'Tis the most beautiful country in the world." He paused and shrugged, playfully. "If I do say so myself."

Cautiously, I broached the subject I suspected he would avoid. "If it's so wonderful, why do you dread returning so badly?"

He sighed, and I worried he was about to dismiss my question outright. "Memories, lass. They haunt me there. But ye, I have no doubt, shall love it."

That was all I needed for now. I didn't want to upset him by pressing further.

"I'm sure I will. Now, what were you saying about your first night there? I interrupted you when you mentioned a castle."

He gave me a curt nod and continued. "Aye. I shall spend the first night there. The next morning, I shall head north to my mother's. She lives in a verra remote part of the country, lass. I doona suspect I shall have any service at all. If ye can sort out what day ye shall be arriving before I leave tomorrow evening, I will make certain to return to Cagair before ye get there. Then we can travel back to my mother's together."

That saddened me, but at least I had a worldwide traveler living in my apartment who could help me with any of my own preparations that I might have questions about.

"Okay. I understand. I'll sit down with my calendar first thing in the morning, and I'll get a flight booked before you leave. Do we need to start your packing tonight?"

He shook his head and pulled me a little closer to him.

"No, lass. I doona wish to waste a moment of my time with ye. I willna need much. It will take me no time to prepare in the morning. All I wish to do tonight is eat, and then place ye right back in my bed for at least another three rounds of lovemaking before daybreak."

An anticipatory shiver of delight ran down my spine at his

words.

Breathlessly I laughed while I glanced down at my phone to check the time.

"Where the hell is that Chinese food? As far as I'm concerned it can't get here fast enough."

He laughed as he leaned forward to pull my face close to him, pressing his lips to mine as we lost ourselves in each other until the buzz from the downstairs intercom pulled us away.

As aroused as I was, I still intended to eat my fill. If our first encounter was any indication, I would need all the strength I could muster to keep up with him throughout the night.

CHAPTER 30

Sleep-deprived and dreading two weeks apart from him, I dropped Ross and Tink off at the airport with so little luggage that I found myself really glad that I wasn't leaving at the same time. I didn't want him to see what a big packer I was.

He'd kissed me thoroughly at the drop-off point and called me as soon as he made it past security.

"We are at our gate, lass. The friend I mentioned pulled through. Tink's papers are set, and she is sleeping in her carrier like the well-behaved pup she is. With any luck she willna cause mayhem on the journey there. Have ye made it home?"

With the phone connected to the speaker system in my car, I continued the drive toward Gramps' house.

"No. I decided to swing by my grandfather's and visit with him a bit. I think it will be best to tell him about my plans before Georgie gets to him. He will be upset if he doesn't hear it from me first."

Ross laughed and I knew I would miss him, even if it was just going to be a few weeks.

"Aye, I suspect ye are right. I'll send ye a text when the plane is about to take off. I canna wait to see ye in a fortnight."

I said goodbye to him as I pulled into Gramps' driveway. I'd not called him beforehand, and I found myself relieved that Gladys' car wasn't parked outside. I knew he'd be more receptive to my sudden appearance if he was alone.

I started to put my key in the lock then stopped on the off chance she actually was here without her car. The last thing I wanted to do was walk in on another family member getting down.

Instead, I raised my fist and knocked on the door. I saw the light switch on in the hallway leading up to the door and stepped back as I waited for him to answer.

"Allanah!"

He said my name with such enthusiasm that it warmed me right through, pushing away any of the melancholy that had lingered because of Ross' departure. I stepped toward him to hug him before stepping inside.

"What a pleasant surprise. It's been quite a while since you've been to my house."

I turned to look at him over my shoulder as we walked toward his den together.

"You don't really love having us over anymore, Gramps. I think you're worried that I'm going to try and move back in here. I promise you, I'm not."

He laughed and patted me on the shoulder. "Did you come to tell me all about your Scotland trip?"

"*Dammit.*" I whispered the curse under my breath before looking at him. "Georgie already got to you? She didn't even know if he was going to say he wanted me to go or not."

"I guess she was pretty certain of it. She called me yesterday evening to tell me that you were taking some time off to follow your boyfriend to Scotland." He paused and motioned to the recliner next to his. "I think it's great, Allanah."

"You do?"

He sat down in his beloved chair and I followed suit.

"Absolutely. I like him."

"You don't really know him."

He made a gruff sound and crossed his arms at me. "I saw a little of him before the race and at the restaurant afterwards. I appreciate how he introduced himself as your boyfriend. He has kind eyes and a firm grip. That'll tell you what you need to know about most men if you pay attention. And all that aside, the way he eulogized Beth warmed me over to him right then and there."

The lump that rose in my throat every time I thought of Beth returned. "I'd forgotten that he spoke at her funeral. I wish I'd been there to hear it."

Gramps reached out to squeeze my hand. "It was lovely, but you were right where you needed to be. Are you excited for your trip?"

I nodded, but the corners of my mouth didn't pull up quite the way I'd expected them too. I was excited. But I was also quite nervous. "Yes."

He frowned at me. "What is it? What's bothering you?"

"I am excited. I'm also quite scared."

He waved his hand in a motion meant to encourage me to elaborate.

"I guess…" I wasn't even totally sure. I'd not thought about my reasons for being nervous, but as had always been the case, my real feelings about things began to spill as I sat in front of my grandfather. "I guess I know that if this trip doesn't lead to him opening up a little more, if it doesn't cause him to let down his guard, I'm not going to be able to stay in this."

When Gramps said nothing, I continued.

"I really like him, Gramps. Like, I *really* like him. I might even love him, but something is up with him. I'm not frightened of him. It's not a dangerous thing. But he's hiding something. Something in his past he is dead set on not sharing with me. I catch it flickering across his expression sometimes. And there are certain subjects, quite a lot of them actually, that he shuts down on. He never tells me directly that he doesn't want to talk about it, but he's adept at giving me the least information he possibly can.

"That's not really something a real relationship can be built on, is it? A lack of trust so profound that you can't discuss the things that make you *you*. I'm hopeful that being with him in the place he grew up will help that, but I just don't know. He's a tough nut."

Gramps laughed at my use of the outdated expression I'd heard him say countless times before as he leaned forward in his recliner, spinning it toward my own so he could gather my hands in his.

"Do you want me to tell you what I think about it?"

I nodded. "Always. You give the best advice of anyone I've ever known."

He smiled at that. I knew he took great pride in his ability to see things more clearly than most people ever did. I supposed it was all the past pain he'd been through, all the tragedies he'd had to overcome that made him that way. His scars had made him wise, and he knew it.

"The kindest men are almost always the most self-loathing. They're kind because they know what it is to be hated by the most important person in their lives, and they don't ever want anyone to feel as loathed as they do."

I frowned. "That's maybe the saddest thing I've ever heard."

He nodded, somberly. "It is. But it's true. Ross is kind. He's good through and through. He was good to Beth. He has been a lifesaver to Caleb. Caleb's girls adore him, and I suspect if you're patient with him, he has the potential to be good to you for as long as you want him to. But here's the thing with men like that: patience is absolutely necessary, but only up to a point. He will never volunteer whatever it is that you need to know. At some point, you will have to be more forceful in your demands for answers."

"That self-loathing he possesses comes from somewhere. It's the result of some mistake, some wrong he's so sure he's done, and his worst fear will be you finding out and hating him the way he hates himself. When you learn his secret, practice empathy if you can. Past mistakes don't always cause future ones."

I stared at the old, wise oracle that had somehow replaced my grandfather, and I couldn't help but smile. "You could charge for this shit, you know?"

He leaned back and belly laughed, pulling his hands away and settling back into his recliner. "I should, shouldn't I?"

I nodded. "How are you so sure about all of that?"

"Let's just say I recognize a lot of myself in Ross. I made a lot of mistakes when I was young; before I met your grandmother. I know what it's like to walk around with that kind of self-loathing. And I know what it's like to finally come face-to-face with the sort of woman who is strong enough to help you overcome it. You're that kind of woman, Allanah."

"Do you really think that whatever he doesn't want me to know is so bad?"

He shook his head without hesitation. "No. I think he's made mistakes. We all do. But he's so innately good that he doesn't offer himself the same grace he would show anyone else. You just remember that whenever you find out what it is, okay?"

I wasn't sure how I could possibly agree to that without knowing, but I nodded anyway.

"And what about you? What mistakes did you make that you didn't want grandmother to find out about?"

He shook his head and clucked his tongue at me. "Nope. Sorry. While revealing my past was necessary for me to have a true relationship with your grandmother, it isn't for me to have one with you. Those secrets were shared with the only person that ever needed to hear them. I've truly let all of that go."

I couldn't fault him for that. I imagined if I lived my life well enough, there would be lots of tales I would never want to share with my grandchildren someday either.

"I can understand that."

"Good."

He stood, making it clear that my visit had come to an end.

"Now, get yourself back home and start sorting out your work schedule. I don't want you to have any possible excuses pop up last minute that might keep you from this trip."

He walked me to the door, giving me a great big hug before gently shoving me outside and closing the door in my face.

"Love you too, Gramps." Laughing, I whispered the words as I walked back to my car.

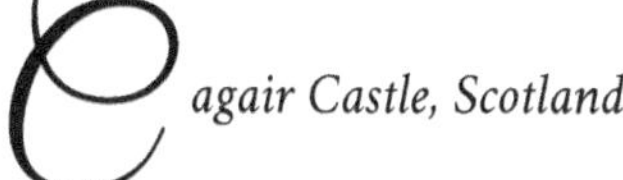

agair Castle, Scotland

Sydney stood on the steps of Cagair Castle waiting for him as he'd known she would be, as he drove up the long driveway leading to the castle's main doors.

The sight of his friend, smiling and waving with her baby in her arms and her husband beside her, was enough to provide some relief to the misery that had settled deep inside him the moment he landed in Scotland. Pulling the car to a stop, he quickly shifted gears and turned off the engine, stretching his legs as he climbed out of the small, compact rental before reaching inside the vehicle to free the over-excited Tink.

"Calm yerself, lass. I know ye are in need of a good run." He set her on the ground allowing her to run free around the castle grounds while he went to greet his friends.

"I really could've picked you up at the airport, Ross. I hate that you rented a car and drove all the way out here after such a long flight."

He dismissed the notion with a wave of his hand as he leaned in to hug her before pulling away to shake Callum's hand.

"Nonsense. The drive allowed me time to think, to ready myself for the difficult journey home. I'm just glad that I get to begin this difficult trip with at least some happiness. How are ye all doing?"

Balancing the babe on one hip, Sydney reached to usher him inside with her other hand, as Callum reached for the baby and answered him.

"I'm pleased ye made it safely, Ross. Orick and I have taken it upon ourselves to cook dinner tonight so that Sydney can see ye settled. The two of ye can visit until then. Whether or not we shall have anything edible on the table is yet to be seen. I'll take the bairn up to Gillian so she can watch him while we finish our meal. I know the two of ye must be eager to visit."

Ross nodded, grateful that Callum seemed to understand and accept Ross' friendship with his wife so wholeheartedly.

Sydney waited until Callum rounded the corner, out of sight from them, before speaking. "You want to stretch your legs for a bit and take a walk with me? It's a pretty day, and Gillian has the gardens looking absolutely gorgeous."

"Ye've read my mind, lass. I doona think I could bear to sit just now."

Giving him a quick smile, Sydney led the way through a series of hallways toward a back entry to the castle. As they stepped through the door, Ross laid his eyes on one of the prettiest gardens he'd ever seen.

He smiled at the sight of Tink, who had already found her way to the garden, frolicking down the garden pathways, her nose pressing itself against every new plant she passed.

"I must admit, there are some things that I shall always miss about Scotland. 'Tis hard to grow anything of such beauty in a city as crowded as Boston."

Sydney laughed and continued to walk ahead of him into the garden, scooping up Tink to love on her. "I'm sure that's true." She paused and waited for him to catch up to her. "I'm so glad you brought her. I've been missing this sweet pup, and I promise I'll take good care of her while you're taking care of your mother. How are you feeling, Ross? I know all of this has to be hard on you."

He nodded. "Aye. It feels wrong for me to say so, but I doona look forward to seeing her. I said goodbye to her a long time ago. I grieved for her a long time ago. I fear that seeing her again will be like tearing open a wound."

Sydney stopped and faced him, pulling him into a warm hug. "I know. I wish this wasn't happening to you. You, as much as anyone I've ever known, deserve a break from tragedy."

He hurried to correct her. "'Tis not true, lass. I have earned any and all of the pain that shall ever come my way."

She rewarded his statement by whacking him hard on the back of the head. "Stop it, Ross. I am so tired of hearing you constantly berate yourself." She paused and shook her head. "Sorry. Me getting after you is the last thing you need, I know. Let's talk about something else."

He smiled, not as upset with her as she seemed to think he would be. He quite admired Sydney's fiery personality.

"Aye. I've something to tell ye. I fear I shall need yer assistance in a few weeks time."

"Okay. Sure. What's up?"

"Allanah is joining me here."

Sydney smiled. "That's the best news I've heard all day. Is she really?"

The knowledge excited him, as well. "Aye, though she willna arrive until two weeks from today. I must travel home before then. I will return to Cagair Castle before she arrives to see her into the past."

"So, have you already told her about all of that?"

Sydney looked far more hopeful than she had reason to be.

"No, lass. 'Tis what I need yer help with. I doona know how to tell her. 'Twas easy when I had magic, for I could prove my words right then. Without it, I fear she will believe me mad. I thought 'twould be easier to tell her surrounded by those who can back up my words."

Sydney nodded. "Probably for the best. If you're fine with it, I might give Morna a call. She's helped make the transition a little easier for some of us in the past. I bet she would be willing to help now. Especially since you're not going to have weeks to get her comfortable with the whole concept of time travel."

He smiled, unsurprised that he and his friend were on the same wavelength. "I've already spoken with her. I needed help with Tink's papers. If 'tis alright, she wishes to meet Allanah. She and Jerry are due to arrive the day Allanah does."

Sydney laughed. Ross didn't miss the way her eyes lit up at the mention of the old, beloved witch.

"Morna knows that she's welcome here any time. I'm glad that she's coming. It's been some time since she's been here. She must've finally recovered from the shock of Jerry's heart attack."

Ross startled at the news. "Heart attack?"

"Yes. Don't worry. He's fine. It was a long time ago now, really. Ross…"

She paused, and he knew what she was going to say before she spoke and held up a hand to stop her. "No, lass. She doesna know about Silva. She doesna know that I ever had magic, nor that I faked my death."

Sydney turned sad, worried eyes on him. "She needs to know, Ross."

He sighed and ran his hands through his hair in frustration. She couldn't know. He couldn't lose her. Not like he did Silva, or Beth, or how he was about to lose his mother.

"I canna tell her, lass. And I need ye to promise me that ye willna tell her either."

"Ross, do you really think I would ever do that? It's none of my business. Of course I wouldn't tell her, but I'm not going to lie to you and pretend that I think it's okay that you haven't. You're in a relationship with this woman. Whether you've told her yet or not, I can tell that you love her. She needs to know. And you need to have it proven to you that no one else thinks you're the monster that you think you are."

"Ye are the only one who knows that doesna think I'm a monster."

Sydney continued to argue with him. "No. No one thinks that. Not me. Not Laurel. Not Kate." Her voice continued to rise with each declaration. "Not Raudrich. Not Marcus. Not even Silva. There is literally no one that thinks you're as terrible as you think you are."

She paused and took a deep breath, lowering Tink to the ground.

No matter her reasoning, Ross knew how wrong she truly was.

"Regardless of yer opinion, lass, 'tis is for me to decide. Aye?"

Sydney surprised him by turning and stomping off in the other direction.

"Yeah, Ross. It is. But if you go and screw this up because you're too bullheaded to move the hell on from what you did, I will have no sympathy for you. Your room is the fourth on the right on the second floor. I assume you can see yourself inside."

She stormed off before he could say another word.

CHAPTER 32

wo Weeks Later

Seeing his mother in such a weakened and confused state had distressed him so much more than he'd expected it to. The years apart had made it no easier for him. The only blessing was that when she remembered him, she seemed ignorant of the time they'd spent apart.

The moments where she knew him, he treasured. He would hold her hand and visit, allowing her to lead their conversations—whatever memories she could recall on that given day or hour.

But the other days, those where she was stuck in her own childhood—a time where no one in her life from that time still existed—were unbearable to witness. Scared, frightened, and alone, only a sleeping elixir from the village healer would calm her. And then it was only for a time.

The evenings alone in his bedchamber were a necessary retreat. Without the time away each night to come to terms with the trials of the day, he wasn't sure he would've been able to return to her bedside each day.

By the time he was due to return to twenty-first century Cagair Castle, he'd never been so ready to leave another place in his life.

He and Callum, who'd stayed with him at his brother's castle for the entire fortnight, rode hard once they departed, only stopping one night of the journey to sleep. By the time they arrived at the stairwell portal, he was exhausted and as eager as he'd ever been to talk to Allanah.

"What time must ye be at the airport to pick the lass up? We should have someone drive ye so ye may sleep along the way. Ye look as if ye might fall over."

Ross dismissed Callum's concern with a quick shake of his head as they settled their horses in Callum's stables before making the short walk to the stairwell. The last thing he wanted was someone else in the car with him. Two weeks without hearing her voice had been torture. He wanted Allanah all to himself for as long as possible.

"Her flight lands at eleven. I shall need to leave within the hour. I'll be fine. If I'm too exhausted to make the drive back here, we can get a hotel near the airport and make the drive in the morning. Thank ye for coming with me, Callum."

Callum nodded, and together they began the downward trek into the twenty-first century.

"O'course, lad. It gave me an excuse to check up on my brother. To see him doing so well has given me a great sense of relief. For the longest time, I thought he would never outgrow the wildness of his youth."

"He takes after Adwen then, aye?"

Callum laughed as they stepped through the illusion of the brick wall in front of them.

"Aye. I was born older than the two of them shall ever be."

Before Ross could respond, the door at the top of the staircase flew open, flooding them with light as Sydney's panicked voice called to them down the stairwell.

"I have been waiting on you two to get back here for days! Ross, get up here right now. We've got a whole lot to talk about."

Confused, he picked up his pace as he climbed the steps.

"What is it, lass? Nothing has happened to Allanah, aye?"

It pained him that his immediate reaction to almost any situation was now worry, but it seemed as if the last year had been a continual onslaught of bad news.

Sydney reached out and put her hand on his arm as she shook her head.

"No. Everything is fine. I've been tracking her flight on my phone, and she's due to arrive thirty minutes early actually, which makes it even more urgent that I talk to you right now." She paused and turned to give Callum a quick kiss on the cheek. "Hey Babe, I'm glad you're home. Can you do me a quick favor though? Go and see to our guests that literally just pulled up in the driveway while I sneak Ross in through the back so I can talk to him?"

In unison, Callum and Ross responded. "Guests?"

Exasperated, Sydney pointed in the direction she intended Callum to go, while grabbing onto Ross with her other hand and pulling him in the opposite direction.

"Callum, you'll see as soon as you get around there. Now go, please, while I try to figure this mess out."

Obliging, Callum took off, and Ross began to stumble along behind Sydney's breakneck pace.

"Lass, what has happened? Ye are frightening me a bit."

"I've been trying to cover for your chicken-shit ass for the better part of two days is what has happened. We have guests that have decided to come, thanks to Morna. Damn her."

A suspicious dread crept up his spine. "What guests, lass?"

Sydney stopped just outside the back door of the castle and released her grip on him long enough to face him.

"Silva is here, Ross. So is Marcus. Morna rarely travels anymore.

She hadn't Silva's baby yet, so she took it upon herself to invite her since she was heading in this direction."

Ross gripped at the doorway as the blood began to drain from his face. Sydney quickly shook her head and reached for his arm again.

"Nope. You can't fall apart here. We need to get you up to your room so we can talk about the plan. Hang on just a minute."

Without another word, they all but ran up to the bedroom assigned to him. The moment they stepped inside, Ross collapsed onto the upholstered bench at the end of the bed.

The thought of seeing Silva again was enough to make him feel ill. But he feared that having Silva and Allanah under the same roof would be too much for him to bear.

"What am I going to do about Allanah, lass?"

Sydney shrugged. "Hell, if I know. This wouldn't be the fiasco it is now, if you'd just listened to me, but I have no faith at all that you're going to do that."

"I need to leave for the airport straight away."

"No." Sydney threw the cell phone he'd left in his direction. "What you need to do right now is text Allanah and tell her that you were delayed and that you're sending friends to pick her up. That way she will get the text as soon as she lands and will know what's going on. Gillian and Orick are on their way to the airport right now."

Unable to think past Sydney's first instruction, he quickly did as she bid, typing out a quick message to Allanah and pressing send before directing his attention back to his panicked and incredibly irritated friend.

He didn't have to say a word before Sydney continued on. "You and Silva need to talk, Ross. You've got to get her on board with whatever you decide to do. That's why I thought that I better go ahead and send someone else to the airport to pick up Allanah. When Allanah arrives here, I'll make sure the two of you have some time alone so you can tell her whatever you decide. Okay?"

At least Sydney had had the foresight to deal with the situation as best as she could. No matter her belief that he was wrong, she'd still come through for him as the wonderful friend she was.

He gave her a soft smile, his mind still racing. "Thank ye, lass. I'll gather my thoughts while I shower. Then I shall go in search of Silva. I know ye want no part in this. Thank ye for what ye've done."

Sydney's expression relaxed and she gave him a quick nod. "You're welcome. You already know what I think you should do, so I'm not going to say anything else about it. Now, I better go and see to the surprise that old witch has sprung on us. I'm eternally grateful for Morna, I truly am, but some days she's really more trouble than she's worth."

Ross gave a soft chuckle as he watched Sydney leave before falling backwards onto his bed with a frustrated groan.

CHAPTER 33

I nearly cried when I landed in Scotland and turned on my phone to see Ross' text. Every day without hearing from him had felt like a week. Not only that, but the amount of effort it had taken to move patients to other therapists and to make certain everything was squared away in such a short amount of time had made for lots of late nights and very little sleep. In addition, I'd been so excited to see Ross that despite the accumulative exhaustion of the past few weeks, I'd been unable to sleep a wink on the plane. The sudden knowledge that not only was our reunion delayed by a handful of hours, but I was also going to have to make small talk with strangers while deliriously sleep-deprived had me in a really bad mood.

Then, to make matters worse, I stood at baggage claim, watching the carousel of luggage from my flight go round and round while virtually everyone but me collected their bags. After half an hour, I knew—my bags hadn't made it to Scotland.

Pulling out my phone, I tapped on Ross' name to call him, knowing that the tone of my voice was so not going to be how I wanted to greet him after several weeks apart. I also knew that my emotions were ruling over my logical brain at this point, and he was about to be on the receiving end of the Allanah that much more closely resembled the one that had knocked on his door because he'd locked Gramps out in the cold than the Allanah he'd seen pretty much every time since that day.

He answered quickly, his own tone immediately apologetic. "Allanah, ach lass, I'm sorry I'm not there. I canna wait to see ye. How was yer flight?"

"The flight was fine, but you didn't even bother to send me the contact info of these people that are picking me up. I'm sure they've been waiting for me for a while now, but my bag isn't here, and I'm going to have to file some sort of report with baggage claim. I need you to text me a phone number so I can call them and tell them it might be a bit."

He sighed. "Ach, lass. That is not something ye needed to be dealing with, I know. I'm sorry. Doona worry about them. I'll call them right now. They are outside in a blue compact car. The lass has some of the reddest, longest hair ye will ever see, and the man..." He hesitated before continuing, "looks like he should be a film star in Hollywood, lass. Ye'll know them when ye see them. I can promise ye that."

"Fine. I'll see you later."

I hung up the phone before he could say anything else and stomped my way over toward the claims office. Thankfully, there was no one in line, and I was able to walk up to the counter right away.

"Good morning to ye. How can I be of assistance?"

I reached into my bag for my claim ticket and extended it in the old woman's direction.

"My flight landed over half an hour ago, and the carousel is now empty. I think my bags have been lost!"

The woman frowned and began to type something into her computer. "I am sorry about that. While it is rare, it does happen. Where did ye fly from?"

"Boston."

"Did ye have any layovers?"

I nodded, knowing that inevitably that was where things had gone awry. "Yes. London."

The woman clucked her tongue as she shook her head regretfully. "Aye. I can see that. It seems yer bags dinna make it on the plane. They should be on the next flight from London, though that doesna arrive for another five hours."

My eyes grew wide. "Five hours? I have people waiting to pick me up now."

She scrunched up her nose. I truly wasn't a violent person but I desperately wanted to pop her in the nose.

"I am sorry, lass. There is nothing I can do. We will hold it if ye wish to pick up yer luggage sometime tomorrow. Or we can have it shipped to the address ye are visiting, but that can take up to five days and will cost ye a rather hefty fee."

I crossed my arms in an effort to keep from launching myself across the table at her. "I'm sorry. What? Your airline loses my luggage, and I'm supposed to pay a fee to have it delivered to me. I don't think so, missy."

Embarrassed, I felt myself flush. I'd never called anyone *missy* in my life. It wasn't cool, and I knew it.

The woman furrowed her eyes at me, and I saw her reach to lay a hand on the phone next to her, as she pointed her other phone in my direction.

"Doona ye 'missy' me. I am doing my job, but that doesna mean I have to accept a berating from ye. Ye are welcome to wait or come by tonight or tomorrow, or ye can pay the fee and have it shipped. The choice is yers, and if ye cause any more trouble or raise yer voice again, I will have no choice but to call security to escort ye off property."

The threat should've been enough to calm me, but it had the opposite effect. Just as I opened my mouth to scream at her, I felt a heavy hand gently touch my shoulder. I whirled toward the sensation in response to the unexpected contact.

A man so tall, muscular, and ridiculously gorgeous stood in front of me that I knew immediately this had to be the man Ross had spoken of.

The stranger didn't immediately address me, instead he spoke to the woman behind the counter.

"We shall return after the next flight has landed for the lass's luggage. Thank ye for yer time and help."

Without another word, the man gently tugged on my arm until I stepped out of line. Once we were far enough away that the person behind me could step up to the counter, he spoke. "Good morning, lass. I'm Orick. I recognize ye as Allanah from the picture Ross sent us. Forgive my intrusion into the situation. 'Tis only I thought it best if we avoided having ye handled by security. 'Twould not be the warm welcome into Scotland that I'd prefer ye have."

I huffed, the knowledge that I was no longer totally alone in a foreign country relaxing me just a little. "You're right. I'm sorry you had to do that. I…we really don't have to wait. I can get back in line and pay the fee."

He shook his head and began to walk away, summoning me to follow him. "I willna hear of it. 'Tis nearly lunch anyway. Gillian and I shall drive ye into the city. We can enjoy a leisurely lunch and a chat, aye?"

Knowing there was really nothing I could do about any of it at this point, I reluctantly agreed. "Okay, sounds good. Thank you for picking me up."

"Not at all, lass. And doona worry about what just happened. All of us at Cagair are quite accustomed to fiery lasses, I can assure ye of that."

"Great." I mumbled under my breath, as I resigned myself to one more day without Ross.

The news of Allanah's delayed luggage was no tragedy as far as Ross could see it. If anything, it meant he had a little more time to get his wits about him, to consider his options, and to work up his nerve to go and speak to the woman he'd been so intent on never seeing again.

He was over Silva. When he thought of her, he no longer felt the tremendous pain and longing he'd felt for so long at the mere mention of her name. Still, he couldn't deny the truth of what was once between them and how important to him she'd once been. How important she always would be. No matter how much he wished she wasn't.

The shower had done wonders for him, but Allanah's angry phone call had set him on edge once again.

He couldn't blame her for being angry. Travel is trying even when everything goes right. Not only had she landed without luggage, she'd also been expecting a different set of circumstances upon her arrival there. He would've been none too pleased himself.

Sighing, he sat back down on the bed in the spacious room, twisting to look through the paned window onto one of the many grassy expanses just beyond the castle.

Was Sydney right? Was his best course of action to tell Allanah about Silva the moment she arrived here?

Perhaps so, but he couldn't bear the thought of it. What if the knowledge made her want to turn right back around and return to the States. It would break his already shattered heart. The first trip to see his mother had tried him beyond what he knew he was capable of. He truly wasn't sure he could make himself return without Allanah by his side.

Silva. What would he say to her? How would it feel for him to see her again? What would she think about his new relationship? Would she threaten to tell Allanah if he decided he didn't want to?

Too many questions coursed through his mind. Questions that would only be answered if he simply got on with it and went in search of his ex-wife.

Running an anxious hand through his still-damp hair, Ross rose from the bed and set about the dreaded task.

Busy noises echoed down the long bedchamber hallway of the castle, the excited sounds of everyone visiting down below.

The thought of walking into the room where everyone was gathered and getting Silva's attention caused his feet to slow. They suddenly felt as if they were filled with lead. He startled at the sound of his name being called from behind him.

Silva. He'd know her voice anywhere. It was forever embedded into his mind and heart.

He turned toward her, all of his nerves drifting away as he lay eyes on her.

She looked different somehow. Tired. In truth, downright exhausted. But at the same time, there was a peacefulness in her eyes, and her smile was genuine as she walked toward him.

"Ben has been asleep for half an hour, but I was waiting for the sound of a door closing in the hallway before stepping outside in the hopes it would be you and I'd be able to catch you."

He walked into her arms as she extended hers toward him,

quickly falling into an embrace as familiar to him as the sound of her voice.

"Ye did lass. Ye caught me." He stepped away and returned her smile. "Is Ben yer son?"

She nodded, and he noticed that her eyes glinted with pride at his name. "Yes. Would you…" She hesitated, and he hurried to reassure her.

"Aye, lass. I would love to see him."

She nodded again and turned back toward the door she'd come out of. She kept her voice low as she spoke. "We will have to be quiet, but he's a pretty sound sleeper. I'm sure we'll be fine."

Ross took a deep breath as he followed Silva into the bedchamber, his eyes quickly moving to rest on the small packable crib set up next to the four-poster bed. As he approached and gazed down at the sleeping child, who even at first glance looked so equally like both his mother and father, all he felt was joy.

The anticipatory resistance that had lodged itself in his chest melted away, and a peace settled over him.

Before him lay the child of the woman he'd once loved more than anyone, and yet he felt no jealousy, no remorse for how things now were, no regret that she or the child lying between them wasn't his.

While he would never forgive himself for the pain he'd caused her, he now knew for sure that they were both exactly where they needed to be. Their love for one another had been necessary, and their eventual love for others inevitable.

Love. The word sprang up in his mind, once again taking him by surprise, but this time it lingered, and it settled itself deep into his heart. And he knew it was true.

He'd once loved Silva.

Now he loved Allanah.

And this love was different. Greater. He knew so much more now. Not only more of himself, but more of the world. He now knew what loss was. He knew what he wanted. And somehow, all of those things made the love that was so surely burning inside his chest more pure than his love for Silva had ever been.

The second she arrived, he would lay out his feelings for her.

"What are you thinking, Ross?" Silva's voice pulled him from his thoughts and back into the moment.

"He's a handsome wee lad, lass."

She smiled again, nudging her head toward the doorway. Quietly, they tiptoed from the room.

"You look really good, Ross. Are you…are you good? Part of me was worried you'd be angry that we came here. I was hesitant, but Morna was so insistent we just felt we couldn't say no."

To his surprise, he was able to answer her effortlessly. "Aye. I am better than I have been in a verra long time."

She reached out to squeeze his hand. "I'm sorry about your mother, Ross. Griffith has kept us informed. I even went to see her myself a while back, but she didn't remember me."

He sighed. He'd not thought of how hard this had to be for Silva until now. In so many ways, she'd been more of a child to his mother than he had. She'd been there in the time following his supposed death when he had not.

"She would now. She often finds herself back in the months before I…" He paused, knowing she understood. "I left. We've spoken of ye often. Ye know that she loves ye, aye?"

Silva swallowed and her voice was broken as she answered. "And I her." She looked at him, her eyes glazing with tears before she continued. "Sydney told me a little bit about Allanah, Ross. I'm so, so happy for you."

He was happy for himself too, but he still didn't know what sort of arrangement he should make with Silva. He was ready to tell Allanah that he loved her, but that didn't mean he was ready to tell her all of his secrets.

"Silva, lass, ye willna say anything to her about us, aye? She doesna know about ye. She doesn't know about any of it."

Silva frowned at him. "Then you should tell her. It won't matter in the least to her if you love her, Ross."

He sighed. Why could no one save him see that it absolutely did matter? "'Tis not true. She wouldna want me if she knew all I'd done."

Silva stared hard at him, the same frustration burning in her eyes that he'd seen in Sydney's earlier. After a long moment, she spoke. "Let me give you a piece of advice."

Thoughtlessly, he interrupted her. "I'd rather ye dinna."

She laughed and shook her head. "Tough. You're going to get it anyway. Learn from your past mistakes, Ross. Quit trying to control and dictate what you think the women in your life can and can't handle. Secrets never keep for long. Your last one didn't, and this won't either. Believe me, the only way this can go wrong for you is if she finds out from anyone other than you."

Ross sighed, the truth in her words sinking in for the first time. She would have to know. He just wasn't ready for that to happen yet.

"Fine, lass. I know ye are right. I swear to ye I will tell her, but not this night, and not tomorrow. I'm already losing my mother. When I tell her, I know the way she'll look at me, even if she does decide to stay. I've seen it in yer eyes before. I doona wish to see that yet. I doona think I could bear it. Not just yet. I will tell her. But in my own time, aye?"

Silva nodded and leaned in to hug him once more. "Of course. This is no longer my story, Ross. It's yours. I just want you to be happy. That's all I've ever wanted for you."

CHAPTER 35

My lunch with Gillian and Orick turned into an all-day tour of the city after the flight carrying my luggage was delayed leaving London. By the time we finally pulled onto the long driveway leading to Cagair Castle, it was close to ten o'clock at night, and I'd officially gone thirty plus hours without sleep. I'd not had a drop to drink all day, and I felt thoroughly drunk and unsteady on my feet as I stepped out of the car and onto the grounds of the castle.

"I'll see these up to yer room, lass. I'm sure everyone is already abed."

I followed Orick and Gillian inside the main doors of the castle, appreciating but not really capable of truly taking in the grandeur of the building, as I walked up the set of stairs that led to a long corridor of doorways.

As soon as I stepped into the hallway, Ross stepped out of a door a few yards down from me. He immediately crushed me to him, pressing his mouth against mine.

"Ach, lass. It felt as if ye would never get here."

He pulled away, looked me over, and grinned. "Ye look..." He hesitated, seemingly knowing better than to criticize me after seeing the expression on my face.

"Like I got run over by a truck? I know." I pointed to the room behind him. "Is this us?"

He nodded.

My feet barely able to move, I trudged inside and collapsed on the large bed as Orick set my bags down inside the doorway. I heard Ross thank Orick and Gillian before he closed the door and walked over to me.

"Long day, aye?"

Still in my clothes, I kicked off my shoes, pulled my hair out of the ponytail it was in, and scrambled to get underneath the blankets. I'd never been so ready to sleep in my life.

"You have no idea." I yawned as my eyelids began to close. "I'll talk to you in the morning, okay?"

And before I heard his response, sleep found me.

---

*W*hile it certainly wasn't the greeting he'd expected, he couldn't blame Allanah for her exhaustion. Simply pleased that she was now there with him, he joined her in the bed, pulling her close as he joined her in sleep. His words could wait until morning.

She pulled him closer as he scooted near her, and her head quickly moved to his chest.

"I...I..." Her words were jumbled as she drifted to sleep. "I'm sorry I was such a cranky bitch earlier. I love you, Ross."

Shocked, he glanced down at her, but her eyes were tightly closed, and the softest hint of a snore was already escaping her.

He smiled, happiness flooding him. At least he knew now that his own declaration was likely to be reciprocated.

J woke at dawn, warm, content, and still snuggled into the crook of Ross' arm. I truly hadn't intended to fall asleep so quickly. I'd wanted to talk to him, kiss him, and speak to him about how the time with his mother had been, but all of my desires had gone racing out the window the moment I'd crawled into bed. Sleep hadn't been an option. My body had simply insisted that I needed it. Right then. Right there. My intentions be damned.

It was fine, though. I knew Ross would understand. And now that I was here, we had all the time in the world to talk and be together as much as we wanted.

Careful not to wake him, I shifted away from his arm, scooting from the covers to go in search of the bathroom. The first door I opened was a small closet, and I took the liberty of removing one of the plush robes and a pair of slippers from inside before trying the next door.

Stepping into the bathroom, I laughed at my appearance in the mirror before turning toward the shower to turn on the spray of water. The way I looked now made my smudged eyeliner and lipstick after sex seem utterly ridiculous. Today, after way too many hours without a shower and the stress of traveling weighing on me, I looked truly terrible.

Thankful that all of that was about to be washed away, I stripped away my clothes and stepped into the warm water. I closed my eyes and reveled in the sensation of the warm droplets rinsing away the grime of my journey. I was so lost in the pleasure of the shower that I didn't even hear Ross enter the bathroom until he spoke next to me. I jumped and turned to see that he had his eyes covered tightly with his hands.

"If ye doona wish for me to see ye lass, I'll leave. 'Tis only that I thought if ye wanted, I could join ye."

I quickly cupped my hands under the water so I could throw some at my face and give my makeup a good scrub. Of course, I wanted him in there with me. Any excuse to look at him naked was good by me.

I tapped on the glass so he'd open his eyes. When he did, I smiled at him and waved him over. "Get in."

Grinning, he removed his underwear and opened the glass door as I stepped deeper inside to make room for him. While there was room for both of us to stand, we couldn't easily do so without touching, and my arms went around his waist instinctively as he stepped under the water.

Looking up at him under the spray, I stood on my tiptoes to kiss him. "I've missed you. I'm sorry I was so short with you on the phone yesterday and then fell asleep the second I walked into the room last night."

He laughed and pulled me into another hug. "Doona worry about it, lass. Ye doona need to apologize again."

I frowned and stepped back out of the spray so I could look at him. "Again? I didn't realize I'd already done it once."

He raised his brows, and there was something mischievous in his gaze. "Aye. Did ye know ye talk in yer sleep?"

I argued with him. "I do not."

He shrugged, and I smiled in response. I'd missed that shrug immeasurably.

"Mayhap not usually, but ye did last night."

I waved him toward me so I could hold him without getting blasted by water.

"What did I say?"

"Ye mean, besides yer apology?"

I nodded against his chest.

With his arms around me, he leaned down to whisper into my ear. "Ye said that ye loved me."

Nausea rose up, threatening to make me hurl right there in the shower. I was thankful that my cheek was pressed against his skin so he couldn't see me blush. Surely, I hadn't said that.

Then again, I knew I'd never been more tired than I'd been last night. Maybe in my delirium, I actually had.

"I...I..." I faltered. I had no idea what to say to him.

"Doona worry, lass." He kissed the top of my wet hair. "I am quite in love with ye, as well."

CHAPTER 36

Shortly after Ross' shower confessional, we moved back to the bed where we made love for the next hour before falling back asleep until the middle of the day. Hearing him say that he loved me had been the balm I needed to soothe my anxious mind. It meant that slowly, his walls were coming down. It meant that maybe—just maybe—I didn't need to press him just yet. Perhaps, he would simply open up with time.

Close to noon, I woke to the sound of a paw scratching at the doorway. Eager to see Tink, I slipped out of bed, threw on a robe, and hurried to answer the door. She jumped into my arms as soon as she saw me, and I stood and scrunched her up against me for a snuggle while she panted and licked the side of my face.

"Where were you last night? I've missed you."

Ross heard the commotion and sleepily lifted his head to speak. "Sydney offered to take her so that we might have some time alone. Bring her to the bed, lass."

Tink let out a small yip, seemingly eager to see her master as I returned to the bed and set the dog onto the mattress. She bounded over to him and smothered him in kisses.

He laughed and turned his head away from her to speak to me.

"How are ye feeling? Any more rested?"

I nodded. A night of sleep, followed by a shower and morning sex had done wonders for me. "I feel great. I'm ready to go and explore the castle, I think."

His expression changed strangely, his brows pulling together as if that were the last thing on earth he wanted to do. Confused, I amended my words.

"That is, if we have time to do that before we leave for your mother's."

He gave his head a slight shake and then forced a smile. "Aye. O'course. We shall stay one more night here before we begin the journey. Lass, I need to speak to ye about something, just to prepare ye for the rest of the day."

"Okay?"

I stood long enough to lift the covers and slip back inside the bed. He scooted closer to me and leaned in to kiss my cheek.

"I'm sure Gillian and Orick told ye, but the castle has been overrun by guests. 'Twill be many introductions today and more conversation that I care to have. I'm worried it might be overwhelming for ye."

I cocked my head to the side and lifted a brow in confusion. "Why?"

Still laying down, he pulled his shoulders up in a half-shrug. "I just have a sense that 'twill be, lass. I know all the people here. They can...they can be a lot to handle."

I reached to kiss him in reassurance. "When I'm not sleep-deprived and upset about lost luggage, I truly am pretty good with people, Ross. I'll be fine. In fact, I'm pretty excited to meet those who've known you forever."

He shook his head again, and I could see the worry lines in his forehead deepen. "Only a few in the group have known me forever."

"Okay." I pulled away from him and rose from the bed, moving to my suitcase to pull out some fresh clothes. "Don't worry, Ross.

It'll be fine. We will socialize today, and then we will have the whole drive tomorrow for the two of us to talk on the way to your mom's. I've never seen you like this. I had no idea you had such social anxiety. Just take a breath."

I couldn't understand his hesitation and worry. Nervous energy rolled off him like the smoke from a steam engine. I bent to pick up his jeans at the foot of the bed and tossed them in his direction.

"Come on. Let's go. I've never explored the inside of a castle before."

In response to my enthusiastic 'let's go,' Tink tore away from Ross and leapt off the bed in her eagerness to set out on an adventure. Glancing over at Ross, who had pulled the covers up over his head, I rolled my eyes and opened the door to the bedroom.

"Fine. You sleep all you want. I'm going to stretch my legs for a bit."

With Tink setting off at an incredibly quick trot, I hurried after her, barely registering Ross' plea that I wait for him. I ignored him and continued on.

*G*roaning, Ross listened to the sound of Allanah continuing down the hallway after Tink. He knew she'd ignored him, not that he could blame her. How could she possibly understand his desire to keep her away from everyone at the castle as much as possible?

Eager to catch her, Ross pulled himself from bed and yanked on his pants before reaching for the shirt closest to him.

He had to find her before she spoke to anyone. Sydney and Silva knew better than to spill his secret. But there was no telling what Morna would do. She was always a wild card.

ink seemed to know exactly where she was going, which made me wonder if perhaps the pup had stayed here at the castle with Sydney while Ross had gone to visit his mother before my arrival.

Of all the people here at the castle, I was most looking forward to meeting the mysterious Sydney. Ross spoke of her often, and always with such admiration that I, on occasion, found myself feeling slightly jealous of her. There was a reverence in his tone when he spoke of his dear friend, and more than once he'd mentioned that he owed her a great deal. Why? I hadn't the slightest clue, but I hoped that simply being around Sydney might give me a little more insight into all of the parts of Ross he still refused to let me see.

Just as Tink reached the front door and twisted her head to look back at me expectedly, I remembered something that Ross had mentioned about Sydney. She was a cook. Perhaps, I could find her in the castle's kitchen. With no real knowledge about castles to pull from, there was still some small part of my mind that seemed to believe kitchens were often found in the basements of such magnificent structures. I'd probably seen it in a movie or television show. With that in mind, I gave Tink a slight shake of my head, urging her to follow me instead as I wandered around looking for steps downward.

It didn't take long, and the moment I stepped down into the stairwell, I knew I was headed in the right direction. Wonderful, spicy smells were wafting up toward me, a sure sign that someone was cooking below. As I continued downward, I could hear a set of mumbling voices. Not wishing to appear as if I was eavesdropping, I intentionally made my steps slightly louder until one of the strangers called up toward me.

"Callum, is that you? Are you back with the groceries for tonight?"

Reaching the last step, I rounded the corner of the doorway and stepped onto the landing of the basement floor where three women —two near my age, the last much older—stood in a half circle smiling at me.

"No." I waved, nervously. "I'm…" I hesitated. I didn't need to introduce myself as Sue here. Among these strangers who were unlikely to bump into anyone that had known me growing up, I could use my given name. I smiled, happy to be able to say the name that felt so much more like me. "I'm Allanah."

The older woman approached first, her eyes bright and friendly, as she walked forward with her arms spread wide. Rather than shake my hand, she pulled me straight into one of the biggest and warmest hugs I'd ever received in my life.

"I'm Morna, lass. 'Tis a pleasure to meet ye."

She pulled away and turned to introduce me to the other two women. Following Morna's lead, they stepped forward to greet me.

They both had long, dark hair, much like my own, but one wore an apron, and she moved in to hug me first.

"I'm Sydney. I'm so glad you finally made it here. Lost luggage is the worst."

"It really is."

As she stepped away, the last woman moved forward. Her gaze was direct and odd, and I couldn't help but feel like she was thoroughly looking me over. Unsure of how to proceed, I slowly reached out my hand as I wondered if maybe she didn't wish to be as familiar as both Morna and Sydney had been.

Seeing my hand move toward her seemed to pull her out of whatever zone she'd been in. I saw her give her head a gentle shake before she waved my hand away and leaned in for a hug.

"I'm Silva. It's nice to meet you."

Morna spoke up from behind Silva's back, pointing to the table in the back of the room.

"Come and sit with us, lass. We shall get a treat for the wee pup, and ye can join us for a cup of tea."

*W*here could Allanah and Tink possibly have wandered off to so quickly? The tower was empty. The sitting room and dining hall were, too. As he moved toward the castle's front doors, the sound of laughter reverberated up from the basement.

The kitchen. Holy hell.

Five minutes apart from him, and she'd already been thrown in among the group.

With anxiety building, he headed toward the kitchen, eager to steal Allanah away from the woman he knew was most likely to say too much.

He could tell who was there with her before he entered the room. The voices of Sydney, Silva, and Morna were each as distinct as Allanah's. Dread settled into his stomach as he made his presence known.

Morna beamed at him, hopping up from her seat at the table they were gathered around and moved toward him at an astonishingly fast pace. Rather than hug him, she surprised him by reaching for his arm and pulling him back up into the stairwell, her voice low as she whispered. "I've been working on a spell to make this all easier on ye and the lass. She's just consumed it in the tea Sydney brewed for her. She will fall asleep at the table within the next minute. Best ye carry her up to bed and let her sleep for a time."

Horrified, he stared at the old witch. "Ye drugged her?"

Morna glared at him and shook her head. "No, lad. I doona drug anyone. Ever. I spelled her. She will dream of all that she needs to know and wake knowing of the magic and the time travel as if there was never a time when she dinna know it. Ye willna need to explain a thing."

His eyes wide, Ross continued to stare, the possibility of how wonderfully easy it would all be if Morna's spell worked, settling in his mind.

He could see no reason why it wouldn't. She was as powerful a witch as he'd ever seen.

"Will she know that something has happened to her? That her reality has changed?"

The old witch scrunched up her nose and gave a slight nod. "Aye. 'Tis likely she will know something, but I've added a calming tonic to the potion. She will accept it all easily."

"I…" He stuttered, unsure of how to continue. Having her sleep all day had multiple advantages. Not only would it keep him from having to convince a panicked and disbelieving woman that magic and time travel were real, but it would also dramatically cut down on the number of hours she would have to interact with the guests of the castle.

Morna laughed, patting his arm as she spoke. "Just say thank ye and get ready to catch her as she slumps over in her chair. Ye are due an easy break, lad. 'Tis the least I could do."

CHAPTER 37

*H*ad I suffered a stroke? An aneurysm? Confused, yet puzzlingly calm, I blinked my eyes and stared up at the ceiling of the bedroom Ross and I had slept in the night before. One moment I'd been sipping tea, chatting about Sydney's baby with Morna and Silva, and the next moment I was flat on my back wondering what the hell had happened.

Slowly, I moved my hands and patted myself all over. Everything felt fine. Nothing hurt. I could move everything. I didn't feel nauseous. My head wasn't aching. Slowly, I pushed myself up, twisting to look out the window next to the bed.

Dark.

How had a whole day passed in a second?

Had Ross' magic returned?

What?!

I scrunched my brows together and closed my eyes as the original thought, and my question of it after, surged through my mind at once. Why had anything to do with magic crossed my mind?

Because it exists. Because Ross used to possess it. Because the old witch downstairs still does. Because everyone under this castle has been touched by it.

The thoughts coursed logically and surely through my mind as I sat there.

Did I know all of that this morning?

No. I was certain that I did not.

Did I doubt any of it now?

Also, no.

Never in my life had two different belief systems combined so succinctly in my mind. I knew that all of this knowledge was new. I knew that for the majority of my life, such a possibility had never crossed my mind.

At the same time, I also knew that for whatever reason, it absolutely did now. I knew that magic was everywhere. That somehow, I was now a part of it, that my boyfriend had been born hundreds of years before.

The strangest part of it all, I was weirdly okay with it. It didn't feel as if my world had been upended or like the foundation of my existence had somehow been shaken. It just seemed as if some barrier in my mind had been suddenly stripped away, and a whole new realm of knowing existed.

Had I dreamed it all? If so, I didn't remember my dreams. The timespan between sitting at the kitchen table and now truly felt like seconds.

Was this what happened to whatever cognizant part of our souls remains after we die? I was pretty sure I wasn't dead.

Dozens of questions coursed through my mind as I opened my eyes again and gazed around the room.

Oddly, even as more questions began to build, an even greater realization occurred to me. None of it really mattered. The truth was the truth, and that was enough.

I looked over to the bedside table and reached for my phone, shooting out a quick text to Ross as I rose from the bed and walked toward the bathroom.

"Get up here."

By the time I made it out of the bathroom, he was sitting at the end of the bed, his brows furrowed and his arms crossed as he looked at me anxiously.

"How do ye feel, lass?"

I shrugged. I wasn't sleepy, but I had never felt more relaxed in my entire life. "Like I just left a day at the spa."

He laughed and pulled me to him. "Good."

I could sense that he wanted to ask me something. While I didn't know the question, I had a sneaking suspicion of what it was about.

"So…you were born in the seventeenth century, huh? That's pretty interesting."

He leaned away from me just enough to look into my eyes. "Aye, lass. Ye are truly fine?"

I nodded. "I'm not sure exactly what happened to me today, but yes, I feel fine." I stepped away and stretched my arms over my head. "Would you like to tell me what happened?"

He stared at me hesitantly, and I could tell by his expression that he wasn't entirely sure either.

"What…what do ye know now, lass, that ye dinna before?"

For the next half hour or so, I told him all of the newfound knowledge that had suddenly been dumped into my mind: his former magic, Morna's current magic, time travel.

When I finished, his gaze was still apprehensive. "And that is all, lass?"

I nodded. "Yes. I don't know the specifics about anything. It just feels as if I was given the cliff notes on some other dimension I didn't know existed."

He laughed. "I suppose ye have. As for what happened, 'twas Morna's doing. 'Twas in the tea ye drank this morning."

I nodded. "Ah. I'd begun to suspect as much. So, what's the plan now?"

"Well…" Ross stood and moved toward the doorway. "If ye are

up for it, everyone awaits us at dinner downstairs. After that, we should get a good night's rest, for the journey to my mother will take us days, and I am sorry to say that the road there shall be quite unlike anything ye've experienced before."

I grimaced. Thoughts of horses and sleeping on the ground filled my mind. "I don't suppose there's any sort of magic that will make that a bit easier, is there?"

He laughed again. I could see relief that I now knew about the magic in his softened expression, and I wondered if this was the big secret—the huge thing he never wanted to talk about. While I knew it had to be part of it, I suspected there was more to it—more that he still didn't believe I should be privy to.

"No, lass, though I will make it as easy for ye as I can. Come morning, I will rise before dawn and journey back with Callum to prepare everything for our journey. While I'm away, ye should call yer family, mayhap Caleb as well, and tell them that we will be out of touch for some time. That is why I couldna call ye. 'Twas not really a lie when I said her village was verra remote."

I snorted. "That's for sure. Okay. Sounds like a plan."

He reached for my hand to lead me downstairs.

"If it's all the same to you, I don't think I'll be accepting any more offers of food or beverage from Morna."

He winked at me and paused in the doorway to kiss my hand. "I would advise ye to do no less, lass."

CHAPTER 38

By some grand stroke of luck, I managed to call Gramps while both Georgie and Caleb were with him. It hadn't taken long after Ross and I had walked in on them for Georgie and Caleb to make their relationship more public—at least where Gramps was concerned.

I spoke to Gramps, trying to get his attention among the raucous voices around him.

"Hey…Hey, listen to me. I want to talk to you guys a minute. Why don't you all gather around the table and let me video chat all of you real fast?"

That seemed to get the attention of the group, and they quickly agreed before hanging up to reconvene at the table. A handful of minutes later, the sound of their video call came through.

I happily answered, eager to see their faces for the last time in what I knew might be months.

"Sue!" Georgie's expression was elated. "How's it going? Turn your phone around and give us a quick glimpse of your room in the castle."

Tapping the button that would switch directions of the camera, I panned up to show them the tall ceilings and the intricacy of the design in the room. When I flipped it back around, all three of their jaws were slightly open.

"It's gorgeous." Gramps grinned at me. "You finally got your luggage, I see."

For the first time, the irony of my panic over the lost luggage crossed my mind. I would have no use for any of it in a matter of hours.

"Yes, I did. Hey, I don't have a lot of time, but I wanted to call you guys and let you know that I probably won't be able to talk to you for a while. We are leaving for Ross' mother's today, and apparently there's no cell reception where she lives—no internet either."

Georgie frowned at me. "What? Sue, are you sure? I've traveled all over the world, and there are very few places anymore that don't at the very least have internet."

I shrugged, knowing that I couldn't begin to tell them the truth.

"That's what Ross says. I'm assuming he would know."

Caleb stayed quietly in the background. He knew that Georgie and Gramps would want to get their fill of conversation in with me.

Gramps spoke up again. "That's just fine. Communication is far too easy these days, if you ask me. You just go and support Ross while he takes care of his ailing mother. We will all be fine, I promise you."

Finally, Caleb spoke. "He's right. We'll take care of everything here. The girls will miss you both, but they're doing well. Just call us as soon as you guys make it back to where there's cell reception."

I sighed, suddenly feeling sad that I wouldn't be able to see or speak to them. I'd not gone more than a few days without speaking to Gramps in my whole life.

"I will. I don't know how long we will be there. It all just depends on..."

Gramps held up his hand to stop me. "We know, sweetheart. There were lots of times when Georgie was out exploring the world that we wouldn't hear from her for months. It will be fine. We love you."

Fighting back tears, I knew I had to get off the phone quickly if I didn't want to turn into a blubbery mess for the rest of the day.

"I love you guys, too. I'll talk to you as soon as I can."

I ended the call and took some time in the bathroom to gather my composure. When I stepped back into the bedroom to find that Ross still hadn't returned from readying things with Callum, I decided to go and find someone to visit with.

The first person I came across was Silva. She stood out in the hallway, just a few doors down from ours, her baby cradled against her chest as she tried to soothe him.

She smiled at me and I approached her as she spoke.

"I don't understand it. Once I'm able to get him to sleep, he sleeps hard, but until then—no matter how completely exhausted he is—he fights it."

I grinned as I looked down into her arms at him. He had plump cheeks and beautiful green eyes.

"He just doesn't want to miss out on any of the fun."

She laughed and continued to try and soothe him. "I suppose so."

We both grew quiet then, an awkward silence settling between us as she gently bounced him up and down and paced in semi-circles around me. I nearly turned and walked off in the other direction when she finally spoke.

"I..." She hesitated and I smiled at her to encourage her to continue on. "I know it's not really my place to say so, but Ross is a really great guy. I'm so glad that he's found you."

I felt the heat rise in my cheeks a little as I blushed. I was quite glad I'd found him, too.

"He really is. Although, I'm not sure he knows that."

She laughed a little and then sighed as the baby slowly settled down in her arms. "No. He definitely doesn't. For some reason that

I will never understand, he seems determined to believe nothing but the worst about himself."

Her expression as she spoke was genuinely irritated, and I realized that she must have known him a long time. She knew him too well—her observations of him too close to my own—for it to be otherwise.

"You and Ross are quite close then?"

She looked taken aback by my question, so I tried to elaborate further. "It's just that Ross doesn't let many people in enough for them to be so astute in their take on him."

She lifted her brows quickly, as she nodded and waved me toward the doorway nearest us. I obligingly followed her inside so she could lay the baby down to sleep.

"I've known him for years. And he may not let people in, but his cards are really all out on the table. It doesn't take much time around him for his poor opinion of himself to leak through."

That much was true. He grimaced at every kind word that was ever said to him.

She was staring at me strangely again, much like she had in the kitchen the day before. Curiosity getting the better of me, I simply had to ask her. "What is it? Why do you always look at me like you're not sure whether you want to hug me or hit me?"

She laughed as together we walked from the room. "I'm sorry. My expression shows everything. I can assure you that I don't want to hit you." She sighed before continuing. "Have you seen the tower room yet? Do you want to join me up there for a chat?"

When I nodded, she began to lead the way as she talked. "It's only…I'm protective of Ross. I'm worried for him. Not because of you. I can tell you're great. Because of him. He's sure to do something to try to make this thing with you implode, and I desperately want to pin you down and make you promise you won't leave him when he does."

I chuckled uncomfortably, unsure of how to process the oddity of this interaction as I followed her up a set of spiral stairs.

As we reached the top and entered a beautiful room surrounded by paned windows that provided a stunning three-hundred-and-sixty degree view of the castle, I spoke.

"Why exactly are you so protective of him?"

She moved to one of the curved benches that lined the walls and motioned for me to join her. "Ross was my best friend for a very long time. I just don't want him to suffer any more pain than he already has."

Perhaps she was referring to Beth's death, but something inside told me that wasn't it. She'd said that she *was* his best friend, which meant she no longer was. And since I'd never heard mention of her name before I arrived here, I didn't imagine that the two of them were in much contact anymore. It was possible she knew nothing about Beth.

As far as I could tell, the statement was another small thread for me to pull on. Another hint at what Ross seemed so intent on keeping to himself.

"What pain has he suffered?"

She sighed again, and gave me a small shrug. "The only thing Ross hates worse than a kind word is being the subject of gossip. He would never forgive me if I said anything. He will tell you in time, I'm sure. I'll just say this: we all go through terrible things, but most of us aren't as hard on ourselves as he is. He doesn't only suffer the pain of the moment, or the loss, he continually carries the pain of the judgment he places on himself. It makes it so much worse. It's never-ending for him."

I found the thought to be immeasurably sad, but I knew she was right. I'd seen it in him too many times before. If you looked past his friendly smile and beautiful eyes, you could see the pain there, the worry that anything good was going to vanish in an instant, and that no matter how it happened, he would be at fault.

I brushed away a rogue tear that had spilled onto my cheek. "If it makes you feel any better, I can see the unspoken hurt that just festers in him, and while I wish he would trust me with it,

I'm doing my best to be patient with him. I promise you I won't run."

She shook her head at me. "No. Don't make that promise. It may not be one you can keep. He may do something that you feel you can't move past, and you always need to feel as if that's okay. All I ask is that if he ever hurts you, just know that it's not because he doesn't love you. His poor decisions are almost always caused by the self-hatred he's somehow been unable to get rid of for most of his life."

A sudden voice called up to us from the bottom of the stairwell. Sydney.

"Ross and Callum are back. You two better come on down so we can all eat a quick farewell lunch together."

With a heavy heart, I set off down the stairs. There was no way that Silva and Ross had just been "friends."

No matter how much I didn't want it to be true, part of the joy I usually felt when I looked at Ross was gone as I watched him enter the dining hall.

Whatever secret Ross held onto was big. Silva wouldn't have said a word to me about it otherwise.

After my conversation with Gramps, I'd been so sure I would be able to move past whatever it was that he didn't want me to know.

Now, I wasn't so sure of that at all.

CHAPTER 39

Something was bothering her. What had happened in the few hours between the time that he'd left her in bed that morning and the time he'd joined her at lunch, Ross didn't know, but something was different between them.

All day, throughout the ride toward his mother's, she'd been quiet. And her fascination with how strange things were in a century so different from her own seemed muted to him.

He'd planned for them to camp outdoors on their first night of the journey, but by the time dusk fell, he knew that would do nothing to help the lass's mood.

"There is a village not far off the path ahead. I canna say for sure that the place I have in mind will still be there, but I believe there is a rather lovely inn. At least, there used to be. Why doona we stop and get warm for the night? They should have a cooked meal available as well."

Riding on the horse in front of him, her head barely brushing his chest, she quickly nodded. "Sure, although I thought you said we were camping?"

He didn't want her to protest if he said he was stopping for her benefit. Instead, he played up his own fatigue.

"Aye, but I now believe this would be better. Stopping in a village will allow me to rest the horse in a proper stable. And I am not as accustomed to riding as I once was. My arse and legs ache dreadfully. I doona know if I would be able to walk come morning if I had to sleep on the ground."

She gave a soft chuckle, and it lit up some hope in him that perhaps her mood was lifting somewhat.

"I am always going to be in favor of sleeping off of the ground."

Blessedly, the inn he had in mind was still running, and he delighted in watching her awe grow as they entered the first real village she'd seen since they'd traveled into the past.

"Wow. It's so dark without street lamps. Everyone's eyesight must be terrible."

He laughed and bent to nuzzle his lips into the side of her neck. "I doona know about that, lass, but I do know that I am glad that I no longer live in this time."

He pointed to the stable in the distance. "If I dismount here, do ye think ye can ride her to the stables while I go in search of the man I need to pay for a night's lodging for the horse?"

She twisted to look at him nervously. "I can try."

Pulling the horse to a stop, he quickly dismounted and gave the mare a gentle pat.

"Ye shall be fine. She's an easy ride. It shouldna take me more than a moment."

I was beyond grateful for Ross' change of heart. Not only had my worries from my conversation with Silva built throughout the day, I was in so much pain from being on the back of a horse for hours on end, I was near tears.

My desire to practice patience with Ross was now entirely gone. We still had several days on the road before we reached his mother's, and once there, I would be apart from everything and everyone I knew for months. I needed answers. And I needed them now. It would be better to have the conversation behind closed doors than out in the middle of nowhere.

Thankfully, Ross was right about the horse. She proceeded in the direction of the stables without me having to do much of anything to get her there. Ross had run ahead to the small house that sat close to it. By the time I reached the stables, he was already on his way back outside with the man I assumed owned them.

It didn't take long for Ross to see the horse settled and even less time for him to secure us lodging at the one inn in the small village.

The inn was endlessly fascinating to me. Lit only by a large fire in the corner and an alarming number of candles, once inside it had a surprising amount of comfortable amenities.

The bed in the room we were shown to was more comfortable than I ever would've imagined. And the food the innkeeper brought up shortly after we settled in was delicious.

I'd found it odd that he'd asked me to wait outside while he procured our room, but as we sat down at the small table in the corner, he explained why.

"They think we are married, lass. 'Twas the only way 'twould be suitable for us to share a room, and I dinna wish to risk ye protesting if they asked us."

I bit into the loaf of bread that accompanied our stew as I spoke in between mouthfuls. "I'm not a moron, Ross. I would expect that in this time."

He nodded, before frowning at me and leaning back in his seat. "What is it, lass? Something is the matter and I can do nothing to solve it until ye tell me what 'tis."

I reached for the bitter, stout mug of ale and took a sip to wash down the dry hunk of bread in my mouth before answering him. "I think we need to talk."

He nodded. "Aye, Allanah. I agree. Talk to me, lass."

I didn't know how to begin. I didn't know how to press him without making him pull away. "You know how you often avoid certain topics?"

His expression shifted to one of confusion. "Do I?"

"Yes. You do. It seems that we can talk about anything as long as I don't mention Scotland, your youth, your past, any time leading up to your arrival in Boston, really. I have so many questions that I want to ask you, but you make it clear that I'm not allowed to. I'm in love with you, Ross, but I feel as if I know nothing about you."

He protested immediately. "I have never said that ye couldna ask me anything."

I huffed and pushed myself away from the table as I began to pace the room.

"You didn't have to say it, Ross. It's clear in the way you change subjects or give me details so vague that it would be fine to share them with a total stranger. I'm an open book, Ross. Ask me anything. I'll tell you. I don't have any secrets. There's no part of my past so painful that I won't tell you about it."

He sighed and looked down at his feet. "Then ye are lucky, lass."

"Stop it, Ross. If I'm the person you love—if this is real—then there shouldn't be anything so painful that you can't tell me either."

Slowly, he looked up, his eyes boring into me. "Fine, lass. Ask me anything and I shall tell ye. I can be the open book that ye wish. Just ask."

Surprised by his willingness, I relaxed a little, making way for some hope that perhaps I'd overreacted to everything Silva had said.

"Really?"

He nodded, somberly. "Aye. What do ye wish to know?"

While I believed his intention to tell me more about himself, I also knew that I would have to tread carefully. He wasn't accustomed to sharing anything with anyone. If I jumped right in with my toughest questions, I knew he would retreat.

"Why did you move from your time to mine?"

He stood from the table, walked over to the bed, and sat down as he motioned for me to do the same. When he did, he faced me and gathered my hands in his.

"The first time I fled out of fear. I left because I dinna wish to fulfill my duty as one with magic. I was meant to be bound to a laird on an isle far from my home. I couldna do it. My need for free will was too strong, but I would have been unable to deny the pull of my destiny had I stayed in my own time, so I left and built a life for myself in yer time."

Progress. That had been easy enough. I continued on.

"The first time? That implies there was a second. What about that time?"

"I couldna outrun my destiny forever, lass. I went back briefly to help out those I should've been bound to. 'Tis a verra long story and one I swear to ye I will tell ye in full another day. 'Tis then that I lost my magic. I couldna stay in the past, but I needed to start anew. Laurel offered me her apartment, as well as funds to help me get started, and so, unable to pass up such a generous offer, I moved to Boston."

Just that little bit of information made so many things click into place inside my mind. I leaned forward to kiss him, hoping the gesture would show him how much this meant to me.

"You told me the night we rode in the limo that you didn't think you would ever return to Scotland. Why? What do you dread so much about being here?"

He didn't answer me right away, and I realized as I watched him that I wasn't sure if he had really thought about the reason himself. Eventually, after a long moment, he spoke after giving me a shrug.

"There is nothing wrong with this place, or even this time. Much more good than bad happened to me here. I suppose 'tis only that I regret the choices I made here. Those choices hurt people I cared for. When I fled this time to live in yer own, Raudrich was forced to take my place at the isle. 'Twas a position not destined for him, and it upended the life he had always intended to lead. When I am here, I canna help but remember all the mistakes I have made, and it pains me."

I squeezed his hand, gently. "You know that we all have mistakes we don't want to be reminded of, right? You're not the only one that's messed up. That's kind of a signature human trait."

He shook his head and looked at me with sad eyes. "Not mistakes like the ones I've made."

I thought of the little I knew of Raudrich thanks to Morna's revelatory tea. "It seems to me that things turned out alright for Raudrich. Maybe all your decision did was allow things to turn out exactly how they were meant to."

He shrugged again. "Mayhap so. Though I doubt it."

I desperately wanted to press on, but I could see he was nearing his limit, and the last thing I wanted was to upset him when he was trying so hard to please me. Deciding to change the subject, I broached the last thing that had been picking at the edge of my mind all day.

"Okay. I just have one last question for you for tonight. But can we please agree that you'll be more open to real conversations like this in the future? I have to be able to talk to you. And I have to know that you're willing to trust me with all of you."

He nodded and lifted my fingers to his lips to kiss them. "Aye, lass. I promise. What is yer last question?"

"I guess it's not a question. Just a suspicion I have that I'd like you to confirm. You and Silva were a thing once, weren't you?"

He visibly jerked next to me as something close to panic appeared in his eyes. "What? Did she tell ye that, lass?"

I shook my head, startled by his reaction. "No. It was just the way she kept looking at me, I guess. Look, it's so not a big deal if you guys were. We all have exes. She just seems extremely fond of you, but in a way that was noticeably different than the way Sydney is fond of you. I just noticed it is all."

He sighed and his expression softened. "Ah. I see, lass. No. Silva and I are friends. Always have been."

I narrowed my eyes at him. I'd been so certain of it. I'd honestly thought it was the easiest question I wanted to ask him.

"Really? Because I'm really not the jealous type, Ross. You swear you guys never…" I paused. "Not even a little bit?"

His jaw tightened. "Aye lass, I swear. I doona even know why ye would ask such a question."

He removed his boots and slipped into bed without looking at me. Slowly, I removed my own shoes and climbed in beside him, a cold and uneasy sensation hanging over me. He'd never spoken to me in such a way before, dismissing me not just because he didn't want to talk, but in a manner intended to make me feel stupid.

Regretting that I'd pushed him, I rolled to turn into his arms. "I'm sorry. Thank you for letting me pry for a little bit."

He too, seemed to regret snapping at me and hurried to pull me into the crook of his arm before bending to kiss me and then trailing his lips up to whisper into my ear. "'Tis fine, lass. Now how would ye feel about exhausting ourselves just a wee bit more? 'Twould surely assure a pleasant night's sleep."

I reached my hand down to stroke his already-present erection. "I think I would feel pretty good about that."

Growling, he pulled me into his arms once more.

*W*ith dawn just beginning to show herself on the horizon, Ross still lay awake in the small bed with Allanah sound asleep beside him. Regret plagued him as he held her.

Why had he lied? Why had he sworn an untruth when he'd been presented with the perfect opportunity to be free of the chains of this secret?

There was no good reason for it, he knew. Perhaps it was only that he was cursed to make the decisions that were the worst for him.

Whatever the reason, he knew it would come back to haunt him.

His choices always did.

CHAPTER 40

The rest of the journey went smoothly. While I'd been hesitant, a few nights spent camping under the stars weren't nearly as dreadful as I'd expected them to be.

Over the last three days of riding together, I learned more about Ross and who he really was than any other time that I'd spent with him. It seemed that Gramps had been right indeed. Once pressed, he opened up. As he did, it was as if a dam had been broken. Without me even asking him, he would regale me with stories of his childhood growing up amongst the very landscape we rode through.

I shared stories, too. I talked of my parents, my first heartbreak, of how I began to build my profession, and what I wanted in my future.

We learned that there are so many things we agree on. We both want children. We are both happy to remain in Boston or at least close to it. We both prefer the deli on the east side of our apartment complex to the one on the west. And we also learned, just as importantly, that the things we disagreed on really weren't that big of deal. Our taste in music varied greatly—our preference for future potential vacation spots even more so.

By the time we arrived in the village where his mother lived, I was certain I'd never had a more enjoyable few days in all my life. All of the anxiety and apprehension I'd felt the day I sat down to visit with Gramps was now gone.

Ross leaned forward on the horse, his cheek pressed warmly against my own as we neared the castle gates, and I gently reached up to place my hand on the side of his cheek.

"Our time here willna be easy for me, lass, but I canna tell ye how pleased I am that ye are here."

"Me too, Ross. There's nowhere else in the whole world I'd rather be."

It was the truest thing I'd ever said.

wo Months Later

One thing I found to be very different in this time than my own was how easily one could settle into a routine. Something about the lack of distractions, the end to the incessant buzzing on our phones and overpacked calendars, allowed a natural rhythm to take place day after day. While I knew that when the time came to return home, I would be ready, I couldn't deny that I quite enjoyed the change of pace, especially since my days took an interesting turn shortly after our arrival.

During our first month, there were still times when Ross' mother seemed to know him. When she did, he never wanted me by his side. She always reverted back to a time when he still lived in the village with her, and there would be no way to explain my presence without causing her distress. I understood completely, but it meant that my days were left empty without much purpose, and it had quickly driven me stir-crazy.

Thankfully, purpose fell into my lap on our tenth day in the village.

I'd been walking back toward the castle after leaving Ross with his mother, and I'd noticed an old man hobbling with such apparent pain that I'd been unable to walk past him without offering assistance. After learning that he'd injured himself in a fall, my physical therapist instincts simply couldn't be denied.

Within two weeks, I had a handful of 'patients' in the village, none of whom had ever stretched anything a day in their life. I was halfway concerned that they were all going to believe me a witch for the relief I was able to help many of them find.

After the first month, the health of Ross' mother began to decline further. For weeks, she'd not known him and still he stayed by her side. When she was frightened, he would comfort her. And when she was happier, he would go along with whatever—or whoever—she needed him to be at that time.

The waiting wore on him. I could see it in the way the whites of his eyes were always red and strained when we met up in the evenings for dinner. But I also knew that despite his heartache, this was exactly where he needed to be. If he'd not done this, if he'd not come here to be with her at the end, he never would've forgiven himself. The last thing Ross needed was to have more self-induced guilt to carry around with him.

"I'll be glad when she finally dies, and I feel like the worst sort of wretch for saying so."

They were the first words Ross had said since entering our bedchamber after dinner a half hour ago. When I looked up at him from the fire I sat in front of, I could see tears in his eyes.

"Ross." I stood and moved over, wrapping my arms around him in a hug. "You are not a wretch. She's not there anymore, and it's a cruel, cruel disease. Of course, there will be some relief when she goes. She won't be in pain. She won't be frightened. It's entirely normal for you to feel that way."

He kissed the top of my head and I felt him shrug against me.

"Mayhap so. Do ye think ye could do something for me tomorrow, lass?"

"Of course. What is it?"

"Griffith has asked me to join him for a ride at daybreak. He believes I need a morning away from all this."

I nodded in agreement. "He's right. You definitely need to go. A ride in some fresh air will help clear your head. You've been with her every day since we got here. And she's not known you for weeks now."

"Aye." He squeezed my hand. "I know ye are both right. Would you sit with her in the morning? The healer has others in the village he needs to tend to, and the young woman who usually tends to her when he is away has just gone into labor. I doona wish for her to be alone in case…" He hesitated as his voice broke. "In case…"

I lifted my palm to his cheek. "Of course. I'll go over there as soon as you guys ride out, and I'll sit with her until you return."

He kissed me, slowly leading me to the bed, in need of a few minutes of comfort where his heart wouldn't feel quite so heavy.

---

*S*he was sleeping when I entered her home, though a candle still burned next to her bedside, and I knew the healer was not long gone from checking on her at first light.

Her face was gaunt, her eyes sunken into her head, and her fingers so slim they were alarming. She rarely touched food anymore, and I knew as I settled into the well-worn chair beside her bed, that it wouldn't be long before she passed.

Hours passed while I listened to her breathing, and as I sat silently next to her, I thought of all the things I would say to her if she were well.

I thought of how I'd thank her for raising such a good man, of how I'd assure her that we would be back to visit again soon. As I did so, tears spilled over my cheeks.

I didn't know this woman—not really—but I knew I was bound to her by the love we both shared for her son. It pained me to know that once she was gone, Ross would have one less heart loving him in this world.

I brushed away my tears, not wanting Ross to walk in and see me crying. As I closed my eyes and pressed my palms against my eyelids, I heard her shift in the bed. I hurried to move my hands away so I could look at her.

Her eyes finally flickered open. To my surprise, she was smiling at me, her hand laid open beside her as if she wished me to take it.

Hesitantly, I did, just that.

For a moment, she said nothing. She simply stared at me with a smile. Then she reached over with her other frail hand and gently patted the top of the hand I had resting on her other one.

"Silva, lass. 'Tis good to see ye."

I froze, surprise pricking its way down my spine with an unsettling sense of foreboding, though I knew I couldn't deny her by telling her I was someone else.

"It…it's good to see you, too."

She pulled her brows in and tilted her head to the right a little as she looked at me. "Why have ye changed out of yer dress? I thought mayhap ye would wear it as ye left."

"My…my dress?"

"Yer wedding dress, lass. Why 'twas the most beautiful wedding I've ever seen. And I finally have a daughter I can call my own."

She smiled again.

My stomach turned over, and my blood ran cold.

CHAPTER 41

G riffith was right. He'd spent far too many days surrounded by the sadness of all that weighed on him. The ride had done him good, though he was ready to be back at the castle and in Allanah's arms.

They'd ridden farther than he expected, and dusk was nearing as they rode into view of the village. He hoped the healer had returned after seeing to his other patients so that Allanah hadn't had to sit all day with his mother.

As they passed through the castle gates and near the stables, he could see Allanah's figure in the distance.

What was the lass doing? She held out a bag in front of her and appeared to be screaming at the stablemaster.

Unnerved by the sight in front of him, he pulled on the reigns of the horse, dismounting quickly so he could run to her.

"Allanah, lass, what are ye doing? Has this man harmed ye in some way?"

She whirled on him, the bag nearly smacking him across the face. Her eyes were red, her cheeks streaked with tears, and she was shook all over.

Before Allanah could say a word, the stablemaster spoke beside him.

"All I've done to the lass is refuse to sell her one of the laird's horses."

"Horses?" Confused, he turned back to look at Allanah. "Why would ye wish to buy one of the horses, lass? What is the matter?"

"I'm leaving, Ross." She screamed the words at him, tears still running down her face. Her chest rose and fell in quick succession, and he feared she might faint if she didn't calm herself enough to catch her breath.

"Allanah, lass." He reached for her, but she jerked out of the way.

"Don't you dare touch me!"

Mouth agape, he shook his head in confusion. "Ye must tell me what has happened. Is it my mother?"

She shook her head. His question forced her to speak. "She's no worse than she was this morning."

She stormed past him in the direction of the horse he'd dismounted. He ran to block her path.

"Lass, 'tis near dark. I'll not allow ye to ride out on yer own. Ye must tell me what has ye so upset."

"You lied, Ross! You were married to her for God's sake!"

His legs nearly gave way as her words sunk in.

How had she possibly found out?

"Wha…how…" His words failed him.

Her jaw tight, she ground out an answer to his unfinished question. "How did I find out? Your mother thought I was Silva, Ross. She asked me why I'd changed out of my wedding gown."

He closed his eyes as the horror of it washed over him. "Lass, I can explain. I should've told ye. I'm so sorry. I…"

She held out a hand to stop him. "I don't care, Ross. I could've dealt with so many things, but you directly lied to me. You swore. I'm leaving."

Panic coursed through him as he moved to grab the reins of the horse she reached for.

"I canna bring ye back now, lass. My mother could pass any day."

She stopped long enough to look at him. "I know. And I'm so, so sorry about that. But I can't stay here. Not tonight. Not ever again. I'm leaving. Now."

He sighed, his heart aching as if she'd just reached inside and ripped it from his chest. His own tears were spilling over now, his voice raspy as he pleaded with her.

"Ye canna leave tonight, lass. I just told ye that I canna take ye back now."

She raised the hand still clutching the bag of coins she'd tried to pay off the stablemaster with.

"You're not taking me back anywhere, Ross. I'm leaving right now. If you take one more step to stop me, I'm going to swing this bag of metal into your head so hard it knocks you right onto your ass."

He let go of the reigns and stepped aside. There was no bluff in her tone.

"Please, Allanah." He dropped to his knees. His tone desperate and hopeless. "Please forgive me."

Without a word, she mounted the horse and rode away from him. From his right, Griffith stepped back toward his own steed.

"I'll follow her, lad. I'll see her safely to Cagair Castle, doona worry."

Sobs wracked his chest as he watched his heart ride away from him.

oston, Massachusetts, USA

I didn't spend a single night at Cagair Castle when I made it back to the present day. Instead, I had Orick, the only person I actually saw upon returning to Cagair, drive me to the airport the second I made it back through the stairwell. Within twelve hours of crossing over into my own time, I was back home in Boston.

I didn't tell anyone I was back. While I knew there was a possibility Georgie would be at the apartment, I figured it was just as likely that she wouldn't be, and I desperately wanted some time alone to process my anger and heartache.

When I unlocked the door of my apartment to find the place dark and quiet, I allowed myself to drop to the floor and cry.

While I'd been a hysterical mess upon leaving Ross, the hard ride home had forced me to stifle my emotions for the time being. Griffith was a good companion. He rode silently throughout the trip, allowing me to set the pace, all while making sure that we had a safe camp the one night that we did stop to actually sleep.

But now, back home in the safety and warmth of my own bed, I let everything go. I cried for hours. My chest had never been so sore before. I ached for him, for the betrayal I felt at his lie.

I didn't care that Ross had been married before. In truth, it made perfect sense, especially after the way Silva had acted toward me. What I simply couldn't abide was the lie. It wasn't something he'd simply decided to not tell me. It wasn't one of the topics he always seemed to skirt his way around. He'd looked me right in the eyes and swore to me that he and Silva had never had any sort of relationship.

Part of me had recognized the lie in that moment, and I knew that made it all the worse for me now. Because the truth was, I wasn't only angry at Ross, I was also furious with myself for allowing my heart to get in the way of my gut.

It wasn't only the lie. It was also the fact that I couldn't help but wonder if perhaps losing Silva was his biggest regret, that maybe that was the thing that plagued him so acutely.

He'd hinted at such a truth, actually, the first night I spent in the past with him, when I'd said to him that his mistake maybe wasn't a mistake at all—that perhaps it had pushed things to happen as they were truly meant to. He hadn't liked that suggestion. He'd even disagreed with me, saying that he doubted it.

Why did he doubt it? Was it because he believed he should've ended up with Silva? Was his relationship with me something he'd settled for as his second best option now that Silva was remarried and out of reach for him? Had he truly moved to Boston not to start anew but to try and outrun his desire for her?

It had to be so. In that lens, everything about him made sense, and that realization hurt me worse than any other pain I'd felt in my life.

I'd seen it with him—my future. Each night when I went to lay against his chest, that space there felt like home.

Now, all I felt was loss and confusion.

Eventually, after hours of sobbing, my eyes finally surrendered and drifted closed in sleep.

"Sue? Sue?"

Georgie's voice called out to me as she shook my shoulder. As my eyes slowly flickered open, she widened her eyes at me.

"You scared me half to death. When I walked into the apartment and saw the lights on, I thought someone had broken in until I noticed your purse hanging on the hook. What are you doing here? How could you come back and not tell us?"

Groggily, I pushed myself up in the bed. "I just got back today, Georgie. I just needed some time alone."

She stared at me hard and her expression slowly softened. "What happened? What's wrong?"

With my head in her lap, she stroked my hair. I spilled everything to her, my tears returning as I vented.

When I finished, she lifted my head and stood from the bed before looking down at me, her brows raised and her eyes furious.

"Screw him, Sue. Seriously. I'm going to kick his ass when he shows back up here."

I sniffled and reached for a tissue. "I think I might let you."

"I'm going to order a pizza, and then I'm going to run to the store for some wine and ice cream. I know how to set you right, ASAP."

A drunken night of pizza and ice cream didn't work the wonders that Georgie had hoped it would. Rather than a healed heart, all I ended up with was an upset stomach and a migraine.

Gramps seemed certain that time would heal things, but as days turned into weeks, and weeks into a month, I wasn't so sure.

I couldn't focus on anything. I wasn't eating well. Even work wasn't enough to pull me out of my funk.

One month and three days after I left him, Caleb showed up at my door with crossed arms and a frown.

He got after me the minute I opened the door, taking me aback. "Enough of this. Do you hear me? It's been enough."

I stared at him, blankly, unsure of what to say to him.

He pushed me aside and stepped into the apartment. "I've been listening to Georgie worry about you for weeks now. You haven't been to see the girls since you've been back, and you're not responding to my text messages or answering your phone. You have got to pull it together."

Guilt immediately flooded me, and tears flooded my eyes for the millionth time that week.

"I…I couldn't go and see the girls, Caleb. I knew Hannah would ask me about Ross, and I didn't want to cry in front of them."

"Ah, hell."

Caleb's shoulders slumped as he wrapped his arms around me.

"Don't cry, Sue. I'm sorry. Gosh, I'm an idiot. I thought I would try the tough love approach. I see now that wasn't the best course of action. Look…" He pulled away so I would look up at him. As I did so, he gently brushed away my tears. "I'm never going to tell anyone how long they should or shouldn't grieve over anything, but I do know that nothing gets better with inaction."

He paused and I noticed him staring at something on the table behind me. Frowning, he returned his attention to me.

"How long has it been since you've been through your mail?"

I shrugged. I was well aware of the mounting pile that had accumulated on my kitchen table. I just didn't care.

"That's not you, Sue. You can wallow and cry, but you can't just stop taking care of stuff. Come here, let's go through this mess together."

Knowing I had no other option, I followed him to the table as he sat down and began to rifle through my mail.

"Junk. Junk. Junk. Bill. Bill. Junk." He stilled on an envelope and regarded it skeptically.

"You might want to open this one, Sue. It looks like a letter."

"Who is it from?"

"No idea. There's no return address. There's not even postage from what I can tell. Weird."

Magic. It had to be. If the letter was from Ross, I had no desire to read it.

Cautiously, I reached for the envelope and turned it over. The handwriting of my address seemed too feminine to be Ross'. Curious, I opened it.

A small note, no larger than a Post-It, fell onto the table in front of me.

"Please remember what I said: His stupid mistakes are not a testament to his lack of love for you. They are a result of the self-hatred he carries for himself."

Silva.

Caleb was staring at me, curiously. "So?"

I crumpled up the note and threw it in the trash.

"It was nothing. Let's carry on."

It didn't matter what the cause was. How could I ever truly love someone who didn't love himself? The same problems, the same mistakes, would plague us over and over.

Ross was in the past.

It was time for me to move toward my future.

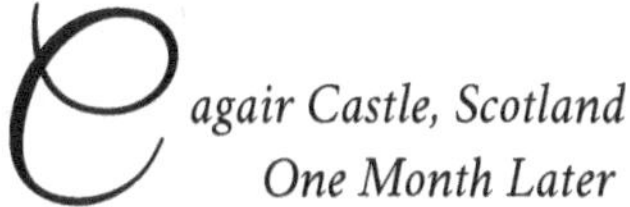

agair Castle, Scotland
One Month Later

Six weeks after Allanah left him, his mother did too. There'd been no sadness on the day she passed, only relief that her misery had finally come to an end.

Griffith helped him bury his mother. And one day later, he set off for Cagair Castle.

The weeks apart from Allanah had given him time to think— time to sort through the ways things always turned out wrong. He'd had to stay for his mother. But now, he would return home to fight for her.

It was his mother who saved him. Perhaps she'd always carried a little bit of magic within her too. For even though her mind no longer knew him, her soul most assuredly did. And on the night before she passed, she'd come to him in a dream.

They sat in the room where she lay dying, but no ailment plagued her. He could smell the sweetness of honey bread rising from the fire behind them. Her eyes were no longer frightened, and her figure was more than just skin and bones. She looked happy and healthy, and peace radiated from her.

"Ross." She'd reached out to him, and he'd dutifully taken her hand.

"What is the one thing ye've desired yer whole life, son?"

"Love."

The answer slipped effortlessly from his lips, surprising him. Was that truly what he wanted more than anything? He knew he wanted Allanah now—he wanted her love—but had that always been his desire? He'd truly never given it much thought.

His mother smiled at him, nodding knowingly. "Then ye must learn to give yerself that which ye wish to share with others. 'Tis as simple and as difficult as that."

With a start he woke in the chair next to her bed. As he gazed down at her, he knew she was moments away from taking her last breath. With tears in his eyes, he crawled into bed beside her, wrapping his arms around her frail frame as he held her until her chest no longer rose and fell in sync with his. He thought about the dream every moment of the ride back to Cagair. With each moment, the truth in it slowly worked its way into his soul. He was not a stupid man. He was not inherently selfish or evil. He was not cursed to make decisions that ruined him and everyone he loved. Instead, he was a man who'd simply denied himself the one thing every living creature needs in order to thrive.

Love of one's self.

No more.

Allanah deserved better from him.

He deserved better from him.

It would take time, he knew. But no matter what, he would win her back.

He simply wouldn't be moving through life without her by his side.

CHAPTER 44

*R*oss was back. He'd been back for a while.

I wasn't sure what I thought was going to happen once he returned. While I knew where I stood—there was no coming back from what happened—I honestly expected him to reach out in some way. I expected him to want to explain.

The lack of contact from him cemented my suspicions. I'd always been second fiddle—someone to distract him from the one woman he truly wanted and couldn't have. He didn't love me. He'd only said it because I'd whispered it in my sleep, and it's hard to keep up an illusion if you don't play along.

It still hurt so much. I was embarrassed to even mention Ross' name to anyone I loved. I didn't want them to know how much I still struggled. I didn't want anyone to see that a man I'd not been dating for all that long had upended my life so completely.

Unfortunately, after Caleb's mini mail intervention, I did too good of a job at pretending I was okay.

So good in fact, that Caleb had taken it upon himself to take over the job Beth had tried to do before her death—match me with someone.

I couldn't say no. If I did, everyone would just assume that I wasn't over Ross, and all of my energy was going into making believe that I was.

The first one was undoubtedly the worst date I'd ever been on in my life. The man was much too old for me, and his dentures literally came loose halfway through dinner.

The second wasn't much better. An hour into the evening, he asked me my opinion on swinging.

And finally, to tie it all up into one big crappy bow, the third man didn't even show up.

When I finally gave up and returned to my apartment, I walked in to find Caleb and Georgie watching a movie on the couch.

"How'd it go?"

I stared blankly at him. "He didn't show up, Caleb."

"Awe." He made a sad face and waved me over. "I'm sorry. That sucks."

"Caleb, who are these losers that you keep setting me up with? Do you actually know any of these guys? And if you do, why?"

He laughed and lifted his palms nonchalantly. "I'm sorry, Sue. I do know them, but I guess I'm just not nearly as good at this as Beth was. Will you let me make it up to you? Let me set you up with one more guy. If it's not good, I promise to never try to set you up again."

I pointed at him. "You promise?"

He held out his pinky and I swatted it away. "It's the last time, Caleb. I'm not doing this again."

"Fine. This one will be better. I have a really good feeling about it."

Three days later, I found myself standing in front of the same Indian restaurant where Ross and I had our first date. Had I known this was where the date was going to take place, I'm sure I would've said no, but Caleb didn't text me the location until an hour before, and no matter how certain I was that this man would be no less of a loser than the others, I still wasn't willing to stand someone up after finding out firsthand how much that sucked.

Sighing, I braced myself and walked inside. The restaurant was empty, which was unusual for this time of evening. I was quickly shown to a booth and offered a glass of water.

As the waiter walked away, I felt the weight of a hand on my shoulder.

I twisted around and looked into the eyes of the one man that was still almost always on my mind.

"Ross. What are you doing here?"

He shrugged. "I…I was supposed to have a blind date."

Anger boiled up in me as I surged from my seat. "You have got to be freaking kidding me. Caleb tried to set us up again? I'm out."

I tried to storm around him, but he grabbed my arm and spun me, his grip too tight for me to pull away.

"No, lass. Please stay. 'Twas not Caleb's doing." He paused. "Well, he helped, but 'twas my idea. We've the restaurant to ourselves. And I swear to ye, I shall block the door if I must. Ye left before we could speak so many months ago. Ye must hear me out now."

I didn't want to listen to him. Whatever his explanation, I knew it would rip me wide open again, and the last thing I wanted was for him to see me cry. "No, Ross. I can't do this."

He didn't release his grip on my wrist. "Please, lass."

His tone was so desperate, and there were tears in his eyes.

Reluctantly, I nodded, and he released me as I moved to return to my seat.

He sat down across from me and began almost immediately. "We doona have a meal coming our way, lass. The kitchen is closed. I just needed ye here to talk."

"Great." I mumbled the response under my breath. The one good thing about finding out my supposed blind date was going to be here was that I at least knew I was going to get a fantastic meal.

"Lass, I have made so many mistakes in my life, but none so great as not giving ye the trust and honesty ye deserved. There is no good reason for why I lied to ye about Silva. The only explanation I can give is this…"

"I know why you lied, Ross." I'd not intended to interrupt him, but the words had slipped out before I could stop them.

He crossed his arms and leaned back, surprised. "Ye do?"

I nodded. "You're still in love with her, Ross. You didn't want me to know about her, because you didn't want me to know that she was the one you really wanted."

He shook his head and reached to grab my hand across the table. "No, lass. That is not why I lied to ye. Not at all. I loved Silva, aye. But I doona anymore, and I havena for a long time. The only one I love is ye, Allanah. I love ye so much that being apart from ye has caused my heart to ache in a way I dinna know was possible. And trust me, lass, I've ached much in my life."

My lips began to tremble. I expected an excuse, but I never anticipated another confession of his love.

"If that's true, then why did you lie?"

"Allanah, I faked my own death and left Silva in the past because I was frightened of my destiny on The Isle of Eight Lairds. I abandoned and broke the heart of the woman I'd sworn to love and protect for my entire life. Is that the behavior of someone ye deserve to be with? Is that the action of someone ye want to be with?"

"You what?"

"Aye. I was married to Silva when I was meant to join the men at The Isle. I couldna do it, so I left. I left without explanation. 'Twas the most horrid thing I've ever done. I couldna tell ye the night that ye asked me, lass. I couldna bear the thought of ye thinking of me the way I thought of myself."

Silva was right. I could see that now, looking into the pained expression in his eyes. He'd not meant to hurt me. He just didn't know how to keep from hurting himself.

"Do you still think that way about yourself, Ross?"

He shook his head. "No, lass. My mother had one last lesson for me before she died."

I gave the hand that held mine a gentle squeeze. "I'm so sorry, Ross."

He shook his head again.

"No, lass. Ye were right. There was naught but relief felt that day. For me and for her."

He paused and stood, walking around the table to scoot into my side of the booth. I turned to face him.

"Allanah, please forgive me. Please take me back. I will never lie to ye again. I doona wish to move forward without ye. All those dreams we spoke of on the road to my hometown—I want all of them, lass. And I doona want them with anyone but ye."

I kissed him, my lips pressing hard against his with months of repressed yearning.

"I love you, Ross."

"And I ye, lass. Ye will never know how much."

He was wrong. I knew how much because it was the same love I had for him.

Consuming. Healing. Whole.

Two weeks after we got back together, I told Caleb he could rent my apartment to someone else since Georgie was moving in with him, and I was moving in with Ross. He'd squealed with delight and happily confessed his part in Ross' plan. While the idea of bringing me to the Indian restaurant had been Ross' idea, the horrid dates leading up to that had been Caleb's—a hope that I'd be so worn down after three terrible dates, that I would at least give Ross the opportunity to talk.

I suppose it worked. And God, I was glad it had.

A year later, Ross compromised—booking a vacation to one of the places on my list that was certainly not on his—Las Vegas. Two days into the trip, we married. Tink carried our rings down the aisle on a pillow.

I called Gramps an hour before the ceremony, and a Cher impersonator held my phone up so Gramps, Gladys, Georgie, Caleb, and his girls could watch our wedding via video chat.

Tired of Vegas after the second night, we booked a last minute honeymoon trip to the one place that no longer held any ghosts for either of us.

Scotland.

* * *

Sign up for text messages or my newsletter to be notified when the next book in the series, *For All Time, releases.*

SUBSCRIBE TO BETHANY'S MAILING LIST

When you sign up for my mailing list, you will be the first to know about new releases, upcoming events, and contests. You will also get sneak peeks into books and have opportunities to participate in special reader groups and occasionally get codes for free books.

Just go to my website (www.bethanyclaire.com) and click the Mailing List link in the header. I can't wait to connect with you there.

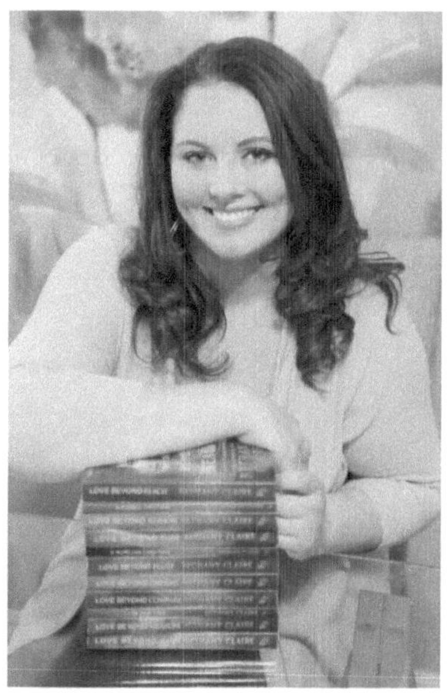

BETHANY CLAIRE is a USA Today bestselling author of swoon-worthy, Scottish romance and time travel novels. Bethany loves to immerse her readers in worlds filled with lush landscapes, hunky Scots, lots of magic, and happy endings.

She has two ornery fur-babies, plays the piano every day, and loves Disney and yoga pants more than any twenty-something really should. She is most creative after a good night's sleep and the perfect cup of tea. When not writing, Bethany travels as much as she possibly can, and she never leaves home without a good book to keep her company.

If you want to read more about Bethany or if you're curious about when her next book will come out, please visit her website at: www.bethanyclaire.com, where you can sign up to receive email notifications about new releases.

ACKNOWLEDGMENTS

First, I'm eternally grateful to all of my readers for continuing to read these books. You're the reason I write, and your support means the world.

To Rori Bumgarner, Karen Corboy, Elizabeth Halliday, Johnetta Ivey, Vivian Nwankpah, and Pamela Oviatt, thank you, thank you, thank you for continuing to hang in there with me and for providing such keen eyes and astute insights.

To Mom, thank you for the time and hard work you put in to each and every one of these books. And for talking me down when overwhelm and self-doubt sets in. I truly do think I have the best mom in the whole world.